WAR OF THE DRAGON

JESSICA DRAKE

DYNAMO PRESS

Copyright © 2018, Jessica Drake. All rights reserved. Published by Dynamo Press.

This novel is a work of fiction. All characters, places, and incidents described in this publication are used fictitiously, or are entirely fictional. No part of this publication may be reproduced or transmitted, in any form or by any means, except by an authorized retailer, or with written permission of the publisher. Inquiries may be addressed via email to jessica@authorjessicadrake.com.

If you want to be notified when Jessica's next novel is released and get access to exclusive contests, giveaways, and freebies, sign up for her mailing list here. Your email address will never be shared and you can unsubscribe at any time.

Created with Vellum

1

Tick, tock. Tick, tock.

I stared at the ornate clock on the mantelpiece, as if I could urge its silver hands to spin faster through the sheer force of my glare. Unfortunately, the gears within seemed immune to my agitation, continuing to turn at the same consistent, dependable rate the clockmaker had designed. One slow, dull, infuriating second at a time.

"Relax, Zara. Tavarian will be back soon."

"Soon?" I jumped up from the settee to pace Tavarian's sitting room. *"He's been gone for hours, Lessie."* Ironic that my spunky, impulsive dragonling was telling me to calm down. Usually she was the impatient one in our relationship, but the more time I spent sitting idle, the more restless I became.

"So what?" Lessie argued. *"As far as I'm concerned, he can stand to be gone a little longer. I don't know about you, but I'm enjoying the luxury of a little time and space to myself. We've been running and*

flying and fighting non-stop for weeks. This is the first time we've had a breather."

I exhaled through my nostrils and forced myself to stop pacing the carpet. Lessie was right. Between multiple kidnappings, rescue attempts, espionage missions, and several harrowing brushes with death, the two of us had been through quite an ordeal. I couldn't fault Lessie for her exhaustion. A large part of me wanted to do nothing more than find a thick, heavy blanket to curl up under and hide from the world.

But I couldn't do that, not when worry gnawed at my brain. The bulk of our dragon rider force had mysteriously disappeared just when Elantia needed them most. Jallis and his dragon were likely among them, while my best friend Rhia, whom I had left in a camp to the north, was right in the path of the invading army. Our country was on the verge of being conquered. These weren't exactly problems I could hide from, not when I knew the enemy would come knocking at the gates of Zuar City any day now.

We might be on a floating island, but in this age of airships and cannons, no one was safe.

"He's back," Lessie said, interrupting my tension-filled musings. *"His airship just landed."*

I raced out the door before she'd even finished speaking, my spelled boots silent on the parquet floors despite my utter disregard for stealth. I beat the surprised stewardess to the door and gripped the porch railing as I watched a carriage approach via the winding road that led to the landing strip on the other side of the island.

"Tavarian." I almost rushed toward him as he disembarked, then forced myself to stop. He was handsome as ever in his tailored grey suit, his inky hair secured at the nape of his neck to leave his arresting, angular face unframed. But his skin was paler than usual, and shadows dodged his silver eyes, reminding me that he, too, had been through quite an ordeal. He'd spent weeks trapped at the Traggaran court, dodging assassination attempts while trying to get an audience with the king, then immediately rushed back to Zuar City as fast as he could to defend me at my court-martial. I'd had plenty of time to rest while locked up in a dormitory room awaiting trial, but Tavarian hadn't.

"Zara." Tavarian gave me a warm smile as he scaled the steps with his long-legged stride. "I'll debrief you in the dining room in thirty minutes. I'm absolutely starved."

"Of course." I moved to the side, allowing him to step past me and through the door. A whiff of his bergamot and leather scent teased my senses as he passed, and my cheeks heated as I remembered our kiss. Had it really only been a few hours since I'd thrown my arms around him and found myself in a passionate, heated embrace with a man I'd once thought as cold and emotionless as Salcombe? It seemed like weeks, or even years. And where did that leave us now? Was Tavarian truly interested in me, or had we just gotten caught up in a moment of passion?

This is the last thing you should be thinking about, I told myself as I followed him inside and shut the door. But I couldn't help it as I stared at Tavarian's retreating back, watching the way his coat clung to his broad shoulders even as the hem billowed out behind him. Even now, with exhaustion clinging to him, those shoulders refused to slump. I wished I had half his strength.

"Don't be ridiculous," Lessie huffed, and I jolted in surprise. *"You've twice Tavarian's mettle. The fact that you're still standing after all you've been through is a testament to the strength of your will. You've made it through ordeals that others with five times the amount of training would have failed."*

"And how would you know that?" I asked, only half-teasing. Lessie had the vocabulary of a full-grown adult—one of the perks of listening to human conversation for hundreds of years while trapped in her egg, waiting for the right rider to come along—but at six months old, she was still fairly naïve and inexperienced.

"Because the other dragons have said the same thing," she said stoutly, unperturbed by the doubt she sensed in our bond. *"And as your dragon, I heartily concur."*

Unexpected tears pricked at the corners of my eyes, and I stopped in the middle of the hallway, surprised by how much the sentiment touched me. I had no idea the other dragons had any opinions of me, much less favorable ones. But it made me even more determined to figure out where they'd gone and rescue them if I could.

I rushed up the stairs to my bedroom and freshened up, then joined Tavarian in the dining room. Lunch was an array of cold meats and cheeses with bread and fruit. The servants also left a bottle of red, but neither of us made any move to touch it. The situation we were in could drive any man to drink, but we needed to be clearheaded if we wanted to come up with a viable strategy.

"Well?" I asked once we'd both piled our plates and gotten in a few mouthfuls. "How did the council meeting go?"

"Not very well," Tavarian admitted. "We have been trying to formulate a plan to deal with the invasion, but we are crippled by our lack of information. No one seems to have any idea why our dragons and riders have not arrived. Even the dragon courier who comes from the western front every day never arrived yesterday, and no one has seen him yet today, either."

My stomach turned into a ball of lead, and I was forced to push my plate away. "So, it's official, then. The dragons and their riders are missing."

"The council is reluctant to admit it, but at this point I must concur," Tavarian said gravely. "Without them, our prospects are bleak. The best the council was able to come up with is to marshal our remaining forces and station them a day's march from Zuar City to meet the invasion before they reach the capital. It's an absurd plan, which will only result in our forces being slaughtered. I told the others as much, but they are determined to fight the Zallabarians to the last man."

"Oh?" I raised an eyebrow, clenching my fists against the anger pounding in my blood. "Are they going to be on the front too, then?"

Tavarian snorted. "If only they were that brave. No, the chancellor and my fellow council members are preparing to evacuate and govern from the southwest as long as possible, and then move to one of our overseas territories if that becomes necessary. They intend to govern in exile while they figure out how to take back the country."

"And what exactly are they going to be governing if Zallabar takes the entire country?" I asked through clenched teeth. "Are you making similar preparations as well?"

Tavarian's eyes flashed. "Of course not. I have lent the councilors one of my airships, but I will be staying behind. I thought you knew me better than that, Zara."

"Sorry," I muttered, averting my gaze. Was that hurt in his eyes? I turned back to look at him again, but the cool mask was back in place, and I buried a sigh of frustration. "I'm just furious we've even come to this point. We've been complacent as a nation for so long, secure in the power of our dragons and the knowledge that we've been the conquerors for as long as we can remember. When I was down in the city, helping the citizens prepare for invasion, I could tell most of them were still in denial that we were really in any danger. They don't seem to realize that if we don't do something, we're all going to be speaking Zallabarian in twenty years."

Tavarian nodded. "Unfortunately, I'm not sure there is anything they *can* do. The number of soldiers required to hold back such a large host is far more than what we have available. It is possible to mobilize the men in the towns and villages and fight back, guerilla-style, but that will be very bloody and costly, and the chances of success are still slim. It might be best for the civilians to lie low while the respective governments sort out their problems."

"So basically, you're saying we should all just submit and hope the councilmen will get their shit together and save us all?" I couldn't believe what he was saying. "We might as well start hanging Zallabarian flags from all our government buildings right now."

"I am saying that just as I think it is foolish for us to throw our soldiers onto the pikes of the enemy when there is no hope of defeating them, it is foolish for our citizens to actively resist, at least not without a solid plan in place. I have experienced guerilla warfare firsthand," he said darkly, his silver eyes swirling with some evil memory, "back when Muza and I were still together. We were quelling an insurgency in one of the colonies, and the locals were fighting back with ambushes. It was a horrible, bloody business with many dead and mutilated on both sides, despite the advantage of our dragons, and Muza in particular was disgusted." His face softened with sadness and regret. "Perhaps this is the universe's way of repaying us for our hubris."

The ball of lead in my stomach eased, melted away by a wave of sympathy. "You and Muza did the best you could under the circumstances." The fact that the two of them lived apart, separated by thousands of miles of ocean because they couldn't bear being forced to fight wars they didn't believe in, spoke highly of their integrity. "But whether or not you think Elantia deserves this, we can't allow our country to be taken. Who is to say that Zallabar is going to stop here? After all, they took Dardil without hesitation. Once they have our territory and resources, they might very well decide to conquer the rest of the continent as well."

"I agree—" Tavarian began, then stopped when a servant rushed in.

"Apologies, my lord, but there's an urgent missive for you." He handed Tavarian a thick cream envelope sealed in wax stamped with Elantia's symbol—a dragon eating its own tail, representing the infinite power of Elantia. Ironic, really, considering the state of the nation now, but I pushed that thought out of my mind and waited on tenterhooks as Tavarian tore open the letter.

"Well?" I asked after a minute had passed. "What does it say?"

He arched a brow, and I flushed a little, remembering that just a few months ago, I wouldn't have dared push him to share his correspondence with me. After all, he was a lord, not to mention my benefactor and head of the house I'd pledged myself to. But after all we'd been through, I figured I'd earned the right to push him a little. Especially considering what was at stake.

"It's a letter from the chancellor's aide," he said, pushing it toward me. "They are leaving Dragon's Table now, and the chancellor implores one last time that I join them." His lips curved into a lopsided smile. "I think I'd rather take a trip to the western front, if it's all the same. Will you join me?"

The knot that had formed in my stomach at the mention of him leaving again loosened, and a spark blossomed there instead. "Hell, yes," I said. Since the missing dragons had come from that direction, it was possible we'd run into them, or at least find some clues as to what had happened to them.

"Excellent," he said. "We'll be leaving in three hours, so I suggest you pack and complete any errands you need to run before we leave."

2

Finished eating, we both left the sitting room, Tavarian to do who knew what, while I checked on Lessie. She'd recently eaten as well, and was flying in restless circles above the grounds, clearly anxious to get going.

"Come down," I called, an irrational fear in my gut despite no signs of danger. "You're an easy target, flying around like that!"

Lessie swooped down, then landed in front of me with a disgruntled huff.

I threw an arm up to shield my face, and coughed as her wings kicked up a cloud of dust around me. *"Be a little more considerate, would you?"* I scolded.

"Sorry," she said, a little sheepishly. But then she tossed her head and eyed me with a gleam in her fiery irises. *"Since when have you become such a worrywart, Zara? Dragons are meant for flying, not cowering in our stables just because we're worried an enemy might come by."*

"I'm just thinking about that airship ambush," I muttered, shoving a hand into my hair. I still remembered finding Ragor and Ullion in the forest, broken and bloody and battered from a shrapnel cannon strike during what was supposed to be a simple training exercise. Not seeing any airships when I'd spotted the Zallabarian force back in Dardil was heartening, but it made me wonder if they'd truly given up on using the airships, or if they were saving them for another purpose. What if they'd built an armada of them, and had used them to take out all the dragons at once?

"That can't be what happened," Lessie insisted, but I could feel the chill in her bones at the thought of her fellow dragons being slaughtered.

"Then what did?" I argued, frustration making my words harsh. *"What else could cause an entire fleet of dragons to disappear? Do you think they all lay down in a field somewhere for a nap and just haven't woken up yet?"*

"Dragons can hibernate for long stretches of time if necessary," Lessie said with a sniff. *"But no, I don't think that's likely. I just don't want to believe they're all dead. Is that so hard to understand?"*

"No." I sighed. *"No, of course not."* I wanted to believe they were alive too. I wanted to believe that Jallis and Rhia were safe, and that Lessie wasn't one of a handful of dragons left alive on this planet. But what had happened to the dragons? Could it be their disappearance had nothing to do with the Zallabarians? Why else would they have failed to arrive?

Knowing I was just chasing my thoughts in circles, I mounted

Lessie and flew by the Treasure Trove to tell Carina that I was leaving again. Needless to say, she wasn't even remotely happy about my decision, but she knew finding the dragons was paramount if we were to stand a chance against the Zallabarians, and in the end, it was better that Lessie and I do something productive rather than sit around and wait for the invasion force to arrive.

"I still think you should leave," I told her as she scribbled something in the ledger.

"Not gonna happen." She barely glanced up from the thick book on the counter, and I noticed she'd nearly run out of pages. A smile tugged at my lips despite our grim circumstances, and I remembered the days not so long ago when we'd stared forlornly at the mostly empty pages of the book, trying to juggle our finances and conjure enough coin out of thin air to keep ourselves afloat. I honestly wasn't sure where we'd be today if I hadn't found Lessie's egg in Tavarian's vault, which had led to Captain Marcas recommending our shop to the higher-end clientele that now patronized us regularly despite being a ground-dwelling establishment. The sky-dwellers living on Dragon's Table and the floating islands many dragon riders called home only came to the ground on business or to seek amusement and cheap thrills. I was proud we were one of the few places that lured them from their luxurious mansions and spectacularly manicured grounds.

"There's no way I'm leaving the shop unmanned just so criminals can bash down the doors and plunder all our hard-earned inventory," she went on, oblivious to my train of thought. "Even with all the preparations we've taken, looting is bound to happen once the city's under siege. Brolian and Kira are already reinforcing the doors and windows, and we've taken on a few more employees to help us guard the place." She glanced up at me, finally catching the look on my face. "What?"

"Nothing—" I said, then shook my head, blinking back a sudden wave of tears. "I'm just thinking you're a giant idiot, and I'm going to miss you so much."

Carina jabbed a finger in my direction, her eyes narrowing to slits. "You are not allowed to talk like that," she insisted, marching around the counter. "You and I are going to see each other again, so don't act like you're going away for good."

"Of course." I wrapped my arms around Carina and hugged her tightly, partially to hide my tears. Despite Carina's words, I knew after everything I'd seen that there was a very good chance I might never see her again. But what really made my throat ache and my eyes burn with unshed tears was both her stubborn refusal to accept the inevitable and her unfailing optimism. She only thought of criminals looting the store, and not Zallabarian soldiers storming the city and destroying everything we owned. Though I wanted to shake her shoulders and scream at her about all the dangers until I was blue in the face, I didn't want to shatter the illusion. There was no point in dashing her hopes, and even if I did warn her, Carina still wouldn't leave. This shop was as much a part of her as Lessie was to me. If the Treasure Trove went down, so would Carina.

Then you just have to make sure it doesn't, I told myself fiercely.

I finished my goodbyes to Carina and the other ground dwellers, then took off for Dragon's Table, a letter clutched in my hand. I didn't know if Rhia was on another mission, or if she was fighting the invaders, but on the off-chance that she'd eventually return home, I wrote a letter updating her on all that had happened and where I was headed now. I knew the chances of her being at her family home were slim to none, but my heart still plummeted when the housekeeper opened the door and informed me she wasn't home.

"Is that Zara at the door?" a female voice called, and I straightened at the familiar voice of Mrs. Thomas, Rhia's mother. She appeared at the door, peering over the housekeeper's shoulder at me with wide blue eyes and flushed, rounded cheeks.

"Yes, it's me, Mrs. Thomas." I smiled, getting a better look at her as the housekeeper moved aside. She wore a sensible dark blue day dress that hugged a plump, hourglass figure. Silver hairs threaded through her chestnut hair, the same color as Rhia's own flowing locks, and they shared the same heart-shaped face and generous mouth. "I came to deliver a letter to Rhia in case she makes it back to Dragon's Table before I do."

"Oh." Her face crumpled a little, and an ache squeezed my chest. I knew she'd been hoping for news of her daughter. "I was hoping perhaps you'd seen her recently. I haven't received a letter from her in weeks."

As a civilian, Rhia's mother was likely out of the loop. "I did see her, not that long ago," I said gently, and then told her about my run-in with her near the Traggaran Channel, and everything that had happened since then. I didn't mention my fear that Rhia and Ykos would get dragged into the battle against the Zallabarians, since they were likely in the direct path of the force marching relentlessly toward Zuar City. Part of me selfishly hoped that my friend would take cover somewhere and wait for the army to pass by, but I knew that wasn't Rhia's way. She would fight to the death to defend our country, as she should. I only wished I knew where she was, so I could draft her into helping me instead.

Rhia's mother seemed heartened at the news that I had seen her daughter alive and well, but she still sniffled, wiping away tears from her red-rimmed eyes. "Well, at least she wasn't at the western front," she said. "When I heard all those horrible rumors swirling about the city, I was worried something terrible might have befallen her."

Still, there was terror in those blue eyes, even though she tried to hide it with her watery smile. She sent me on my way with a small package of pastries and a warm hug, wishing me luck on my journey. I promised her I would send any news of Rhia her way, though I didn't have much hope I'd receive any since I was going the opposite direction.

"I wonder what it would be like if I had a mother who worried about me," Lessie said thoughtfully as we flew back to Dragon's Table. Her own mother and father were long dead, having laid her egg several hundred years ago. *"Part of me is envious whenever the*

other dragons talk about visiting with their own parents. It would have been nice to meet them at least once."

I blinked, surprised at both the train of thought and the forlorn note in Lessie's voice. *"I know what you mean,"* I said, stroking the side of her neck as we glided past a small, puffy cloud. *"I can't tell you how many times I've stared up at the ceiling at night, trying to imagine the sound of my mother's voice, or my father's smile."* I didn't have anything to remember them by, not even pictures, so I'd had to conjure their faces completely from imagination. I'd told myself that I'd inherited my thick lashes and curling hair from my mother, and my eye color and stubborn nature from my father. But in reality, who could tell? For all I knew my hair came from some cousin or aunt, and I resembled my father more than I did my mother. Family traits expressed themselves in all sorts of funny ways.

"Part of me thinks that perhaps it's best I don't have a mother," Lessie said after a long moment. *"That way if I die, there will be no one to mourn me."*

I was about to tell her not to be silly, that I would mourn her, when I realized that was stupid of me. Of course I wouldn't mourn Lessie— when she died, I would die, too. What would happen to us then? Would we simply cease to exist, or was there some afterlife that awaited us? Would we soar off into the stars of some heaven together, or did dragons and humans have separate afterlives?

"There better not be," Lessie growled. *"When we die, we go to whatever paradise or hell awaits us together. I don't care which god I have to fight."*

I laughed. *"Let's focus on staying alive and fighting our enemies in this life. We can worry about fighting afterlife enemies later."*

"Fair enough," Lessie said, and I could feel her smile in the bond, echoing my own. I hoped this sudden turn in mood was a good sign, because we were going to need all the optimism we could get to survive what was coming.

3

Tavarian's errands ended up taking longer than we thought, and by the time we finally took flight, the sun was sinking below the horizon, painting Elantia in streaks of red and gold. As it slowly disappeared, leaving behind a dusky twilight, stars appeared overhead. I found it curious that even though we were so much higher in the sky, the stars were still no closer than they'd been on the ground. To the heavens, it didn't matter whether you were a ground or sky dweller—to us, they were forever unattainable, frosty and distant, yet the guiding light we used to navigate both our lives and the world we lived on.

Tavarian put a hand on my shoulder. The touch sent an electric thrill racing through me, but it quickly fizzled out when I turned around and looked up into a face that was borderline haggard.

"You need to sleep," I said.

The corner of his mouth twitched. "That bad, eh?" He scrubbed a long-fingered hand over his angular face. "I thought I'd keep you company."

My heart warmed at the offer, but the practical side of me rejected the notion wholeheartedly. "In your state, you'd probably end up snoring on my shoulder, and we both need to be alert for what's coming." I nudged him toward the staircase that led below decks. "Get out of here and catch a few hours in the sack. Your crew is more than capable of handling the ship, and Lessie and I will let you know if we see anything of importance."

For a minute, I thought Tavarian would resist, but then he nodded and stepped away. My heart sank a little in disappointment as I watched him retreat, and I told myself to stop being an idiot. Why tell someone to leave if you wanted them to stay? I hadn't been lying when I'd told Tavarian he needed to rest, but that wasn't the only reason I'd pushed him back. Despite the passionate kiss we'd shared earlier, I wasn't sure if getting involved with someone during wartime was a good idea. Although I had every intention of getting out of this alive, there was always the possibility one of us could die. I needed to keep my head clear and my heart untangled so neither of us would trip ourselves up if we were forced to make hard decisions.

Who are you kidding? I asked myself. I was already hopelessly tangled up inside. The sheer relief and happiness I'd felt when Tavarian had walked into the courtroom, strong and alive and oh-so-*vital*, had made my heart swell to three times its size and my stomach do flip-flops. Despite my better judgment, I'd grown to care for the man.

"Hey." Lessie nudged me with the tip of her snout. *"Can we go for*

a ride? I want to scout the area and see if there are any dragons nearby."

"Sure." We'd be able to see much better in the sky than from the deck of the airship, and I needed something to occupy my thoughts that didn't involve the handsome, enigmatic man who was likely stripping down and sliding rough cotton sheets over lean, muscular flesh...

"You're not doing a very good job putting him out of your mind, are you?" Lessie asked, highly amused.

"Shut up," I grumbled. I pulled my riding leathers on and notified the crew I was heading out, then hopped onto Lessie's back. As we took off, the wind rushed over my face and through my long hair, immediately quieting my mind. There was something so peaceful about flying. The feel of the air streaming around us, of Lessie's massive, powerful form shifting and moving as her wings beat on either side of me while clouds darted past us, could be both soothing and intoxicating, depending on my state of mind. It would be so easy to just allow my mind to go blank, to just take in the sights and sounds and sensations as my worries floated away, out of reach.

Instead, I leaned forward in the saddle and adjusted my goggles. As much as I'd love for this to be a pleasure outing, it wasn't. It was a mission, and we had work to do.

Lessie and I flew for several hours, twilight giving way to full darkness. The moon was large and bright in the sky, making it easier for us to scout our surroundings. I zoomed in with my goggles as we flew in increasingly wider circles, scanning the skies and the ground for any sign of our fellow dragons and riders. Lessie mentally put out intermittent calls every few minutes, asking for any dragons in the vicinity to respond.

"Zara," she said urgently. *"Someone answered!"*

I gripped the pommel of my saddle hard, my heart pounding in my chest. *"Who?"*

A pause. *"His name is Temerion. He lives there, with his rider."*

Lessie pointed her snout to indicate the direction, and I focused my goggles. Several leagues away, a stone castle jutted from a sea of trees with purple diamond-shaped leaves.

"There?" I echoed. Even in the darkness, the castle was clearly old and in need of repair, with cracked stone walls and windows, and battlements that looked like they hadn't seen either action or a good broom in hundreds of years.

"He's invited us to land. He and his rider would like to speak to us."

Casting a glance back at the ship, I gauged the distance. It was about thirty minutes behind, so we had some time. Taking my unspoken cue, Lessie made a beeline for the property, then circled above it several times as we checked for any enemies or dangers before landing in the castle courtyard.

A large, black and yellow dragon ambled out of the stables, his rider at his side. They were both old, the man dressed in a well-made but slightly faded brown tunic, his head smooth and bald as an egg even as his strong chin sported a thick, snowy white beard. His eyes were sharp as they looked us over, but the same could not be said of the dragon. Shock rippled through me as I stared into a pair of milky eyes that had likely once been bright as sapphires. The dragon's nostrils flared as he sniffed us, but those eyes didn't so much as flicker.

He's blind.

"Yes, he is," the man said, reading the look on my face perfectly. "But we still fly together often. Temerion has a wonderful sense of direction, and between his keen senses and my own eyesight we are a functioning pair." He gave me a warm smile. "I'm Bartuck of House Vanar. Who are you?"

Vanar. Was that one of the twelve main houses, or a secondary one? I couldn't remember. "I'm Zara Kenrook of House Tavarian," I said, holding out a hand. "Do you and Temerion live here by yourselves?"

He nodded. "Our military days are long over, and after having our chains yanked around for a decade I didn't see much need to run in dragon rider circles and subject myself to more politics and rubbernecking." He gave me a gap-toothed smile that was somehow endearing. "I go to town whenever I need supplies, but other than that, we're happy to keep to ourselves...at least until recently." The smile faded, replaced by a grim look as he glanced toward the skies. "I may be a hermit, but even I take notice when dragons are flying back and forth toward the Zallabarian border and soldiers are marching through my woods. What's going on?"

"The kingdom is under attack," I said bluntly, deciding there was no point in beating around the bush. Bartuck's mouth flattened, but he didn't seem surprised. "An invasion force of Zallabarian soldiers has been sweeping through the land via Dardil in the northeast, swallowing up our towns and villages as they make for Zuar City. At the rate they're going, they'll have conquered Elantia within the week."

Temerion gave a snort of alarm at this, and Bartuck's eyes widened. "Within the week?" he sputtered. "Surely they can't be that powerful. How have we not beaten them back yet?"

A woman appeared at the door before I could answer. "Sir," she said, giving us a gentle smile. "Would you like me to put on tea for your guests?"

Bartuck blushed. "Yes, of course, how very rude of me." He waved me inside. "Please, come sit down while you tell me what's been happening. I'm sure you are weary from your travels."

I would have refused, but it seemed rude to make an old man stand in his own courtyard in the dead of night, so I followed him inside. It was only a little before nine o'clock at night, so I supposed it wasn't so strange to see that the servants were still up and about. For some reason, I'd been surprised to see he had servants, but then again, of course he'd need someone to help him around the castle. He might be a self-styled hermit, but he was still a dragon rider, and all dragon riders came from money.

Except me. But even that wasn't quite true. I might have grown up poor, but that didn't mean my parents did. Which house had they come from? And why did none of my other family members claim me?

The woman—who I gathered was the housekeeper—settled us in the parlor, and I gave Bartuck an abbreviated version of current events while we sipped tea and nibbled on biscuits. As I relived the horrors and trials of the past few months, the confections turned to ash in my mouth, and I quickly lost my appetite as anger and fear roiled in my gut. I left out my personal experiences, including my time in Traggar and my misadventures with Salcombe, but even what little I did tell him alarmed the old man.

"The entire dragon fleet...missing?" He sagged against the faded upholstery of the sofa, his face ashen. "Surely that can't be possible. Just the other day I saw a scout flying at full speed over the forest."

"Well they've either disappeared or deserted en masse," I said, then winced at the bite in my voice. "Sorry. I didn't mean to snap at you. I'm just..." Terrified, I wanted to say, but buried it. "Frustrated."

"No wonder." The man's eyes looked bleak. "My son, Rurian, was fighting at the western front. He could be amongst those who went missing."

My heart ached for him. "Lessie and I are searching, looking for any clues as to where the dragons might have gone. I was hoping either you or Temerion might have seen something, but..."

"But Temerion is blind," Bartuck finished, "and we don't leave the house much."

I sighed and stood. "I'm sorry to have brought such terrible news to your door. I advise you and your dragon to evacuate if you can, and hide any dragon eggs you might have in case the invaders come searching for them."

"Evacuate?" the old man echoed, shaking his head. "I'm not sure where we could evacuate to. No, I'm afraid this old man and his dragon are safer where we are. We do have two dragon eggs, and they are already well protected, but I will take precautions to make sure that if the enemy comes to us, they will not find them." His gnarled hands clenched into fists, and for a moment I imagined them as they would have been forty years ago, strong and healthy as they clutched a blade or aimed a crossbow from dragonback. Another rider might have called those his glory days, but from the way Bartuck had spoken of his military service, I had a feeling he didn't think of them fondly.

"Fair enough." I felt each and every one of my twenty-two years in my bones. Dragon's balls, I was too young to start feeling so old! "Lessie and I appreciate your hospitality, but we should get going now."

"Wait." The old man held up a hand as he got to his feet. "Sit there a moment. I might have something that can help."

He shuffled out of the room, and I sat down, trying not to fidget with impatience. How long had I been here? Had Tavarian's ship already passed us? I hoped to hell that it wasn't so far ahead that we'd lost sight of it.

The man returned a few moments later with a black velvet box, patchy and faded, much like everything else in the castle. But my treasure sense lit up the moment I laid eyes on it, and I sat up straighter at the loud, clear peal of sound.

"What *is* that?" I asked.

"A protection amulet," he said, opening the box to reveal a

golden chain with a large, white, oval gem. The stone was housed in a gold filigree festoon, and together they looked rather like an ornate mirror, albeit opaque. "It has been worn by the women in my family for generations, and my wife wore it before she died. I tried to get Rurian to take it with him, but he refused to wear something so feminine." His eyes shone with tears as he lifted the chain with trembling fingers. "I'm hoping it will protect you instead, so you can find my boy."

I swallowed against a lump in my throat as I took the chain from him. Ninety percent of the "amulets" brought into my shop by enterprising treasure hunters were absolute rubbish, but my treasure sense told me this was the real deal. The tiny gem was warm in my hand, the kind of warmth I only felt from magical objects. It was a valuable piece, and a family heirloom besides—definitely not the kind of gift I should be accepting, especially from a stranger.

But the terror I'd seen in the man's eyes had faded, replaced by something even worse—hope. He was placing that hope on me, on the chance that I would find his son, his only living relative, and bring him back. And though I had no idea if we'd find Rurian dead or alive, I knew I couldn't extinguish that hope by refusing the only bit of help he could offer.

"I'll bring this back to you," I told him, clasping the necklace firmly in my hand. "And your son along with it, if I can."

"Thank you," he said fervently. "That's all I ask."

He helped me clasp the amulet around my neck, careful not to allow the chain to tangle in my hair. I thought about asking him exactly what sort of protection the amulet offered, but I was out of time and didn't want to be regaled with stories. Besides, I told myself as I took my leave, I'd find out soon enough, wouldn't I?

I hadn't really taken the amulet as protection. I'd taken it as a promise, and it was one I'd do my damnedest to keep.

4

"*Well, that was disheartening,*" Lessie said as we took to the skies again. "*Temerion told me he is able to see through his rider's eyes when he needs to, and that he's gotten along well enough without his own eyesight, but I can tell he misses it. Humans don't see the world the same way we do.*"

"*We don't?*" I asked, my curiosity piqued. Lessie had told me she'd spied through my eyes once or twice in the past, but I'd never tried to return the favor. "*What's the difference?*"

"*We see more colors than you do,*" she said, a bit smugly, "*and at much farther distances. Things are crisper, sharper...I suppose you'd have to try seeing through my eyes to really understand it.*"

"*Hmm.*" Closing my eyes, I reached through the bond, deeper than I usually went. Lessie listened in on my conversations quite frequently, but I rarely bothered to do so with her, so I wasn't as familiar with the inside of her head. The moment I entered, I was overwhelmed with sensation. Thoughts not my own swirled around me as I experienced what Lessie was feeling.

An icy cloud brushing my wingtip.

The persistent warmth of banked fire deep within my chest.

The sensation of the harness and saddle rubbing against my scales.

An annoying itch behind the middle spike atop my head.

Smiling, I opened my eyes and reached up to scratch that itch. I was rewarded with both a rumbling purr and the relief and satisfaction I felt when I scratched one of my own itches. It startled me that I had to lengthen my entire torso just to reach the spot—Lessie had grown quite a bit since the first time we'd flown together. The day would come soon enough where she was too big for me to reach that spot while I sat in the saddle. I knew from my lessons on dragonlore at the academy that dragons grew throughout their lives, but how long would this rate of growth continue? When would her body decide it had had enough, and slow down to a more manageable growth? I thought of Odorath, Major Falkieth's dragon, who was the size of a small building. Kadryn was about half that size and hadn't grown much since we'd met him. Perhaps Lessie would slow down once she'd matched him.

Lessie snorted at the thought. *"I'd like to be at least a little bit bigger than him before I slow down,"* she objected.

I rolled my eyes. *"You don't need to be bigger than Kadryn. I've seen the way you boss him and the other dragons around. You're already the alpha."*

Lessie huffed, but I could sense her smug pleasure in the bond. *"We've caught up,"* she informed me.

I blinked, looking at the airship that loomed ahead of us. I'd been so distracted by the experience of being inside Lessie's head that I'd completely forgotten I was supposed to be trying to look through her eyes.

We landed on deck for some rest, then spent a few more hours circling around, calling out to any dragons in the vicinity. Exhaustion dragged at me, but my worry that we might miss something kept us both awake, scouring the land for any sign of battles or struggles.

Unfortunately, we encountered nothing but miles of forest and farmland—rolling hills and valleys blanketed in darkness and starlight. The invasion force had not yet swept through these lands, leaving them untouched and peaceful. But I knew they wouldn't stay that way for long. The second Zallabarian army at the western border would come marching east, ravaging these lands and swallowing up any towns and villages in its path.

Finally, when the faintest tinge of dawn began to crest the horizon, Lessie and I returned to the ship. Tavarian waited for us on deck when we arrived, divested of his coat and waistcoat and dressed only in a rumpled white shirt and trousers.

So much for my idea of him stripping down and sleeping naked.

His black hair was loose, I noticed, and there was a pillow crease on his cheek that was oddly adorable, especially in contrast to his sharp, angular features. But his silver eyes were clear and alert, and the shadows that had dodged his face had all but disappeared.

"Did you find anything?" he asked, not bothering to inquire as to where I'd been. Of course he knew what Lessie and I had been doing. He likely would have been searching the area as well if he'd had his Muza with him. The idea that he was forced to travel via airship rather than dragonback...there was something in me that found the idea vaguely offensive.

"No. We ran across an old man and his dragon living in a castle, and warned them about the invasion, but they hadn't seen anything helpful."

"That's too bad." His gaze drifted to the horizon. "We're closing in on the border mountains, but we'll need to land soon and find someplace to hide the airship. It's best not to travel during daylight hours."

He went to consult with the captain, and twenty minutes later, we'd landed in the middle of a large clearing in a vast forest of high, ancient trees that easily shielded both the ship and Lessie from view, while still having enough space between the trunks that Lessie could move about fairly unencumbered. The clearing abutted a small pond, and there were tracks of varying sizes, indicating local animals used it as a watering hole, but I wasn't too worried. Lessie generally scared off any predators in the area.

While the crew bustled around the ship, securing it for the day and establishing watches, Tavarian went below decks to conference with the council via a magical device used to communicate over long distances. I debated following him down so I could collapse onto my bed, but I felt hunger gnawing on Lessie through the bond, and I realized I could eat as well. The tea and biscuits I'd had at the old dragon rider's house had long been burned up by hours of flying, and I absolutely hated sleeping on an empty stomach.

"Let's go hunting," I told Lessie. I unsaddled her, then hopped onto her bareback and took off through the forest. The thick trunks were the color of molasses, and the plum-colored leaves shielded us from the rising sun, allowing only a bit of dappled sunlight to penetrate to the forest floor. The wind sighing through the leaves was the only sound, but I imagined if I'd been walking by myself, I would have heard birds trilling to each other as they rose for the morning and small animals rustling through the underbrush.

Despite Lessie's size, she was surprisingly swift on the ground, and silent enough that we were able to surprise a herd of trogla. Their slender legs allowed them to run faster than most animals, but Lessie was still able to take down two and drag them into a small clearing, where she happily tore into the carcasses after flash-roasting a haunch for me.

The meat was far more than I could eat in one sitting, so after I'd filled up, I returned the remainder to Lessie, then sat on a large, flat rock and opened up my treasure sense. Immediately, something pinged very loudly, and I was startled to realize it was right beneath my feet. Had I been so tired I hadn't noticed until just now?

Using my talent, I visualized the space below my feet, and got a hazy image of a temple filled with priceless artifacts. Excitement sparked in my blood, and Lessie lifted her head, sensing my change in mood. If only I had my excavating tools...

"Do you want me to help you dig?"

I glanced toward the trogla carcasses, both of which had mostly been reduced to a pile of mangled, spat-out bones. *"Are you sure?"*

Lessie nodded. *"I'm done with these."* She pushed the bones aside. *"Just tell me where to dig."*

I found a spot I thought marked the entrance to the temple, then pointed it out to Lessie. Her large claws cleaved through the packed dirt with ease, and in less than twenty minutes, she'd made a hole large enough for me to stand in.

"Hang on a second." She stopped, and I climbed in, not wanting her to accidentally damage anything. *"I think maybe if we—"*

My sentence was cut off with a shriek as the ground abruptly gave way beneath me. Lessie's roar of surprise and fear echoed as I landed hard on a cracked stone tile floor, and I winced as the impact bruised my tailbone.

"Zara!" She scrabbled frantically as she fought to widen the hole to come in after me. *"Zara, are you all right?"*

"Stop!" I cried, terror gripping me as visions of the entire ceiling

collapsing on me slammed into my brain. *"It's okay, Lessie. Stand back. I'm fine, just a little startled."* And bruised, I thought as I gingerly got to my feet, but I wasn't seriously hurt, so I left that part out. Lessie could sense my pain anyway and knew the difference between banged up and gravely injured. Taking slow, deep breaths, I worked to steady my pounding heart. Light from the hole I'd fallen through illuminated the dusty space around me, revealing faded mosaics and cracked tiles. A motif of lightning bolts and thunderclouds beneath my feet clued me into the temple's god, but the scenes on the walls of a god darting around on a cloud, terrorizing humans and enemies with gusts of wind and bolts of lightning thrown from his hand, settled it. This was a temple dedicated to Sarlin, the ancient god of storms and thunder.

Now that my head had cleared, the chimes and pings of various artifacts became noticeable once more. There was nothing around me but some ancient pottery and statues—some cracked and broken while others remained perfectly intact—but these things were all too large and heavy to take, so I left them where they were, stepping around them gingerly as I ventured into the darkness. As I drew farther away from the light, I dug a matchbook from one of my belt pouches and lit one to help illuminate the space. The first thing that caught my eye was a bejeweled bowl, and I instinctively reached for it, drawn to the sparkle of deep green gemstones.

My fingers barely grazed the surface when a flash of golden light lit the room, blinding me. I stumbled back, nearly knocking the bowl from the stone table it rested on, reaching instinctively for the dragon blade that hung in a makeshift sheath from my belt. I closed my hand around the handle in the center, feeling the reassuring weight of the metal pressing against my palm. In half a second, I could have it spinning in my hand, the blades fully extending as I moved, slicing through whatever had produced that flash of light.

But...what if it wasn't a person? What if I'd activated some kind of spell?

"Put that thing down," a male voice drawled. I blinked rapidly, clearing my vision, and spots of light danced before my eyes as a figure came into view. Tall, handsome, with golden skin and eyes like lapis lazuli, dressed only in a leather kilt that hung to just above his knees, displaying lean, powerful legs. His torso was bare except for a winged torque that rested on his broad chest, and thick, cinnamon hair curled around a wickedly handsome face, the ends barely brushing his shoulders.

"Who..." I sputtered, gaping at the display of masculine perfection. "Who are you?"

Those lapis lazuli eyes flicked lazily to the bowl I'd just touched, then back at me again. "It's generally not a good idea to touch a god's sacred ritual bowl, unless you're planning on performing said ritual," he said. Those eyes glittered as he looked me up and down. "Somehow, you don't seem like the religious type."

I scowled, examining him again as I looked for clues. The winged torque on his neck, the messenger pouch strapped to his belt, the wings attached to the ankles on his lace-up sandals..."You're Caor," I said. "The messenger god." Once, I would have accused him of being a normal man playing dress-up, but after spending my time around Tavarian and handling magical artifacts, I knew the distinctive sensation of power. It hummed in the air around him, far more potent than any mage or artifact I'd ever encountered.

He blinked at me. "You know the old gods." It was not a question.

"It's my business to know you," I said. *So that I can properly price and sell your art and artifacts,* I decided not to say. Despite the very real danger in this situation, I couldn't help the thrill that raced through my blood. Dragon's balls, I was talking to a god!

Caor arched an eyebrow. "I suppose it is, since you make your living stealing from us."

I winced. "I didn't know you guys were real, and the people who built these temples are long dead. How was I supposed to know I was stealing from anyone?"

The god's eyes blazed with anger. "Your ancestors should have taught you our ways. Instead they buried our existence in the sands of time, much as our temples have been buried beneath the roots of forests that were mere saplings when we walked the earth."

My own eyebrows rose. "Is that why you guys weren't here when the dragon god came to our world and nearly destroyed it?" I challenged. "Where were you exactly when our cities were being razed by dragon fire? Or were you all just too weak to stand against him, so you cowered and hid and left us to our fate?"

Caor bared his teeth. "Humans turned their backs on us—" he began to snarl, then abruptly stopped. He smoothed his face into a pleasant expression and cleared his throat. "I must remind myself that neither you nor anyone alive today remembers those times," he said, more calmly. "We did, in fact, send a champion to help your race fight Zakyiar, but your mages mocked and killed him. Everything was fine before we blessed humans with the power of magic, and with the rise of mages, you all decided you didn't need us anymore. It only made sense to leave you to your own fate after you repeatedly pushed us away."

I sensed there was a *lot* more to this story, and that Caor's account was pretty one-sided. I desperately wished I knew more about the gods. There were very few records about them, and most centered around their mythology. Everyone had assumed that they were mere legends conjured by the minds of people who wanted something to believe in, something to explain why the world was the way it was, rather than accepting that everything was random and that there was no point to life. Of course, one could argue that the existence of dragons proved that gods were real...but some argued that Zakyiar, the dragon god, had not been a real god, but simply an extraordinarily powerful specimen of his kind. That he had been vanquished was proof he was not indestructible, as the gods had always been portrayed.

"That sounds pretty stupid of us," I said, trying to placate him. I had no idea what sort of abilities a messenger god had, but I knew I didn't want to be on the wrong side of his ire.

"It was!" Caor tossed his head. "And now you've forsaken us completely and are riding around on these idiotic dragons. They might be fun to fly, but they can't do much aside from breathe fire. They can't shift the weather or shake the Earth or create miracles the way we can."

Lessie's snarl of outrage echoed through the chamber, and Caor looked up. "Oh, is that your mount?" he asked. "I suppose I've offended her."

"Just a bit." I crossed my arms, annoyed. "Is there something you want with me, or did Sarin send you down here to tell me not to touch his ritual bowl?"

"As a matter of fact, there is." Caor leaned his shoulder against the wall, partially covering a mural of Sarin gleefully pursuing a nymph through the forest. "The gods may have turned their back on humans, but they do still watch what is going on every once in a while. Recently, we've felt a stirring in the ether from the dragon god. He is exerting his influence on this plane, trying to claw his way back from the land of the dead to the living. And while most of the gods don't care, I've always had a soft spot for humans, so I came down to check on things."

"With me?" I asked, skeptical.

He shrugged. "You do visit our temples rather frequently. Even if it's just to steal."

I cringed. Couldn't really argue with that.

"Well, you're right that the dragon god is exerting his influence in my world," I said. "My old mentor, Salcombe, found one of the pieces of his heart, and has been working feverishly to recover the rest. He's always been selfish and cold, but it's almost as if madness has taken hold of him, and he'll do anything and everything it takes to get the remaining pieces. He already has two of them, and is on the trail of a third one." I shivered, remembering our last encounter. We'd fought, and his enhanced strength and speed, gifts from the dragon god, had enabled the once sickly old man to deal a blow to my head that would have killed me if I hadn't received medical attention at camp.

"Two?" The corners of Caor's mouth turned down. "With that many in his possession, he may be able to locate the remaining pieces without your help."

I stared. "Just how much do you know about me?" I demanded.

He quirked a brow. "I'm a god. We have our ways."

"Then why am I even talking to you?" I snapped, thoroughly annoyed. "Surely you know everything by now and have the perfect solution to this mess." I understood why the gods had been upset with us—I would have been pretty pissed, too, if I'd sent someone to defend the human race and the humans had killed him for his trouble. I wondered just who this mysterious savior had been, and why we'd killed him rather than accept his help in a time of dire need.

Caor huffed. "If that were the case, then life in this world would be pure bliss and there would never be any problems. And where's the fun in that?" He winked. "This new development is the most interesting thing that has happened in years, and the gods will be watching with interest to see how this unfolds."

I folded my arms across my chest, trying to contain my ire. "Perhaps you all might consider giving us lowly humans a helping hand. After all, if the dragon god wipes us all out, there is no chance that humankind will ever worship you or the other gods again, is there?"

"True," he conceded. "But as I said, none of the major gods want anything to do with you faithless humans, and especially not someone who has desecrated our temples," he added.

"Are you serious? That's ridiculous," I grumbled. *You'd think two thousand years is enough time to get over a grudge,* I added silently.

"Two thousand years is a mere week compared to the long life of a god," Caor said blithely, and I jumped. He could read my thoughts? "However, I am not as stuffy and hardheaded as my peers, so I may pop in to give you a hint or a spot of encouragement once in a while." He flashed a sparkling grin at me.

"Gee, thanks." But despite my sarcasm, hope bloomed in my chest. Ever since this mad quest had begun, I'd always felt one step behind Salcombe, constantly being jerked around even as I fought to thwart him. Now that I had a god on my side—albeit a minor one—could it be that the tables were about to turn? "Any chance you'll be giving me one of those hints now?"

"Not quite yet." Caor made a flourish with his hand, and a gold ring with a diamond-cut ruby appeared between his thumb and forefinger. "However, I will give you this for now." He plucked my right hand up and slid it onto my ring finger, and my skin tingled as a buzz of power rippled through me. My treasure sense blared loudly—perhaps half as loud as it did when I sensed a piece of the dragon heart nearby, which was quite an accomplishment considering I'd never felt anything as powerful.

"What does it do?"

"It will keep me informed of your status," he said cryptically. "Good luck, Zara Kenrook. You're going to need it."

And with that, he vanished.

"Hey!" I shouted. "Get back here! I have more questions!" But my voice echoed off the lonely dirt walls, and I sighed, knowing my words had fallen on nonexistent ears. I placed a hand to my forehead as I leaned against the wall, suddenly woozy. Had I imagined the incident? But no, the ring on my right hand was very real. I rubbed the thumb of my opposite hand over the glittering red stone, marveling at it. A gift, from a real god. Or was I expected to give it back when this was all over?

"Zara!" Lessie's voice broke into my thoughts. *"Are you all right?"*

"I'm fine," I assured her, pushing off the wall. I gave a regretful look at the treasure strewn about the hall, then made my way to the entrance. There would be no more treasure hunting in temples, not if I actually wanted Caor's help. *"Did you hear all of that?"*

"I heard the part about how the gods hate dragons," Lessie growled as I gripped a handhold to hoist myself up. When I'd made it halfway, she reached in and gently grabbed me around the waist, lifting me out. My knees wobbled as they hit the ground, and I took in deep lungfuls of fresh, forest-scented air. *"If that's how they feel, we don't need them, Zara. We've been doing just fine on our own."*

I gave her a droll look. *"You know that's not true, Lessie."*

Her eyes flared. *"Well, they've certainly been no help so far. My* brethren are missing, half our country has been conquered, and Salcombe is still running around unchecked. What good are they if they can just sit by and let these things happen?"

"I can't argue with that," I said, stroking the side of her neck. Beneath her anger, I sensed her quivering fear. She'd been terrified when I'd fallen down the hole, to a place where she'd been unable to reach me, and I couldn't blame her. After being separated for weeks, back when I'd been stuck behind enemy lines in Traggar, she was loath to let me out of her sight again. "But we're desperate, Lessie, and we could use all the help we can get. That alone is enough for me to give them a chance."

I glanced back to the hole, wondering if I should tell Lessie to cover it up. But the moment I had the thought, the hole closed before my eyes, swallowing the dug-up dirt and rippling until the surface looked smooth and untouched. It was as if we'd never been there. I glanced at Lessie.

She huffed. "So, he can manipulate the dirt. I'm still not convinced."

I laughed. "Let's get back to camp. I have a feeling Tavarian's going to want to hear all about this."

As I expected, Tavarian was very interested in my encounter with the messenger god. He was startled when I first mentioned it, but once he'd accepted the idea, he grilled me mercilessly about the experience, wanting to know every detail about the god's appearance and manner, exactly what he'd said, and even more importantly, what he hadn't.

"Fascinating," he said, sitting back against his chair. We were in the ship's formal dining room, picking at the remnants of the plain but perfectly edible fare the crew had cooked up. "For all Caor's claims that the gods are angry at humans and want nothing to do with us, I think the truth is the opposite. It is quite possible that just as the dragon god needs an agent to work his influence in this world, the old gods also need humans. Belief is a very powerful thing, and in the case of the gods, that power could be quite literal. If humankind has ceased to believe in them, it is possible that they are no longer able to influence our world the way they once did."

I frowned. "You think we have that much power over them?" If that was the case, it certainly explained why the gods hadn't just destroyed us all in a fit of pique. I wondered if, by the time the gods had sent their champion, humankind's belief in the deities had already waned enough to weaken them significantly. But then again...how did the gods get their powers in the first place, if they were the ones who created humans? Surely there was more to their strength than just belief, or Caor would not be able to appear to me. Or was this like the chicken and egg argument, and it was impossible to definitively prove which came first?

I pinched the bridge of my nose, trying to stave off the headache brewing behind my temples. Thinking about this might be interesting, but it wasn't productive. It didn't matter how the gods came into being. What mattered was what they were doing now and if they were going to help us.

"I think the gods were helpless, and there was no champion," Lessie

chimed in, sounding more than a little smug. *"Like you said, the lack of humans' belief probably stripped them of their powers, which is the real reason they're so angry at us. Caor probably made up that whole story just to save face."*

I relayed Lessie's theory to Tavarian, who nodded. "That's quite possible. I wish we could go to the state archives, so I could dig through the history books from that time period, and what lore we have available on the old gods. But even if we could, this is hardly the time. We need to focus on the war."

"Agreed." It was ironic, now that I'd switched gears to focus on saving my country, the gods were trying to push me back to the dragon heart quest. Was putting it aside the right thing? What choice did I have? Tavarian and I were the only ones searching for the missing dragons. If we didn't find them, then Elantia's legacy, the very thing that had given us power for so many centuries, would be lost. And so would we.

5

After breakfast, I retired to my cabin for some much-needed sleep while Lessie napped in the forest, well-concealed by the towering trees. I'd been asleep for little more than an hour when a shout filled my head, rousing me from a muddled dream.

"Zara! Come quick! There are enemy ships flying overhead!"

Her words drove all sleep from my brain, and I immediately shoved my feet into my boots and raced up the stairs. Gripping the ship's railing, I stared up at the sky as eight enemy ships, flying in formation, soared over us.

"They seem to be headed for Zuar City," Tavarian said grimly. "Which alone would be bad enough. But *that* is what truly concerns me."

He jabbed a long finger toward the sky, and my eyes nearly popped out of my sockets. Was that a *dragon* bringing up the rear?

"Lessie, have you tried contacting them?"

"No," Lessie said, and the growl in her voice surprised me. *"That's Leeras, and I've never trusted him. He's always been a snitch and a tattletale. For all we know, they're working for the enemy, and reaching out will expose us."*

I blinked, surprised not just because Lessie had once again shown she was capable of wisdom far beyond her baby years, but because I hadn't thought the same. Shame creeped up my cheeks in a red flush. What if I'd told Lessie to reach out to the dragon and given away our position? There was no way we could fight off eight airships, no matter how well-trained our crew was. Tavarian might have magic, but I had no idea what the extent of his abilities were. He'd never been formally trained, so he wasn't as skilled as a mage who'd been raised by a mage family.

I relayed Lessie's words to Tavarian, who frowned. "The dragon rider must be a former cadet, then," he said. "Likely a prisoner who has changed sides to spare his life, as Lessie suspects." He shook his head, disappointment written all over his face.

I stared at the dragon's retreating back, still stunned at the possibility. "It didn't even occur to me that some of our dragons would switch sides," I said dumbly. "But I guess dragon riders are just like anyone else. Some of us are brave, some of us keep our heads down and do what we're told, and some will do whatever they need to save their own skin." My upper lip curled in disgust, and I could feel Lessie's echoed sentiment in the bond. "Do you think there are more like him, then? Did the Zallabarians kill all our loyal dragons and keep the ones who agreed to serve them?"

"I wouldn't rule it out," Tavarian said grimly. "Which makes it even more important to find out what happened."

The sound of the passing airships faded, but my mind continued to buzz, making it impossible for me to consider going back down to sleep. Instead, Tavarian and I stayed up on deck, keeping watch for any other sign of both enemy ships and dragon riders. But we saw neither friend nor foe, and when night fell again, the crew roused and took us up into the sky.

Lessie had catnapped through most of the afternoon and had far too much energy to stay on deck. Besides, the ship moved faster when she wasn't weighing it down, so we took to the air again, circling around the ship as we'd done the night before, searching for clues. This time, Lessie stayed silent, and it broke my heart a little that she was forced to treat her own kind with suspicion. She was far too young for all of this, and yet she rose admirably to the occasion, fearlessly facing down any enemy in our path and trusting my decisions. We made an excellent team, and I knew we would only get better with more experience.

But would we ever fly alongside other dragon riders again? True, there was always Muza and Tavarian, and if the worst came to pass, we could always retreat to that mysterious island. But I hated the idea of Lessie and me being the last dragon rider pair in the world.

You're getting ahead of yourself, I scolded myself. *We don't know what actually happened to the other dragons. For all you know, they're in hiding somewhere.*

I sincerely hoped the dragons had merely gone to ground somewhere, out of reach of Zallabar's nasty airship cannons. But knowing the Elantian army and the stubbornness of our officers, I doubted that they were all safely tucked away in some mountain. If they'd had a confrontation with the enemy, at least some of them would have died. Leeras's rider was Fillian Hallis, a fellow cadet who had been sent off with Rhia to the front while I'd gone to the Traggaran Channel. That meant he'd been part of the fleet that had disappeared. I wished we could have captured him and forced him to tell us what happened, but perhaps we'd get lucky and come upon another survivor.

"Zara!" Lessie's voice was equal parts excited and terrified. *"Look, ahead!"*

I did, and terror gripped my throat, cutting off my air. Several hundred yards away, a juggernaut of an airship loomed ahead of us, bristling with cannons on either side. *"Up!"* I barked, and Lessie shot into the cloud cover above, obscuring us. My heart pounded painfully in my chest as I wondered if the ship had seen us. If even one of those cannons struck us...

"We can't just sit here and do nothing," Lessie protested. *"Whatever that airship is intended for, it can't be good. We need to disable it somehow."*

I sucked in a lungful of icy air. *"You're right,"* I said. *"But we have to do this carefully."*

We waited a few long, tension-filled moments, and then I had Lessie gingerly stick her head beneath the clouds to see where the airship was. Icy drops of moisture clung to my skin, and I shivered uncontrollably.

"It's passed us," she informed me. *"Shall we follow?"*

"Yes."

On silent wings, Lessie dropped below the cloud cover so we could keep the ship in sight. Unfortunately for us, the moon was still far too bright, but we stuck as close to the clouds as we could, keeping far above the ship and managing to keep the moonlight from shimmering against Lessie's iridescent scales. As with the other airships we'd seen, this one was held aloft by a giant gas balloon, so Lessie and I carefully approached. We slowed a few hundred feet away, high enough that we were out of the cannon's range yet still too far away to strike.

"Slowly now," I said as we glided closer. I tensed, knowing that the men would detect the fall of Lessie's shadow the moment we hovered over the ship. Lessie inhaled deeply, and I could feel her scales warming beneath me as she stoked the fire deep within, her chest ballooning with the effort. A few seconds later, we drifted over the prow of the ship. There was silence, and then shouts from the men below. *"Now!"*

Lessie opened her mouth and spewed a great gout of fire directly at the balloon. The canvas immediately caught fire, and we turned tail and sped off in the other direction as fast as we could. Gunfire followed us from the soldiers' muskets, but we were out of range long before any bullets could even hope to graze us.

"Go, go, go!" I shouted, urging Lessie faster. My words were swallowed by a deafening explosion, and Lessie faltered as the heat and force propelled us forward. For a harrowing moment,

we spiraled out of control, and I gripped the pommel tightly as my ears rang and my skull reverberated from the force of the explosion. A few interminable seconds later, Lessie's wings snapped up, and we steadied into a glide.

Panting, we turned to see the ship plummeting to the ground, screams coming from a writhing ball of fire. To my relief, it landed in the middle of the winding road below us, far enough away from the tree line that I wasn't worried about the possibility of a forest fire. We hovered for a moment, watching as the broken ship burned. No survivors crawled or walked from the wreckage. We'd killed everyone on board.

"Should we go down and have a look?" Lessie asked.

I shook my head. *"We don't have time to wait for the fire to go out."* Hopefully it would destroy everything on board. A ship that large had to be carrying supplies, probably weapons, too. *"We've already lost Tavarian's ship again."*

Lessie and I hurried to catch up with Tavarian's airship, and we continued our search through the night. Just as the first rays of dawn touched the horizon, the military camp came into view. My heart lifted at the sight of the tents and buildings, which remained intact. Could it be that we still held it?

"No," Lessie said sadly. *"Take a closer look."*

I zoomed in with my goggles, and my heart plummeted. Emblazoned on the sides of the tents and the flag flying from the headquarters building was the Zallabarian national emblem. The camp had been taken.

Lessie and I returned to the deck of the ship, and I rushed to Tavarian, who was already on deck. "Just in time," he said. "I'm ordering the crew to land now."

"The camp," I said, pointing toward the tents. "It's been taken."

"I know. We'll land someplace safe, out of sight."

We moored the ship in the safety of a nearby forest a few miles from camp. Lessie was absolutely exhausted, and immediately parked herself beneath a row of trees and fell asleep. Part of me wished we could do a fly-by over the camp and get a better look, but with the sky growing lighter by the second, I knew we couldn't take the risk.

"Well, now what?" I asked, throwing up my arms. "We've made it all the way here and we still haven't figured out where the rest of the dragons went."

"Perhaps we could capture an enemy soldier," Tavarian mused. "We could force him to tell us what happened."

"Y-you don't need to find a soldier," a male voice called from the ground. "You have me."

6

Tavarian and I whirled around as an Elantian soldier limped into the clearing, his face contorted with pain. His uniform was tattered, and I winced at the bloody bandages wrapped around his exposed right thigh. His dark brown hair was a mess, his jaw was covered with several days of beard growth, and the skin beneath his blue eyes was dark and heavy with lack of sleep. He gripped a battered sword in his right hand, but it might as well have been a twig for all the use he could make of it—the man looked as if he might collapse at any moment.

"Drop your weapon." Tavarian was in front of me in an instant, but it wasn't necessary. Lessie had awoken, and she swiftly planted herself between the newcomer and the ship, a low growl rumbling in her throat. From our position on the deck, I could still see him, and he immediately dropped the sword, his face going white.

Lessie leaned in and sniffed him. *"He smells like blood and death,"* she informed me. *"But...I don't think he's an enemy."*

I frowned. *"How can you tell? He could be lying about being Elantian."*

Lessie gave a mental shrug. *"Just something about the way he smells. I'm a good judge of character."*

I snorted but gave her the benefit of the doubt. Lessie had liked Tavarian from the start, even when I'd suspected him of wrongdoing, so there was that. "Lessie says he's trustworthy," I said to Tavarian.

To my surprise, Tavarian relaxed, but only a little. "State your name and rank," he ordered.

"Lieutenant Louis Barlay," he answered in a shaky voice. He looked Lessie in the eye again, and his legs quavered beneath him. "I'm afraid I'm going to need to sit down."

He collapsed where he stood, unconscious. Cursing, I vaulted over the ship's railing and landed in a crouch, sprinting over to him. A quick check of his pulse confirmed he was still alive, but it was too slow for my liking. "He's lost a lot of blood," I called back to Tavarian.

Tavarian ordered the crew to bring the soldier aboard. They carried him to the infirmary, where his uniform trousers were cut away so they could get a better look at the wound. "It's infected, my lord," the cook, who also seemed to serve as a medic, said in a worried voice. The stench of gangrene filled my nostrils, and I nearly gagged at the sight of the infected flesh, which was turning a vile shade of black and yellow.

"Leave us," Tavarian ordered. The cook obeyed without hesitation, shutting the door behind him. Taking a deep breath, Tavarian laid his hand directly on top of the nasty wound and closed his eyes, muttering a foreign language under his breath. His hand began to glow with magic, and the lieutenant groaned, his body jerking beneath him.

Tavarian ignored him, continuing to work his magic, and I grabbed the man's hips to keep him still. The power from Tavarian's hands rippled through the room, causing the hairs on my arms to stand on end. His murmured words were similar to the chanting healers used. Healers were a lesser class of mage who specialized in treating the sick and wounded—as I understood it, they didn't have as much power as regular mages, and could only focus their magic on one specialty. But they were just as rare, which was likely why Tavarian hadn't been able to bring one along. But then again, he didn't need one, did he? Had he learned how to do this from listening to healers? Or had he found the spell in a book somewhere?

I wasn't sure how long Tavarian kept up the chant, but when he lifted his hands, the glow faded away to reveal baby pink skin. There was no sign of the awful infection. The lieutenant groaned again, his eyes fluttering open. They widened at the sight of us standing over him, and when he sat up and saw his newly healed wound, his eyes nearly bulged out of their sockets.

"How—"

"My healer took care of your wound," Tavarian said abruptly. "You've been asleep for quite some time now."

"Are you sure? It felt like only a few moments ago." He passed a hand over his forehead, which was no longer clammy and feverish. "When I saw your ship land with that dragon, I only thought to bring you the news. I didn't imagine you would actually be able to save me." He gripped my hand, his blue eyes shining. "Thank you, miss."

A blush rose to my cheeks. "Don't thank me," I said, pulling my hand from his. "I didn't do anything." I wished I could give Tavarian the credit, but I couldn't betray his secret even if I wanted to, thanks to the blood oath we'd taken.

"Maybe, but if I hadn't seen the shimmering scales of your dragon in the sky, I would have stayed up in the trees and died there." He smiled warmly. "I assume you're the reason she didn't eat me."

"Actually, your gangrene is probably the cause of that," I said, wrinkling my nose. When his own cheeks colored, I added, "Though she did say that she thinks you're trustworthy. Are you?"

"I'm certainly not the enemy," he said. His blush turned even deeper as he glanced down again and realized he was only clad in his underwear. "Would someone be so good as to find me a towel or something. I'd rather not give my report half-naked."

Tavarian opened the door and summoned a crew member. A few minutes later, the lieutenant was brought a spare pair of trousers—not military issue, but they covered the important bits.

Once he was dressed, we adjourned to the salon, where he gave us a report while wolfing down the first decent meal he'd had in days.

"There was a big battle three days ago, about an hour eastward on the mountain pass near the border," the lieutenant told us. "Most of us went to fight, but I was ordered to remain behind with a few hundred soldiers to guard the camp and supplies. I don't know exactly what happened, but I surmise the battle was a total disaster. No one returned. Not the dragons or their riders, or even the cavalry and foot soldiers." A shudder wracked him, and he abruptly pushed his plate back, his appetite deserting him. "The Zallabarians swept in here and completely overwhelmed us. It must have been a thousand to one, their numbers were so great."

"Are they holding prisoners?" Tavarian asked.

The lieutenant nodded. "I was among them for a short time but escaped the next day. That's how I sustained that nasty wound," he said, giving me a grim smile. "As you can imagine, morale is terrible. We thought no one was coming for us, and there are rumors of another army approaching from the north. Is that true? Now that you've arrived, I thought perhaps help is coming."

"I'm afraid it is true," I said gravely, not wanting to beat around the bush. My heart clenched with sympathy for the man and his comrades as his face fell, and I wished I had better news. "A massive army cut through Dardil and is sweeping through Elantia now, heading for Zuar City. Lord Tavarian and I came here to seek out the missing dragons, but we haven't seen any sign of them." I decided not to mention the potential deserter we'd seen. No reason to crush the man's spirit further or make him fear dragons even more than the general population already did.

We questioned the soldier a bit more about what had happened, but he was able to tell us little, as he'd neither been at the battle nor stayed at the camp very long after it had been taken. Tavarian had a crew member see him to a spare cabin so he could rest and recover, while the two of us stayed to decide our next move.

"Given the number of enemy soldiers at the camp, and our lack of knowledge on patrol schedules and routines, it may be too risky to try to capture one," Tavarian said. "I will disguise myself as a farmer and venture out to see if I can talk to the locals and get a better sense of what happened."

"Absolutely not," I argued. "You can't go out there by yourself."

Tavarian raised an eyebrow. "I am quite capable of defending myself."

"I know you are." I remembered the one time I'd seen him in dragon rider armor, his sword bloodied as he'd fought through Salcombe's henchmen to rescue me the first time I'd been kidnapped. "But that doesn't mean you should go out there on your own. The magic earpieces only work at certain distances. What if you go out of range, and something happens to you? I've already lost enough friends."

Tavarian's eyes softened. "I suppose you could come with me," he said reluctantly. "But Lessie would have to stay behind."

"No," Lessie snapped, before I could answer. *"You are not leaving me behind. You promised, Zara."*

"Right." I relayed the message to Tavarian.

"If Lessie insists on coming along, then we will have to wait for dark," Tavarian pointed out. "Time is of the essence, so it would be far more prudent for us to leave now and have your dragon join us once night has fallen. She can guard the ship and crew by day, and fly us back at night."

Lessie was silent for a long minute. *"Fine. But the moment you run into any trouble, I'm coming. I don't care who sees."*

"Agreed," I said, reaching out through the bond to soothe her. *"Don't worry, Lessie. We're not going far, so you'll be able to see and hear everything. I'll let you know right away if we run into any trouble."*

"You'd better," she grumbled.

Tavarian and I went off to change clothing, then met at the gangplank. I looked him up and down as he approached—he'd changed into a plain red shirt and brown trousers, completing the look with suspenders and a wide-brimmed hat. For some reason, seeing him in normal workman's clothes made my stomach flutter—they didn't fit him as well as his tailored suits, but they enhanced his masculinity somehow, the rolled-up sleeves displaying his powerful forearms and the open collar just a hint of the tawny flesh beneath. The only thing that didn't quite match was his skin color. While he wasn't the pasty white of an office worker, he also wasn't as well-tanned as a man who worked the fields all day.

Tavarian returned my appraisal as he stopped to stand in front of me, the corner of his mouth curved up into a smile. I'd donned a blue and white dress I'd packed specifically for this—my time in Traggar had taught me the need for disguises—and wrapped a scarf around my head to conceal my distinctive red hair.

"I forgot how much dresses suit you," he said, his silver eyes gleaming. "I might actually prefer this look to the ballgowns you wore back in Traggar."

"Why? Because they're a more accurate representation of my lowly background?" I kept the words light as I stopped in front of him, but I still felt the sting of his insinuation.

"No, because it's something you chose, not something a madman stuffed you in while forcing you to do his bidding." He offered his arm. "I hope you don't mind pretending to be someone's wife again."

I was still stuck on the compliment he'd given, and it took me a moment to respond. "Not at all," I said, taking his arm. It was solid and strong, and my blood heated a little as my fingers curled around bare skin lightly dusted with hair. I wondered why he was offering his arm, then decided that maybe it helped solidify the illusion a bit more. It was certainly better than holding hands.

We walked down the gangplank together, and I patted Lessie's snout as we passed her. I felt her disgruntled glare on us long after we'd disappeared from her sight, and ignored the twist of guilt in my gut. Putting it out of my mind, I stopped to gather some medicinal plants as we walked, putting them in the basket I'd hooked on my other arm as an accessory. We walked in silence for some time, keeping a watchful eye on our surroundings in case we ran into enemy soldiers. Hopefully they wouldn't think anything of us if we did, but I had my dragon blade hidden in the bottom of the basket, just in case.

"Lessie will adjust in time," Tavarian eventually said in a low voice, mindful of being overheard. "Separation anxiety is completely natural, especially in a dragon's earlier years."

I glanced up at him. "I suppose you'd know better than anyone about that." I squeezed his arm in sympathy. "I can't imagine being away from Lessie the way you are from Muza."

He gave me a sad smile. "Some days, especially the days when I watch other riders fly past, are incredibly difficult," he confessed. "While I don't regret giving up the fighting, I miss flying so much, there are some days I can hardly stand it. But Muza's freedom is worth any price, and it isn't as though I never get to see him."

"Do you ever go to the place where he lives now?" I asked.

"Rarely," Tavarian said. "It is not easily accessible."

"Then how do the two of you meet? Do you have a way of getting messages to each other?"

Tavarian shook his head. "Later," he said as we exited the forest. I followed his gaze to a small farm in the distance, maybe half a mile away. I picked up my pace at the sight, and in no time at all we were at the gate. A lean woman in a checkered red and white dress with an apron over it was chasing chickens in the front yard, and we waited as she snatched one up and snapped its neck.

"That's dinner for tonight," she said with satisfaction, then nearly dropped the dead chicken at the sight of us. "My goodness. And who are you?"

"Mr. and Mrs. Berger," Tavarian said, and my mouth dropped open as he affected a perfect country accent. "We have a sheep farm a few dozen miles away, and were thinking about buying some land in these parts instead." He leaned in a little, lowering his voice. "We only arrived yesterday when we heard there's been some big battle here. Is there anything you can tell us about that?"

The woman glanced around, as if she expected a soldier to pop out from a nearby hedge. "Why don't you folks come into the house," she said briskly. "You look like you could use a glass of milk."

We received not only a glass of milk but also some bread and butter.

"This is delicious," I told her around a mouthful of food.

The woman beamed. "We're the finest dairy farmers this side of the valley," she said. "We took great pride in helping provide the military camp with their weekly supply of milk and cheese." Her smile faded. "Or at least we did before the Zallabarians took it.

Now we're forced to supply them instead. They've paid us more than fairly so far, but..."

"You would rather not serve them at all," Tavarian finished gently.

The woman nodded. "I'm not the only one who feels that way, but not all the farmers in the area share my sentiments. There are plenty who are quite happy to serve whoever is buying, and the Zallabarians are actually paying more than we got from the camp. I imagine they're trying to buy our loyalty, but some things can't be bought." She gave us a gimlet stare. "Now, how can I help you? I can already tell you aren't farmers," she said, glancing at Tavarian's hands. "What few callouses you do have come from a sword, not farm work."

Tavarian cleared his throat, glancing around. "Is there anyone..."

The woman shook her head. "My son and husband are at market today, and there is no one else in the house."

"We're trying to find out what happened to the survivors of the battle, especially the dragons and riders that were up here," I said. "The general had called everyone back to Zuar City to meet the invading force that's sweeping through the country, but only a handful of dragons showed up. Someone told us that there had been a battle here, but we have no idea if the dragons were all slaughtered, or if something else happened. Is there anything you can tell us?"

She shook her head. "We did see dragons flying overhead these past few weeks, but they disappeared a few days ago. Judging by the loud cannon fire we heard from the east, beyond the pass, I'm guessing there was a battle, like your friend said, but I didn't see anything firsthand. We farmers tend to keep to our land and away from all that business." She shuddered. "I'd say that if you want to know what happened, your best bet is to go to the battlefield and have a look around."

We asked the woman a few more questions, then thanked her for her time and hospitality and followed her directions to the mountain pass.

"It sounds like the Zallabarians are actively trying to woo the Elantian population," Tavarian said as we walked along the road. "Which is good for the citizens, but very bad for resistance."

"Yeah." I bit my lip, thinking of Carina. Would the Zallabarians try to loot the shop, or would they allow her to stay open and establish some kind of business relationship with her? I remembered General Trattner and his love of history and antiques. Surely, he would be loath to destroy an establishment like that, but then again, I doubted the army had much use for a treasure shop. I supposed it would depend on whether or not Carina decided to work with the Zallabarians or fight them. I hoped it was the former, but knowing her loyalties, and that she was my friend, I had a feeling she would be one of the few who resisted the occupation.

"Stop that," Lessie snapped, breaking into my thoughts. *"You're acting like we've already lost the war."*

"You're right." My cheeks heated with shame. I couldn't allow myself to think like that—attitudes shaped actions. If I already

thought we'd lost, how could I hope to find the missing dragons? *"I'm sorry. It's just hard."*

"I know." Lessie softened her voice. *"I wish I could be there with you."*

I kept in constant touch with Lessie as we walked, occasionally stopping at farms along the road as we drew closer to the battlefield. Like the first woman, none of them could tell us anything about the battle aside from the horrific sounds they'd heard from afar. And while I was disappointed, part of me was glad they hadn't been forced to experience the horror themselves. Their lives were already difficult enough. Why add more heartbreak and terror?

Eventually, we made it up to the mountain pass. My heart froze when I saw it was heavily guarded by Zallabarian soldiers, but they allowed us to pass after checking us for weapons. My heart beat a little faster as the man peered into my basket, and I was thankful I'd thought to hide my dragon blade in the bushes near the beginning of the path.

"Lessie?" I reached out to her through the bond as we crossed. *"We've made it through."*

No answer. *"Lessie?"* I tried again.

"It's possible that the mountain is interfering with your ability to communicate," Tavarian said when I told him I couldn't hear her. "Try not to worry too much. You should be able to reach her when we cross back over."

He gave my hand a reassuring squeeze, and together, we made

our way down the pass. But the warm, fuzzy feeling his touch inspired evaporated as I got my first glimpse of the carnage the Zallabarians had wrought.

"Dragon's balls," I choked, covering my mouth with my hand. Even from here, the stench was horrific. Bile rose in my throat as my world spun—a world filled with heaps upon heaps of corpses. Bodies from both sides littered the blood-soaked battlefield, and the air was filled with the buzz of flies swarming around them, fighting for any piece they could get along with the crows and vultures. The animals weren't the only living things here. Zallabarian soldiers were digging mass graves to dump the bodies into.

Tavarian's hand tightened over mine, his face uncharacteristically pale. He said nothing, because really, what was there to say in the face of such death? An irrational wave of guilt swamped me as I wished Lessie and I had been here, and yet at the same time, I was thankful we weren't.

"I have to go down there," he said once we'd stopped at the edge. There were only a few more feet of gentle incline left until our feet met the battlefield. "Do you want to stay here? I won't blame you if you do."

I shook my head, squaring my shoulders. "I'm not going to run from this."

"All right."

He released my hand, and together, we walked through the field, scanning the fetid ground for anything that could tell us what had happened here. To my relief, there were very few dragon corpses, maybe ten total, and while each one was a tremendous loss in a dwindling population, at least I could take comfort knowing they hadn't all been slaughtered here. But if they hadn't died in battle, then what had happened? It was hard to believe the entire fleet would have turned tail and run just to save their own hides. Dragons were born and bred for battle—they would have risen to the occasion no matter how bad the odds. We tried to approach the mass graves, but the soldiers wouldn't allow us to get close enough to get a glimpse of the bodies inside.

Please tell me Jallis isn't here, I chanted silently to the gods. If they wanted someone to believe in them, to pray to them, well, here I was. *Please tell me my friends are safe.*

But, unsurprisingly, I received no answer. Shaking my head, I continued my search. Really, what was I thinking? That the gods would change their behavior overnight? I wondered if Caor was watching me from their plane, or if he was hidden somewhere in this one. Could the gods walk amongst us, invisible? But then again, if I were him, the last place I'd want to be was here.

I thought I was doing a pretty good job of keeping it together until I passed by another pile of bodies. A soldier working on the other side jostled something, and one of the dead slid from the top, plummeting straight toward me. Tavarian grabbed my arm, hauling me away just in time, but he couldn't save me from the sight of rotting intestines spilling out of the corpse along with a swell of nasty fluid.

Nausea hit me hard, and the next thing I knew I was on the ground, as far away from the corpse as possible as I vomited every last bit of the bread and cheese and milk we'd had earlier. Tears scalded my eyes and cheeks as my stomach cramped and heaved, and I gasped for air in between waves. I was vaguely aware of Tavarian holding my scarf-covered hair out of the way, and when the last bit of vomit had cleared itself from my throat, he rubbed my back in soothing circles as I shuddered and retched.

"Sorry," I choked out when I was finished. I didn't dare turn to look at him. I was sure my chin was covered in drool and skies knew what else, and that my eyes were red.

Tavarian didn't force me to my feet. He merely handed me a handkerchief, which I gratefully used to clean myself up.

"You don't need to apologize," he said. "I had a similar reaction the first time Muza and I walked through a battlefield. Though it wasn't something quite as terrifying as a falling, exploding corpse," he added wryly. "That was a new one."

A smile twitched at my lips, and I was surprised that either of us could find humor in the situation. Did that make us human, or monsters? "What did it for you?"

His eyes darkened. "The sight of a pregnant mother on her back, a spear shoved through her belly."

My stomach turned again, and I would have thrown up again if I had anything left in my stomach to give. "I regret asking," I said hollowly.

"I'm sorry." Tavarian winced slightly. "I wish you didn't have to see any of this. But now you understand why Muza and I had to separate."

Yes. Yes, I did. If Lessie and I had been forced to endure years of this carnage, we might have had each other for comfort, but would our souls be intact? I understood why so many soldiers who'd endured wars were jaded, why they turned to drink for solace or buried their sorrows between a woman's legs. It was one thing to see all this death, but to be a willing participant in it? Just because I'd killed in self-defense didn't mean I was okay with slaughter on a scale like this. The only redeeming factor in all of this was that the civilians had largely been left unharmed.

Gods, why couldn't I stop shaking?

Tavarian's face softened, and he pulled me into his embrace. I took deep, shuddering breaths as he wrapped his arms around me tightly and held me. He didn't try to take advantage, didn't try to press me with platitudes, he merely anchored me, warming my chilled bones and giving me a solid foundation to hold myself up with until I found my own strength.

"Thanks," I said after a long moment had passed. I wanted to stay in that embrace forever, but a fly buzzed by my ear, reminding me that we were standing in a field of death. I pushed away and gave him a watery smile. "Can we get out of here?"

"Certainly." He offered his hand. "I don't think we're going to learn anything more here. Let's get back to the ship."

"You there!" a male voice shouted from behind us, and we froze. Tavarian and I turned as one to see a Zallabarian soldier striding up to us, a shovel in hand. He jabbed a finger at Tavarian, and my heart shot into my throat. I was terrified that he'd spotted us for the spies we were. "You look like a strong, capable man. Why don't you pitch in and help us dig these trenches, eh? I'll give you a silver coin for six hours of labor."

"I—"

It wasn't a request. He slapped the shovel into Tavarian's hand and propelled him bodily toward the trenches. "Get going," he barked. "We need to get this done by sundown!"

By sundown? I stared in dismay, looking around at the mounds of bodies. There had to be thousands of soldiers here. How many days had they already been working on this? If the bodies lying around were only the ones we could see, there had to be many more already buried.

"Sir," I protested, "what about me?"

He looked me up and down. "Too weak and scrawny," he declared. "Go on home. Your husband will be along."

Weak and scrawny? Outrage sparked in my chest, and I shoved it down before I gave myself away. "That wasn't what I—" I began, then sighed when the man strode off without a word.

Knowing I couldn't leave Tavarian out here by himself, I found a spot on the hillside, away from the corpses, to sit and watch. A few of the workers leered at me as I'd passed by, but they were sharply reprimanded by their superiors and reminded they were not to accost the civilians. Most of the officers and soldiers seemed subdued, far from celebrating their victory. But then again, a large number of the dead were their own comrades in arms. Despite my anger and disgust with all the death and destruction around me, I had to admit that the individual Zallabarians did not seem like inherently evil people. But then again, I knew they weren't. I'd visited Zallabar several times, and while they'd never been on good terms with Elantia, as a whole they were normal, pleasant people, just like any other nation. Even the Traggarans, who were ruled by the revolting King Zoltar III, were mostly decent people. They were just trying to live their lives, like everyone else.

I wasn't allowed to sit around for very long. Barely half an hour had passed before a trio of women came up to me, sporting dresses and aprons. "Come along," the one in the middle said briskly, wrapping her hand around my forearm and tugging me to my feet. "No point in moping around when there's work to be done."

"Huh?" I shook off her grip. "What are you talking about?"

She gestured to the soldiers working the trenches. "These men can't run off fuel, and neither can your husband. We need to prepare the noon meal for them. Come along!"

Bemused, I allowed her to drag me off to a tent some ways away, where makeshift wooden tables had been set up. Several fires roared beneath bubbling cauldrons outside as an army of women boiled meat and stewed vegetables. I was steered to one of the tables, parked beside a mound of celery, and handed a large knife. "Chop," the woman ordered.

So I did. I spent the rest of the day chopping vegetables, until it felt like either my arm was going to fall off or my palm would permanently fuse to the handle of the knife. Dragon's breath, who knew so much food could be cooked and prepared in a single setting, and that so many people would eat it? I barely had a chance to sit down and inhale a bowl of the stew we'd prepared for lunch before I was back at it, helping the women wash a mountain of dishes before going back for another round of prepping and chopping all over again.

Finally, when the men had been fed both lunch and dinner, and my lower back was a mass of aches and knots, I was allowed to collapse beneath a tree. I was so tired I wasn't even hungry, and I picked at my bowl of boiled meat and vegetables, wondering where Tavarian was.

A few minutes later, he plopped down next to me. He smelled of sweat and dirt and death, strands of black hair plastered to his sweaty forehead, his skin flushed from the day's exertions.

"Are you okay?" I asked, touching his arm. It was coiled tight, like a spring, and I wondered if he'd be sore in the morning. Tavarian might be fit, but I had a feeling it had been a very long time since he'd ever had to do hard labor like this, never mind an entire day's worth.

He nodded. "Just exhausted. Did you learn anything from talking to the women?"

"Not much." I tilted my head back against the tree trunk, letting the rough bark scratch against my scalp. "Apparently the fight took place in the dead of night, starting around four a.m., so even those who live close to the mountain didn't see much. And none of them know what happened to the dragons. The normal prisoners of war have been taken to camps further east, including many wounded."

"That is good to know," Tavarian said. "Let's hope they get treatment."

Would they get treatment? I wasn't sure if the Zallabarians would bother. "I did hear the Zallabarians have spent the last years beefing up their army considerably," I continued, trying not to think too much about the fate of those soldiers, "which makes me wonder if they've been planning the attack all along, even before the recent coup." The official word was that the new Zallabarian dictator, Autocrator Reichstein, had deposed the previous ruler because he'd felt the Zallabarian government was too weak and wanted to move against Elantia now. But this new information suggested that Zallabar had already been planning to go to war.

"It's possible that Zallabar was planning to attack a different country," Tavarian said tiredly. "But I agree, it does seem strange."

"What about you?" I asked, nudging him. "Did you learn anything?"

"The men I worked with told me much the same," Tavarian confirmed with a sigh. His shoulder brushed mine as he too leaned back against the wide trunk, and I took his hand in mine, turning it over. Large blisters peppered his wide palms, and I winced at the sight of the reddened, bloody flesh. "I recognized several of the dead bodies as officers I'd previously fought with. I don't understand how the council, myself included, could have been so blindsided by all of this. Our spies in Zallabar fell down on the job as well. If only we'd seen what was happening and prepared ourselves better, we might have been able to prevent all these deaths." His voice sounded tortured, and my heart ached with sympathy even as a spurt of anger filled my chest. For as much as I felt sorry for Tavarian, he was also right. The council had willfully stuck their heads in the sand, like a flock of ostriches, and allowed this to happen.

"You need to have this looked at," I said, prodding at his hand. With all the dead bodies around, even minor wounds could get infected.

"I'll take care of it later," he murmured, closing his eyes, and I knew he was referring to his magic. How handy it must be to be able to heal yourself. But it took energy to perform magic, and he wouldn't have the strength if he was seriously injured. I stood up and found a fairly clean rag, dipped it into a pot of boiled water, then returned to his side to clean his abused hands.

He groaned a little as I pressed the cloth into his hand, and the sound, pain-laced though it was, sent a shiver of awareness through me. Pushing away the feeling, I focused my attention on the task, gently but efficiently cleaning the wounds.

"Thank you," he said in a voice like rough velvet. I released his hand, but rather than pulling away, he gripped me tighter. My heart pounded, and for a moment I thought he was going to pull me in for a kiss. Instead, he gathered his legs under himself and brought us both to our feet.

"We need to get going," he said under his breath. "Before these men find another way to put us to work."

Right. Lessie couldn't very well pick us up from this location. I tried reaching out to her again, but the bond was still eerily quiet. Damn. We needed to get to a better spot where we could talk to each other and where she could pick us up with minimal risk. My muscles twitched with nervous energy, eager to burst into a run, but I forced myself to follow Tavarian's steady pace. Running would only draw attention.

My body remained tense as we traversed the mountain pass once more, subjecting ourselves to another invasive search from the soldiers. I didn't relax until I'd retrieved my dragon blade and we were back in the valley.

"Do you think—" I started to say to Tavarian, when Lessie's voice burst into my head.

"Zara! Are you all right?" Her frantic energy sizzled through the bond. *"I haven't been able to reach you!"*

"We're both fine," I said gently. *"I'm sorry I scared you, but the mountain must have interfered with our connection."*

"I'll say," she said grumpily. *"Did you find anything?"*

Instead of answering, I sent her an image of the battlefield. Lessie's shock and pain hit me with the force of a gale, especially when she saw the dead dragons, but after a few moments it was gradually replaced by suspicion.

"There aren't enough dragon bodies," she said. *"Where are the others?"*

"We don't know," I said. *"Tavarian and I were roped into cooking and helping the soldiers bury the dead, so we haven't been able to do much*

investigating." I briefly told her what we'd learned from talking with the other workers. *"We'll discuss what to do next when you get here."*

"That won't be for some hours yet," Lessie said. The sun was kissing the horizon, but full darkness was still a few hours away. *"Find someplace to hole up and sleep until I can get you. You're exhausted."*

I relayed the conversation to Tavarian, and he nodded.

"We should try to get as much sleep as we can, since we'll be traveling again come nightfall," he said. His silver gaze swept the surrounding terrain. "Perhaps we can find a cave or build a temporary shelter in the woods."

Unfortunately for us, these woods were rather sparse, with no good shelter to be found. Worse, the area was heavily patrolled by Zallabarian troops, and even though we weren't dressed like Elantian soldiers, we still didn't want to run into them. The Zallabarians might be under orders not to provoke the civilians, but that didn't mean we could trust them.

My feet ached when the skies opened up, instantly soaking us in a downpour. "Can't you do anything about this?" I shouted at Tavarian over the sounds of the storm. What was the point of having magic if you couldn't use it to influence your surroundings or make yourself more comfortable?

"I think I would draw a bit too much attention if I used my magic to banish a rainstorm," he said dryly, blinking at me through wet eyelashes. Raindrops slid over his high cheekbones, matting his inky hair, his clothes clinging to him like a second skin.

I raised an eyebrow. "Does that mean you can do it?"

He glanced up at the sky. "I've never tried. However..." He skimmed a hand over the top of my soaked head and ran it down my back. My lower belly tightened with desire, but the tingles I felt weren't merely the product of lust. Magic emanated from his touch, and my skin tingled as sparks skipped down my spine.

He stopped just above the curve of my ass, then removed his hand. "Better?"

I blinked. The rain hadn't let up, yet it wasn't hitting me anymore. The water slid right off my arms, as if Tavarian had covered my entire body in some kind of tarp or oilcloth, repelling the rain so that it sluiced directly onto the ground and away from my skin.

"Yeah." I stared wonderingly at him. "I can't believe that worked."

He smiled crookedly, and my heart flip-flopped in my chest as the expression softened his features. Tavarian bore the weight of his title and responsibilities like a second skin, and yet in these rare moments he seemed almost boyish. "I used this spell when Muza and I would fly in the rain, but it's been so long I'd forgotten it." He ran his hands over his own body, rain-proofing himself as he'd done with me. "It doesn't keep out the cold, but at least we won't get any wetter."

"You can say that again," I said as a chill wind buffeted us. My teeth chattered, and I instinctively wrapped my arms around my midsection for warmth. By unspoken agreement, we set off again, battling the winds, until we happened upon an abandoned barn in the middle of a field.

"This will do," Tavarian said as he shouldered the door open. It swung inward with a hair-raising screech, and I wrinkled my nose at the smell of old hay. "We can bed down here for a few hours while we wait for Lessie."

Tavarian and I did a thorough search of the barn to make sure no one else was hiding here, but the only other residents were a few field mice sheltering from the rain. Most of the hay on the ground floor was too moldy to use for bedding, but we found relatively dry, clean hay in the loft.

"I wish we could start a fire," I said, my teeth still chattering. I drew my legs into my body and wrapped my arms around them, trying to conserve the heat, but my clothes were still too wet and icy from the rain to make a difference.

"We can't risk drawing attention, and I also don't want to accidentally set the hay aflame," Tavarian said ruefully. The sunlight had completely disappeared, driven away by the storm clouds, so his features were cast in almost complete darkness. "However, that doesn't mean I can't warm you up."

He leaned in, hands outstretched, and murmured something as he placed them on my shoulders.

I gasped as a flood of warmth filled my body, and it wasn't just his body heat. His hands glowed with power, and wafts of steam billowed up from my shoulders as he drew the damp from my skin and clothing.

"Relax," he coaxed, his deep voice soothing. He ran his hands slowly down my arms, using his magic to warm me while simultaneously pushing me onto my back. A small voice in the back of my mind cried out a warning that allowing him this close was dangerous, but a tidal wave of desire swept over me, drowning out that voice. Sighing, I relaxed into the hay, allowing my arms and legs to fall at my sides, opening myself to his touch.

Tavarian locked gazes with me, and the air around us shifted, growing charged with unspoken desires. Slowly, he dragged his gaze down, following his hands as they slid up my hips and along my sides, molding to my curves. My breath caught in my throat as they brushed the sides of my breasts, and when his gaze dipped to my cleavage, my face heated as I realized my nipples, aching from both the cold *and* the heat, were pushing through my dress.

He paused, a beat of hesitation. Unwilling to break the spell, I answered not with words but by arching my back, offering myself up to him. His eyes flashed, and he clamped a hand over my right breast. Delicious heat seeped into my skin, and I bit my lip on a moan as his calloused palm rasped against my nipple.

"No." He shifted, and I gasped as he nipped my lower lip with his own teeth. "If we are going to do this, I don't want you to hold back." He covered my other breast with his left hand, heating me in more ways than one. "I want every gasp, every moan. I want *all* of you."

His words ignited a wildfire in me, and when he leaned in to nibble my earlobe, I couldn't hold back the moan that burst from my lips. "All of me?" I gasped. "What does that mean?"

"I think you know exactly what it means," he said, his left hand gliding down my side. A delicious shiver rippled through me as his fingers worked beneath my shirt, their warmth seeping into my chilled skin. I was tempted to let him keep going, to strip me bare so we could take and take from each other until there was nothing left to give.

But my mind refused to shut up, so I grasped his hand and pushed up onto my elbows.

"No." I looked into his eyes as I held his hand between both of mine. "I don't know exactly what it means. I don't know if 'all of me' means my body, my heart, my soul, or all three. And I don't know how long you want it either. What is this between us, Tavarian? What are you thinking when you—"

"Zara." Lessie's voice cut off my train of thought. *"I'm almost there. Where are you?"*

"On a farm. We're hiding in a barn," I answered her as Tavarian scowled.

Lessie immediately sensed the situation through our bond, and I could hear the grin in her voice. *"Am I interrupting something?"*

"No." My voice came out sharper than intended. "Lessie's here," I told Tavarian.

"I see." Tavarian's face was a study in conflicting emotions, but he quickly mastered himself. "We'd better get going, then," he said softly, his face inscrutable once more as he held his hand out to me.

"Right." We climbed down the ladder, and Tavarian re-did the moisture-wicking spell before we stepped outside. It was still raining, but the rain had reduced from the deluge into a steady pitter-patter. Squinting through it, I could just make out Lessie's silhouette as she glided in. She landed right in front of us, and I climbed on first, Tavarian coming up behind me. Another wave of warmth surged through me as he wrapped his arms around my waist, pulling me back against his rock-solid chest.

"We'll finish this conversation later," he said, his lips brushing against my earlobe. Another shiver went through my body, and I shifted in the saddle, trying to get comfortable and relieve the tension between us.

"Where to?" Lessie asked, a welcome distraction.

I glanced over my shoulder at Tavarian. "Should we head back to the airship?"

He shook his head, glancing up at the rain-streaked sky. If his mind was still on our interrupted conversation, he gave no sign of it. "We should take advantage of this cloud cover and search for the missing dragons. It is clear they were not slain here, and they couldn't have disappeared, so they may have been taken into Zallabarian territory."

"All right," Lessie said. She flapped her wings, and with a powerful flex of her legs, launched us into the sky. Visibility was fairly poor in this weather, with little to no moonlight to guide

our way, but between Lessie's superior sight and my treasure sense, we could easily avoid any enemies on land or in the sky.

We flew for several hours in silence, Lessie putting out a mental call to any nearby dragons. Zallabar was a large country, but still, we managed to cover a good third of the distance from the border to the capital without receiving any response. How was this possible? An entire fleet of dragons didn't just up and disappear. They had to be *somewhere*.

"We need to head back," Tavarian said into my ear. Between his body at my back and Lessie's beneath me, I was quite warm. If not for the dire situation, this would have been one of the most pleasant dragon rider flights I'd been on. The feel of his inner thighs squeezing my legs reminded me of my early rides on Jallis's dragon, and the pang of guilt I felt drove away any lingering desire.

How can you be thinking of sex at a time like this? I scolded myself as Lessie turned around. It was one thing to be attracted to Tavarian—nobleman or not, he *was* a handsome man—but it was quite another to act on it while our friends were missing and our country was under attack. Maybe under other circumstances I could consider a fling, but the last thing either of us needed was to be distracted. It was only Lessie who had interrupted us, but what if it had been the enemy? What if Zallabarian soldiers happened upon us one night while we were tangled up together, our minds muddled by lust and our pants around our ankles?

A tumble in the hay isn't worth your life, Zara, I told myself sternly. If I wanted to keep my head, I was going to have to keep my distance from Tavarian. The man did strange things to me with his crooked smiles and talented hands, and I couldn't afford to let myself get wrapped up in him when death lurked around every corner.

We made it across the border just as the first rays of dawn gilded the horizon, and were safely hidden in the clearing by the time the sun was up. The moment Lessie landed, I jumped down and headed for the airship, not waiting for Tavarian to follow.

"Is Lieutenant Barclay awake?" I asked the captain. "The wounded soldier?" I prompted when he didn't immediately answer.

"Oh. Yes! I believe he woke an hour ago." He jerked his thumb to the stairwell. "You'll find him below deck."

I made a beeline for the infirmary while Tavarian got a report from the captain. The lieutenant wasn't in there anymore, but the crew directed me to a cabin just a few doors down, where he was sprawled on the mattress. He was dressed in clean clothes that hid the bandages on his leg, and I was pleased to see some color back in his cheeks, though he was still clearly exhausted.

"Private Kenrook," he said, struggling to a sitting position. He frowned as I grabbed the chair in the corner and dragged it over to his bedside. "Or is it private? The crew told me that was your rank but that seems wrong based on what I've heard of you."

I shrugged—rank didn't matter to me anymore. I couldn't care less what the military thought of me after what they put me through. "You can call me Zara if you like." I sat down and braced my elbows on my knees as I leaned forward. "Lord Tavarian and I just came back from visiting the battlefield."

The color drained from his face, but to his credit, the man squared his shoulders. "And? What did you find?"

I told Barclay what we'd seen and learned, Tavarian walking in halfway through the conversation. He interjected with a few details here and there—mostly stuff he'd observed while digging the mass graves—but aside from that allowed me to do most of the talking.

Barclay sagged against the pillows when I'd finished. "I'm glad to hear you only found a few dragons on the battlefield, but that doesn't really tell us much, does it?" He shook his head. "At least we know for certain that they didn't kill the survivors. Although I wish I knew how many they'd captured, and if any managed to flee."

"We may have to risk flying back into Zallabar during daylight so we can have a better look," Tavarian said. "There could be signs of fleeing soldiers that we missed. We also need to gather intelligence, something best done by sneaking into a town or village and questioning the citizens."

I knew Tavarian was right. But the thought of Lessie flying over enemy territory in daylight, within reach of those terrible cannons, was more than I could bear. Fear squeezed like a vise around my heart as I imagined, not for the first time, those terrible shrapnel cannons punching holes in her wings, sending us both plummeting to our deaths.

"I agree that we need to go to Zallabar to investigate," I said. "But

I won't take Lessie."

"Like hell you won't!" Lessie snapped. *"You promised we wouldn't be separated again, Zara."*

I bit back a growl of frustration. *"I know what I said, but I can't put you in danger like that. It'll just put us both at risk."*

"I don't care. Either we go together, or we don't go at all."

"Let me guess," Tavarian said, amusement coloring his voice. "Lessie insists on accompanying us?"

"Yes." My brow furrowed. I didn't want to go against Lessie's wishes—unlike some dragon riders, I considered her a true partner, an equal in all the decisions we made together. And yet, how could we do this without putting her in danger?

Tavarian seemed to sense my internal conflict. "It won't be easy, keeping her hidden, but if we stick to the forests by day it should be doable. Besides, Lessie can sense other dragons at great distances, something that is invaluable if we hope to find them. She really should come with us."

"See?" Lessie said smugly. *"Even Tavarian agrees I should come."*

I fought against the urge to roll my eyes. "Fine, then we'll take her."

We went our separate ways—Tavarian to inform the captain of the change in plans, and me to my quarters for some much-needed rest. Someone had filled the wash basin with fresh water, so I stripped down and used the accompanying sponge to clean myself up. The smell of sweat and death from spending all day in that battlefield still clung to me, and I desperately wished for my shower back home, where I could stand under the hot spray and scrub the memories, if not from my mind, at least from my skin.

How long until the invasion force reaches Zuar City? I wondered as I slipped on a fresh set of clothes. I didn't dare sleep in pajamas, not while we were in enemy territory. Surely it was only a matter of days. Part of me wished Lessie and I had stayed back to meet the enemy head-on rather than leaving Carina and the orphans to deal with the threat alone. But Lessie and I wouldn't make much difference against such a large force—we were of better use sticking to our current mission.

Flopping onto the bed, I closed my eyes and tried to drift off. Though exhaustion tugged at my mind, I was far from ready to forget the day's events. The sight of all those carcasses, piled on top of each other like slabs of meat in a charnel house, curdled my stomach. That body that had nearly fallen on top of me, the way its guts exploded out of its abdomen when it hit the ground—

Stop, I ordered myself, my eyes popping open. *Think of something pleasant.*

I closed my eyes, and this time a different memory seeped in. Tavarian, gliding his hands over my body, using his magic to warm me. My blood heated as I remembered the way his touch had felt—firm yet gentle, at least in the beginning. But his touch had turned sensual, and the molten look in his silver eyes as he'd gazed upon me, as he'd felt my body react, made my breath come a bit faster.

It would be so easy to get up and seek him out. So easy to tell him I wanted a word, then take him back to my room and strip off his clothing. I could let him push me against the wall, take my mouth and my body, fist his hands in my hair and make me forget about the horrors. So many soldiers found comfort in the arms of their comrades. Was this really so different?

Yes, a voice in my head said sternly. Because Tavarian wasn't just some fellow comrade-in-arms, a warm body I could roll around with one day, then forget the next. He was the man who'd taken me in when he could have had me killed—the man I'd pledged my loyalty to. The man who'd taught me it was possible to fight for your country without compromising your integrity.

He was a man who, if I wasn't careful, I could easily fall in love with.

And he's a distraction, I warned myself. The fact that we'd been ready to rip each other's clothes off when we should have been watching for enemies was proof enough of that. Besides, I'd already told myself that I was going to keep my distance. Why was I still thinking about this?

"Lessie?" I asked. *"Are you awake?"*

"I am now," she said, a bit grumpy. But I felt her irritation slide away as she sensed my own turmoil. *"Is everything all right, Zara?"*

I sighed. *"I'm just so...frustrated. We've been searching for days now and we still don't have any idea where the dragons could have gone. How does a host of over one hundred dragons and riders disappear?"*

"The most likely explanation is the Zallabarians have taken them,"

Lessie said. "Although it seems impossible to corral so many dragons, it's possible they could have done it with the aid of those cannons." A wave of grief and anger rolled through the bond. "Those dead dragons in the field could have served as threats."

"Or the Zallabarians could have figured out how to capture the riders," I said. "With their riders as leverage, they could make the dragons do almost anything, including fly wherever they want them to go." While dragon riders were able to impose their will on their mounts, a dragon could resist under certain circumstances. The impending death of their rider, whose life was tied to their own, was definitely one of those situations where the dragons might act independently.

"Agreed," Lessie said. "There isn't much I wouldn't do to save your life, Zara, even if I had to submit to the enemy for a while. Where there's life, there's hope, after all."

"Still," I said, "I can't understand what the motive would be for the Zallabarians to take the dragons alive. It's a lot of trouble, and very expensive to feed over a hundred of them. Not to mention that aside from threatening the lives of their riders—which will only take them so far—there's no way to control the dragons."

"I don't know, but I know we're not going to be able to puzzle it out while we're exhausted." Lessie gave me a mental hug, and her warmth curled around my soul, as if she were in the cabin with me. "Go to sleep, Zara. We'll need our wits about us if we're going to be traveling in enemy territory."

7

Once I finally managed to fall asleep, I was out like the dead. One moment I was talking to Lessie, and the next, a crew member was prodding me awake.

"Whaa?" My mouth felt fuzzy, as if I'd licked a trogla pelt. "What time is it?"

"Nearly nightfall," the sailor informed me. "Lord Tavarian asks that you pack your bag and meet him in the mess hall."

I did as he asked, and after a quick meal, we were airborne. Since Lessie was carrying us both, we'd packed light—only two changes of clothes, including civilian outfits to blend in, some basic hunting gear, our weapons, and some first aid supplies. We would have to hunt and forage for our own food along the way, though with Lessie to help out, it shouldn't be too hard to get meat, at least.

The clouds, unburdened from yesterday's rainfall, were thin and light, providing less cover than we'd hoped. Thankfully, Tavarian's cloaking spell meant we didn't have to rely on the cloud cover as much as usual, and we struck north, avoiding the battlefield and the areas we'd already covered the previous day. In no time at all, we were in Zallabarian territory, flying across mountains and forests very much like the hidden valley where Lessie and I had trained.

When I said as much to Tavarian, he nodded.

"The hidden valley is only a day's flight northwest of here," he told me, leaning in to murmur in my ear so he wouldn't have to shout above the wind. I shivered a little as the warmth of his breath ghosted along my ear. I'd spent the last thirty minutes studiously ignoring the feel of his body against mine, but now that he was speaking to me in that low, inviting voice, I had to actively fight the urge to lean back against him.

"The hidden valley would be a good place to hide the dragons," I said, hoping he didn't notice the slight breathlessness in my own voice. Was he *trying* to be tempting? Or was this how he always was with women whom he let his guard down around? "Perhaps if we find them, we could take them there."

"Perhaps, but remember, the location has been compromised by Salcombe," he said. "Of course, he may not be a threat now that he no longer needs you, but..."

"Right." I clenched my jaw. Tavarian didn't need to finish the sentence. Salcombe was unpredictable. He might not need me now, but he could change his mind, and he would come for us eventually as Tavarian still held one piece of the dragon god's heart. I wondered where he'd hidden it, then decided it was better not to ask. If Salcombe *did* come for me, at least he wouldn't be able to torture the location out of me.

Then again, if he truly was able to sense it, as Caor had suggested, what difference did it really make?

I rubbed the ring on my right hand with my left thumb, wondering if he was watching me now. Was he annoyed I wasn't making any effort to go after the dragon heart pieces?

"Who cares?" Lessie said, sounding more than a little disgruntled. Clearly, she hadn't gotten over her hatred of the messenger god just yet. *"If he's not going to do anything to help, he has no right to complain."*

"I agree." Still, I felt a little guilty that I'd given up on the quest, even if it was just temporary. Yet, I couldn't be two places at once. As long as Tavarian still held one piece of the heart, Salcombe couldn't resurrect Zakyiar. And though he had those false citizenship papers to protect him, even Salcombe would be hampered in his movements by the ongoing war, which would affect Zallabar and all surrounding countries. Hopefully that would hold him up long enough while we solved the mystery of the missing dragons.

Lessie called out repeatedly to any nearby dragons, imploring them to respond. For over two hours we traveled without seeing or hearing a damned thing, a fact that frustrated both of us. I could feel Lessie's increasing hopelessness. I tried to hold my own emotions back in the bond so as not to drag her mood down further. My experience as a treasure hunter told me that attitude was extremely important—if you set out thinking you weren't going to find anything, you'd overlook important clues that a more optimistic mind would have spotted. Until we saw evidence that indicated otherwise, we had to keep our spirits up. We had to assume the dragons were alive.

Eventually, we crossed a broad river flowing toward the northern sea, a winding river of silver in the pitch-black landscape beneath us. But the river wasn't the only source of light. Tiny yellow pinpricks indicated the presence of civilization—towns, villages, vineyards. As I zoomed in with my goggles, my stomach tightened at the sight of a nearby garrison.

"We need to land," I said out loud, speaking to both Tavarian and Lessie.

"Agreed." Tavarian pointed to a forest about twenty miles from the nearest town, nestled between two towering hills. "That spot should work nicely."

Lessie immediately banked right, heading in the direction Tavarian indicated. She landed a few miles outside the nearest town, just long enough to allow us to dismount. *"Don't do anything stupid,"* she said as she nuzzled my side, the words both warning and affectionate.

"Same to you," I said, rubbing her snout.

She snorted, then took off with a flap of wings, buffeting Tavarian and me with a torrent of grass and dirt-filled wind.

Once Lessie's form faded into the distance, I turned to look at the town. It was a pretty town, nestled right alongside the river, and I could make out the spires of a castle silhouetted against the moonlight. A fairly wealthy town that likely did a brisk business in trade, thanks to its location.

"The sun is already starting to come up," Tavarian noted, indicating the horizon with a tilt of his chin. Sure enough, it was starting to lighten, bringing the grey beginnings of twilight. "If we start walking now, we should arrive at dawn."

We took a moment to change out of our flying leathers and into our civilian clothes, then made the trek to town, once more in our roles as husband and wife. By the time we arrived at the gates, the sky had lightened to a blushing pink, softening the thatched roofs and stone walls of the houses and buildings that lined the streets. A long line of traders, some with carts and wagons, others on horseback or foot, passed slowly through the open gates as they headed to the market, and we seamlessly blended in, just another couple visiting. A sign above the gate pronounced the town's name as Krallitz. Judging by the size and what I'd seen from similar Zallabarian towns I'd visited in the past, I estimated its population at around twenty thousand people.

"No signs of war here," I murmured as we walked through the streets. Even at this early hour the town was busy—smoke wafted from chimneys, wagons rolled and horse hooves clopped, while errand boys darted through the crowds, carrying parcels or messages in their small hands. There were no haunted faces here, and despite the nearby garrison, hardly any martial presence in the town. If I hadn't seen the death and destruction at the border with my own two eyes, I could convince myself that the war was just a bad dream.

"There wouldn't be," Tavarian said softly. "After all, they are invading us, not the other way around."

His words filled me with unexpected rage, and I clenched my hands into fists before I remembered myself. It seemed supremely unfair that the Zallabarians were going about their day-to-day lives as if nothing was happening, as if a few miles away they weren't butchering our soldiers and stealing our lands. A dark, buried part of me wanted to lash out at them, to set fire to their homes and run my dragon blade through their guards and soldiers.

But then again, hadn't we done the same to them? Hadn't we invaded their lands, stolen their own resources, beaten and humiliated them on more than one occasion? For all I knew, my dragon blade, which was an old weapon from the days when dragon riders were still a new force in the world, had been used to subjugate the ancestors of these same people. It would have been one thing if we'd conquered the other countries, brought them under our banner, and improved the quality of life for everyone, but we hadn't done that. Instead, we'd taunted and bullied them, and paid no attention as Zallabar built up their resources to surpass our own.

It was our own arrogance that had brought this upon us, and in truth, the townsfolk here weren't to blame. Just because their leaders had decided to make war on my people didn't mean that they didn't deserve to live their own lives and take whatever comfort and joy they could find.

"It's all right." Tavarian squeezed my hand. "It's natural to be angry at them, even if this war is through no fault of their own.

Soldiers have to dehumanize the enemy, lest they lose their own sanity."

"But I don't want to dehumanize them," I said, knowing and hating how petulant I sounded. "I hate that my heart is so full of hate, even if it was just for a moment. What if I keep going down this path? What if I become just like the enemy?" I thought of my time in Traggar, how the people had spoken of Elantians with such derision, how they'd mounted a dragon head in the town square and cheered. What if I became like *that*?

"But that is what's so wonderful about you, Zara." The warmth in Tavarian's voice took me by surprise, and I glanced up. He looked down at me, an almost tender expression on his harshly handsome face. "You recognize that darkness, and you fight it with every breath you have. That ability is more valuable than any weapon, even ones formed by the finest smithies. It is those who forget that humanity, who allow the darkness to take hold of them bit by bit, who become the very thing they hate."

Tears pricked at the corners of my eyes, and I hid them behind a smile. "I didn't know you were such a wordsmith, Tavarian."

He gave me another one of those crooked smiles. "I do happen to have a career in diplomacy. Words are my primary trade."

I raised an eyebrow. "Is that what this is, then? A negotiation with my sanity?"

"No." He lifted my hand to his mouth. "It's a negotiation with your heart."

Heat raced down my arm and straight into the center of my

chest, where my heart flip-flopped wildly. Was he talking about the feelings between us? Or my feelings regarding our mission? Or something else?

"If the women of Elantia knew you were such an impossible flirt," I teased, slipping my hand from his before I got myself into serious trouble, "they would be throwing themselves at you left, right, and center."

To my surprise, his gaze darkened. "You would think so, wouldn't you?" he said softly.

"Did...did I say something to upset you?" I blinked, confused at his sudden change of demeanor. One moment he was warm, inviting, squeezing my hand as if we were a real couple, and now he was frigid, like an unexpected northern wind cutting through a balmy summer day.

"No." He shook his head, clearing the emotion from his face. My heart sank in disappointment—the blank mask he wore was firmly back in place. "Let's head to an inn and buy some breakfast. Perhaps we'll overhear something useful along the way."

The message was clear—mouth shut, eyes and ears open. I focused on my surroundings, pushing aside my jumbled thoughts and feelings and emptying my mind. Several loud chimes tugged at my treasure sense despite the fact that I'd toned it down, but I ignored them, instead focusing on the swirl of conversations around us. We stopped at the market, where we both purchased jackets, scarves, and gloves for the increasingly chilly weather, then ducked into an inn a block over. The smell of eggs, buttered toast, and jam nearly bowled me over with hunger, and Tavarian and I quickly ordered, eager to fill our hungry bellies. I hoped Lessie was able to find food in the forest. I'm sure she was even hungrier than us, since she'd carried us both through the night.

She's come a long way since her first flight, I thought, pride swelling my chest. We'd only stopped twice for short rests last night, even though she was carrying twice the usual load and was still rather small by dragon standards. But then again, Lessie had always been stronger and smarter than she had any right to be. Spending several hundred years waiting to hatch had given her an edge, and she continued to develop much faster than normal dragonlings.

As we ate, Tavarian and I tried to glean useful information, striking up conversation with our server as well as the patrons sitting at the table to our right. But it wasn't until a group of locals sat down at the table behind us that we heard anything truly interesting.

"Got a letter from my brother yesterday," one of them said. "He says the Elantian conquest is going well, and they just won a great victory along the western border."

"I hear that the army will be reaching the Elantian capital any day now," another one said. "How long d'you think the city will hold out?"

"Less than a day," the first one said with a chuckle. "We have superior firepower, especially now that we have taken their dragons. The idiots don't even carry muskets, I think. What chance do they have against us?"

"Taken their dragons?" a third one said. "What do you mean?"

"It's in the letter from my brother," the first one said, as if it were obvious. "He says the dragons have been routed and captured at the western border."

"Captured?" the second one exclaimed. "What the hell for?"

The first one shrugged. "I dunno. Do I look like the autocrator to you?"

Tavarian and I exchanged looks as the group began to bicker amongst themselves, some of the patrons from nearby tables joining in. My stomach churned with both excitement and dread. This was the first real news we'd heard, the first confirmation that the dragons *had* been taken alive. Part of me had held out hope that they'd somehow managed to escape and were holed up in hiding somewhere, but even though the truth was grim, having some concrete knowledge was still better than nothing.

"Preposterous, the idea of keeping dragons!" a woman said in a rather shrill voice. "What if the beasts escape and rain hell down on our towns and villages?"

"I agree," a man with a reedy voice said. "They should be exterminated, every last one of them!"

"Calm down," another man said, his voice cutting through the cacophony of voices. "My brother's a sergeant, and I've heard similar news from him. He told me the dragons have already been taken to a secure location south, where they'll be kept for breeding." He raised his voice amongst a swell of angry shouts at this. "The army has everything well in hand. Our superior weapons and numbers have already made the conquest a cakewalk. The autocrator clearly knows what he's doing."

There was some grumbling about this, but most of the locals were appeased by the man's words. And why shouldn't they be? Under the leadership of Autocrator Reichstein, the Zallabarians had conquered Dardil and were taking Elantia by storm. They were undoubtedly proud of their country, even as the situation galled me.

"It's actually brilliant," the first man said. "If the military is able to successfully breed the dragons, they'll be able to use their babies to control the older ones. Not to mention threatening to kill or torture the riders. Soon enough we'll be the new dragon riders, and Elantia will be a footnote in history."

Lessie's anger surged through the bond, and I could feel the fire burning in her chest. *"Using dragonlings as leverage?"* she fumed. *"Torturing riders? This is barbaric!"*

"I know," I said, my own anger roiling in my chest. I sucked in a slow breath through my nostrils, trying to calm myself before someone noticed. *"Please, relax,"* I told her. *"I don't want you to burn the forest down and give away your position."*

Lessie's growl echoed in my head, but a moment later, her anger lessened considerably. I met Tavarian's gaze over the table, and though similar emotions showed in his eyes, we didn't say a word. We couldn't risk being overheard, not with these Zallabarians nearby who were obviously thirsty for Elantian blood.

And not just Elantian blood, I thought, remembering what the first man had said. *Soon enough we'll be the new dragon riders.* Was the autocrator planning on using the dragons for war, and conquering other nations? It made sense, yet I still wasn't certain if he could really pull it off. Dragons would go to great lengths to save their riders, and yet they were still a proud race. And never mind the riders, many of whom would refuse to be subjugated like this. How long would they be willing to submit to such degradation before they fought back, regardless of the consequences? Even if the Zallabarians succeeded in breeding the dragons, they couldn't bond with them. Only someone with dragon rider blood could, and even then, only if the dragon accepted them.

I turned my attention back to the remnants of my breakfast. Though the food was delicious, my appetite had vanished. I was about to tell Tavarian we should leave when the door banged open and a group of soldiers marched in.

"Stay in your seats!" the lead soldier—a captain, judging by the braids on his uniform—barked when several people jumped to their feet. "I've got soldiers posted at both entrances, so don't even think of trying to run."

Dread turned my stomach to lead, and I glanced toward Tavarian. Though his face was placid, he had a white-knuckled grip on the back of his chair, and his hand inched toward the dagger he had strapped to his belt. What was going on here? Had someone recognized us? I scanned the room, looking for a familiar face, someone who might know me, but I saw no one familiar.

"Listen up," the captain said, silencing the worried murmurs. "By order of the autocrator, all able-bodied men between the ages of eighteen to forty-five who are not working essential jobs are hereby drafted. Those of you who fit the requirements, line up along that wall." He pointed to the wall on the far left. "The rest of you may leave, but you are to give your particulars to my men outside on your way out."

The sound of grumbling and chairs scraping against the wooden floorboards filled the air as disgruntled customers got to their feet. Sweat broke out on my forehead as I looked at Tavarian again—he definitely fit the profile. Swiftly, he grabbed my hand and pulled me to the door.

One of the soldiers stepped in front of him. "Up against the wall with you," he said in a steely voice.

Tavarian squared his shoulders. "But sir, I am forty-six years old. Surely—"

"Forty-six?" The soldier looked him up and down with a huff. "You look healthy enough to me, and certainly spry enough to grab your lady's hand and dart for the door. Unless you have proof of your age, I suggest you line up with the others." He not-so-subtly placed a hand on the hilt of his sword.

"Please, sir," I said, wringing my hands and giving him my big blues. "The two of us were just married, and—"

"And you wouldn't want your husband to be branded as a draft dodger, now would you, ma'am?" He grabbed Tavarian's hand and wrenched him from my grasp. "Callouses," he said, glancing at his palm. "But you've got an educated accent. What's your trade?"

"I'm a schoolteacher," Tavarian said. "Come fall, I'll have a classroom full of children depending on me."

The soldier shrugged. "Guess they'll just have to find another to fill your shoes. Don't look so glum," he added, slapping Tavarian on the shoulder. "Seeing as how you're educated and all, they'll likely make you an officer."

Tavarian gave him a pained look. "Might I at least be allowed to say goodbye to my wife?"

The soldier looked at me again, and this time he gave me an appreciative once-over, his eyes lingering on my curves in a way that made me want to punch him. "Suppose so," he finally said. "But make it quick."

Tavarian pulled me aside, then drew me close to his chest in a hard embrace. I buried my face in his chest as we staged a tearful embrace, though there wasn't much to stage. I was genuinely terrified. "Don't worry, Zara," he whispered in my ear, and I sucked in a deep lungful of his leather and bergamot scent. "I'll use this as an opportunity to try to ferret out the exact location of the dragons. The moment I have what I need, I'll slip away and rejoin you at Lessie's hiding place in the hills."

Dammit. This is not what's supposed to happen!

I grabbed the front of his shirt, glaring up at him. "You better not die on me," I growled at him. The two of us were supposed to retrieve the dragons together, to survive this adventure so that after we were safe, we could explore whatever this was that lay between us.

Tavarian's eyes flashed as he gripped the back of my head. "The same goes for you."

He crushed his mouth against mine, a hard, fast kiss that immediately set fire to my blood. It was over almost as soon as it began. He whirled away, leaving me with his taste in my mouth and his scent on my skin. Tears of anger and helplessness stung at my eyes as he lined up with the other draftees, and for a split second, I wanted to grab Tavarian's hand and make a run for it, consequences be damned.

Instead, I left the tavern before I could give in to the temptation.

Stop being stupid, Zara, I told myself as I walked through the market, my heart racing. Tavarian wasn't a helpless orphan or an inexperienced cadet. He was a battle-hardened dragon rider, and a mage besides. If anyone could figure out a way to sneak out of the camp after being recruited into the enemy's army, it was him. Besides, we desperately needed intel about the dragon's location. "South" was far too broad an area for us to efficiently search.

In the meantime, I couldn't just spend the next few days moping around. I needed to make myself useful. And that meant a change of plans.

Instead of heading back to Lessie's hiding place in the forest, I went to the first dressmaker's shop I could find, and immediately bought several elegant dresses, a pair of shoes, and a hat. After changing into one of the dresses, I packed the rest of my belongings into a suitcase purchased from a shop up the street, then hired a hack to take me to the finest inn in town.

Looks like all my training with Salcombe is going to come in handy, I thought as I smoothed the skirts of my striped muslin dress. I'd spent weeks pretending to be a noblewoman at the Traggaran court, and I knew that for this particular mission, I was better served acting the part of a wealthy woman than a farmer's wife.

The inn was a large, three-storied building that was charming, though not nearly as fine as some of the places Salcombe and I had stayed in. As I alighted from the hack, handed down by the waiting valet, it briefly occurred to me that the disguise would be more convincing if I had a ladies' maid. But since I couldn't very well hire some girl to go riding around with me on Lessie, I would have to do without.

While the valet unloaded my luggage, I swept inside and approached the front desk. "Good morning," I said to the middle-aged woman behind the counter. "I'd like your finest room." I plucked two gold coins from my rather hefty purse and set them on the counter, thankful Tavarian had insisted I carry half of our funds.

"Certainly." The woman's eyes widened at the sum, which was far more than a single night's accommodations. "How long will you be staying?"

"For the next few weeks," I said. "I assume this will be enough to cover the first week, and I'll pay weekly until I leave. I am waiting for my husband to join me when he is next on leave," I explained at her quizzical expression. "He is a major."

"I see." Her expression cleared immediately. "Is he stationed at the nearby garrison?"

"No," I said, thankful she'd reminded me of it. As the nearest military post, it would be the most likely place for the military recruits to be taken, including Tavarian. "He is with the troops in Elantia."

"Oh, you must be proud, then," she said, her dark blue eyes sparkling. "How brave, for our men to be fighting so far away from home."

"Indeed." I hid my grimace behind a sweet smile. "Although I would prefer him to be by my side, just like any wife."

"Of course." The woman gave me a sympathetic smile, then handed me a key. "Your room is on the third floor. Your luggage will be delivered presently."

"Thank you." But I didn't leave right away. "You know, I was passing by a tavern earlier today and heard quite a ruckus coming from inside from the soldiers. Apparently they stormed the place and rounded up all eligible men for the draft. I wonder if that means that perhaps our campaign isn't going as well as expected, if the autocrator feels we need more men."

The woman shrugged. "Perhaps, but all the rumors and gossip I've heard suggests we are doing fine." She smiled at me again. "My neighbor's son was drafted just yesterday, and she's rather distraught about it, but most of us don't mind. With so many men leaving town, jobs are opening up and wages are rising. Women are being hired more than ever now, for positions that used to be reserved for men. Even the government in Barkheim is hiring women for all kinds of positions, which is unheard of!

My sister lives there, and she was able to get a job as a clerk in the Education Ministry. It really is a wonderful thing."

I blinked—surprised not only at the woman's effusiveness, but that Zallabar had an Education Ministry. Elantia didn't have anything like that, but it seemed the Zallabarians were better organized in more than just warfare. "Well, that is very good for your sister," I told her. "Hopefully she can keep her position once the men return from war."

"That may be a long while yet," the landlady said with a crafty smile. "If the autocrator's campaign against Elantia is successful, I doubt he will want to stop there."

Just how far was the autocrator planning to go? I wondered as I headed up the stairs to my room, which turned out to be a two-bedroom suite. My luggage was already waiting for me by the bed, and I set to the task of unpacking while I thought. Did Reichstein plan on conquering the entire continent? Would he stop there, or would he move to the southern islands, or even beyond, to other continents? Even if we were able to find the dragons and get them out safely, would there be anywhere we could go to escape his reach? The steam vehicles, portable cannons, and experimental airships coupled with Zallabar's large and ever-growing population made their army a force to be reckoned with. Was there any other country out there who could withstand them?

Does it really matter? a voice in my head asked. *If Salcombe resurrects the dragon god, it won't matter which country is in charge of which territory. We'll all be either dead or enslaved.*

Stop it, I told myself. All this constant worrying was unproductive. I needed to focus on one problem at a time. Casting my dark thoughts aside, I stripped off my dress and took advantage of the steaming bath waiting for me, then put on a new dress and went downstairs to the lobby. Perhaps I'd overhear some gossip or find something of interest in the newspaper.

I'd only been sitting down for a few minutes when a young officer walked in. My muscles tensed as he looked my way, but he only gave me a perfunctory smile before approaching the counter. "Excuse me, ma'am," he said politely. "We've had a rather alarming influx of wounded soldiers, and are looking for women to work in the infirmary as nurses. Do you know of anyone who might be suitable?"

"Hmm." The landlady drummed her fingers on the counter. "I think I might know a girl, but she just got a job at the butcher's and—"

"Excuse me." I put my newspaper aside and walked over, a bright smile on my face. "Did you say that you were looking for nurses?"

"Yes, ma'am." He smiled back, taking brief note of my fine clothing and, most likely, my upper-class Zallabarian accent. "Do you know of anyone? Perhaps your maid would be willing to donate some of her time?"

"Oh, I'm new in town, so I can't recommend someone," I said, "but I would be more than happy to volunteer myself."

"You?" The soldier's mouth dropped open with shock, but he

quickly got hold of himself. "That is, I mean, are you certain, ma'am? It's a pretty grim job and not for the faint of heart."

"I am the wife of a soldier," I told him, lifting my chin. "I assure you I am anything but faint-hearted."

A blush crept up the sides of his neck. "My apologies, ma'am. I did not mean to imply you weren't."

"Never mind that," I said. "Can you tell me a little bit more about the position? Where is this infirmary? At the garrison?" Tavarian and I might be able to communicate with each other if I got a job on the premises.

"About three miles from the town center," he told me. "We do have an infirmary at the garrison, but it's overflowing, so we've commandeered a nearby estate that the owner generously agreed to let us use as a temporary hospital. If you'd like, I can have a soldier come pick you up in the mornings and return you here by nightfall."

"Thank you, but I can manage," I said with a gentle smile. The last thing I needed was a Zallabarian military escort. "Please, officer, allow me to help. As I said, my husband is in the military. For all I know, he may end up coming through this hospital at some point, and besides that, no effort is too great for the glory of Zallabar." Those last words felt like sandpaper on my tongue, but I forced them through my teeth anyway. Even if Tavarian wasn't there, an infirmary full of wounded soldiers was still an excellent place to gather intelligence.

"Very well, then." The soldier seemed impressed by my patriotism as he pulled out a written order from his pocket and handed it to me. "I'm very glad to have you on board, Mrs..."

"Mayer," I said, using the name of a Zallabarian trader I'd once dealt with. "Mrs. Amelia Mayer."

"Mrs. Mayer." He bowed. "The address of the estate is in the letter. Please report at six a.m. sharp." He bowed smartly, then left.

The landlady whistled as I opened the letter and scanned it. "Six a.m., eh? That's a bit of an early start for you, isn't it?"

"Not so early," I said with a bland smile. "My husband is an early riser, so I've become accustomed to waking with the dawn."

"Still, it's admirable that you're willing to sully your hands when so many others wouldn't." She glanced down at my hands, and I surreptitiously hid them in the folds of my skirt, painfully aware that they were not a lady's hands. My nails were uncommonly short, for one, and I had callouses from all the digging and climbing and weapons training. Hopefully no one would notice when I showed up tomorrow.

I retired to my room with the newspaper, and in the privacy of my bedchamber, told Lessie about the change in plans.

"I can't say I am happy about this," she complained when I'd finished. *"You've visited Zallabar on more than one occasion, both as yourself and as Mrs. Trentiano. What if one of the soldiers is someone you've done business with in the past?"*

"That's a risk I'll have to take," I said, though privately I wished for Salcombe's fan. Why, oh why had I sold it in my shop? Any item

that could be used to change one's appearance was extremely useful, but because I'd given up thieving, I'd allowed Carina to put it up for sale so I wouldn't be tempted. *And look where that's gotten you.*

"I don't know why I bothered to come along in the first place," Lessie said sullenly. *"You and Tavarian have gone off in separate directions anyway and left me all alone out here."*

"I'm sorry," I said, my chest pinching with guilt. *"I didn't mean for it to turn out this way."*

"I don't think anyone meant for any of this to turn out this way, except perhaps the Zallabarians." The sad smile in Lessie's voice made my heart sink. *"But I know you're just doing your best. Hurry back soon, will you, Zara? It's lonely out here."*

"I will. I promise."

But then again, I'd promised that I wouldn't leave Lessie again, and yet here I was, wasn't I? How many more promises would I have to break before this war was over? How many more sacrifices would I have to make before we would be safe again? I didn't know, and that, more than anything else, kept me tossing and turning well into the night.

8

I managed five hours of sleep before a servant knocked on my door—my requested five a.m. wake-up call, along with a breakfast tray.

I could definitely get used to this, I thought as I sat by the window in the drawing room, sipping my tea and quietly eating one of the breakfast pastries the cook had set out for me, along with fruit. I knew I should probably eat more, since I was in for a long day of work, but I wasn't much in the mood for breakfast. Besides, I'd looked up the estate on a map, and it wasn't that far from the market in that area. It wouldn't be hard to grab food if I needed it.

Though I was tempted to simply walk to the estate, I'd already arranged for a steamcab the previous night to come pick me up, as a lady of my status would normally do. As it rolled along the paved streets, I sat back against the upholstery and took in the quaint beauty of the town. The larger Zallabarian cities didn't look like this—the buildings were larger and more industrial, the air less clear thanks to all the steam and smoke from various factories. Elantia might be primitive in comparison, but our skies and rivers were clear. That would all change once the country was under Zallabarian occupation.

How will the citizens feel about that? I wondered. On the one hand, many would curse the new technologies—after all, change was frightening, and most people naturally resisted. But industry tended to lead to a rise in economy, which meant more jobs and wealth. Would the people eventually welcome Zallabar for the progress it represented? The border villages were already being lulled by their spell.

Whatever the outcome, I knew things were going to have to change. No longer would Elantia be able to rely on its dwindling number of dragons for protection. If we ever won back our country, we would have to not only adopt the same weapons as our enemies but also constantly work to invent new ones, better ones. It was really too bad that no one had yet been able to replicate those airship cannons. They would have made a difference if we'd been able to manufacture enough of them in time.

At this early hour, it only took about ten minutes to reach the estate. Several soldiers were stationed at the gate entrance, and I approached, dressed in another of the frocks I'd purchased, this one a spring green embroidered with tiny flowers. The soldier raised an eyebrow when I handed him the paper with my orders, but after a moment, he waved me through.

"You'll want to get an apron to cover up that dress," he called as I passed. "I'd hate to see you walk out of here stained in blood."

A shiver crawled down my spine at his ominous words, but I forced myself to ignore it. *He's talking about the soldiers' blood, not your blood,* I reminded myself. *He has no idea who you really are.*

I walked up the path to the front entrance, noting the overgrown hedges and unruly flowerbeds. *Whoever owns this estate clearly doesn't take care of it,* I thought as I walked through the front door. The door handle was tarnished, and the marble floor in the foyer sported several cracks. There was no furniture to speak of, and down the hall, voices buzzed and heels clicked across the tile. The smell of antiseptic fluid, soap, and death immediately assailed my nostrils as I followed the noise to a large hall lined from one end to the other with wrought-iron hospital beds.

"Excuse me," I said, catching the elbow of a harried-looking woman. "I'm new here. Who do I report to?" I shoved my orders into her hands.

The woman barely glanced at the paper. "Mrs. Klein is in charge," she said, pointing at a woman bent over one of the beds. She handed the paper back to me and bustled off.

I approached Mrs. Klein a bit hesitantly, not wanting to disturb the patient's privacy. Not that any of them had much privacy to begin with, I thought as I looked around the hall again. Apart from a few beds cordoned off with standing curtains, most of them were exposed. Some of the patients looked reasonably okay, plaster casts propped up against footboards while they slept, while others looked at death's door. The smell of blood and rot laced the air, and my stomach turned as I was reminded of the battlefield once more.

They're still alive, I told myself. *Remember that. These people are still living.*

But they wouldn't all stay that way. Mrs. Klein assigned me to clean up—changing bedpans, replacing soiled linens with fresh ones, helping the more experienced nurses change bandages and mop fevered brows, and so on. Lots of the men had recent amputations, while others suffered flesh wounds. There were head injuries ranging from mild concussions to full-on comas, raging fevers from infection, and a surprising number had burns. Were these from dragon fights, or something else? I wished I could ask, but the burn victims were delirious, in too much pain to have coherent conversations.

"It's terrible, isn't it?" the nurse I was assisting said as she pulled back a bandage. I gagged at the foul odor that wafted from the wound. "Even with all our medicines and advancements, sometimes we just can't treat infections like this. This man's wound was already festering when he was brought in."

The man whimpered in pain as she cleaned the wound and applied a fresh poultice, then bandaged it again. Drops of sweat rolled down his feverish brow and across his hollowed cheeks, and despite knowing that he was the enemy, I felt a twang of pity. The soldier couldn't have been more than nineteen years old. He should be at home with his family, working on the farm or learning his father's trade.

Finished with the bandaging, the nurse gave the soldier a draught to ease his pain, and we moved on. There was very little chance to talk. I was kept in constant motion, running back and forth between the beds, as well as to the laundress for fresh linens. The poor woman couldn't keep up with the demand. We were constantly running out of clean bedding, and I often had to bring back sheets that weren't completely dry, just so we had something to put on the mattresses.

Finally, Mrs. Klein took me by the elbow and pulled me away. "Go to the mess and grab something to eat," she ordered, not unkindly. "I don't need you keeling over from exhaustion."

I passed a hand over my brow. The smells, combined with the moans and screams of pain, had robbed me of my appetite, but now that she mentioned it, my skin was clammy, and I felt a little faint. "Thank you," I said.

"No, thank you." She gave me a brief smile. "It's not often we get volunteers like you."

I stripped off my stained apron and, after stopping by the basin to wash my hands and face, went to the mess. The mess turned out to be one of several salons that had been converted into impromptu dining areas. Exhausted, I sat down at one of the tables with a group of women and spooned some lentil stew from the large pot in the middle of the table.

"You've done well today," one of the nurses said with a warm smile.

I smiled back. "Thanks, but I haven't done much. Just grunt work."

The woman to my left patted my shoulder. "It's that grunt work that allows the rest of us to do our jobs," she said. "And let me tell you, most of the ladies who volunteer only last an hour or two before they either faint from the smells or cry from exhaustion. You're still here, and that means something."

That's because I'm not a real lady. But I didn't say that. Instead I complimented her, then asked the other women about themselves as we ate. Several were nurses by trade, but many of them were like the woman I was pretending to be, soldiers' wives who wanted to do what they could to help with the war effort.

Once the women were comfortable with me, I started digging for information. "Where were these men wounded?"

"There was a battle at the border, in the Shirivan Mountain Pass," one of the nurses told me, confirming my suspicions. "We won, but as you can see, it was not without great cost." She sighed. "Luckily we are close enough to the border that they were able to get the wounded to us by airship, but any farther in and we will not be able to help."

"The troops have medics with them," another pointed out. "And I am sure they will commandeer the hospitals and infirmaries at the towns and garrisons that they conquer."

"I don't know about that," the first one said. "I wouldn't trust the Elantian doctors and nurses not to poison the soldiers, regardless of whatever healing oath they took. Our people will likely need to begin drafting more doctors and nurses and setting up emergency hospitals of their own."

"Well, at least now that the dragons are out of the equation, things will get easier," a third woman said. "Dragon fire is truly an atrocious weapon. We've lost more than half of the men who were afflicted by burns. It's almost as if the stuff eats through your flesh even after you put it out."

"Really?" I asked, doing my best not to roll my eyes. Dragon fire was no more dangerous than any other fire, but of course the Zallabarians would have come up with superstitions to make the dragons sound even more dangerous than they really were. "The dragons are gone?"

"Not gone, precisely," the first one told me. "But nearly all of them were sent to the border for that battle, and we've managed to capture them."

"Capture them?" I asked. "But how can such large beasts be held? I thought they could only be controlled by their riders?"

A brunette wrinkled her nose. "The beasts seem to have a modicum of intelligence and can be manipulated and leveraged against one another."

I asked a few more questions, trying not to seem too obvious, but it quickly became apparent that none of the nurses or doctors had any idea where the dragons were being held. Not that I was too surprised. It would be stupid to make the location public knowledge, and the Zallabarians were anything but stupid. *Unlike my own blasted country.*

After eating two helpings of stew and downing half a liter of tepid tea, I returned to the hall. This time, Mrs. Klein tasked me with feeding the patients. Pushing a cart loaded with a large pot of stew, a stack of bowls, and some spoons, I stopped by each bed, ladled the stew into the bowl, and carefully spoon-fed the patients who were too ill or injured to manage it themselves.

Several of them were too out of it to manage much conversation, but to my delight, more than enough were willing to talk.

"You're awful pretty," a man with a horrific burn on the side of his face told me in between bites. He gave me a lopsided smile, the good side of his mouth curving upward even as the mangled side remained flat. "I hope the sight of my face don't bother you too much."

I gave him a smile of my own. "Of course not," I lied, even though the sight made my stomach lurch. The burns extended down his neck and past the collar of his dressing gown. "I'm just happy you're recovering. Not everyone is so lucky."

"Very true." His gaze flickered, sadness giving way to anger. "I barely managed to dodge the flames, but the two soldiers next to me were incinerated. I was never so frightened in my life." His hands fisted in the sheets. "I don't understand why we captured those dragons. They're horrible beasts, dangerous! They should all be put down, if you ask me, not kept and pampered like pets."

Kept and pampered? I fought to keep my expression neutral even as my brows started to rise. "From what I've heard, being separated from their riders will hurt the dragons almost as much as your burns hurt you."

"Good," he said with a grim satisfaction that stirred my own anger. "When I'm well again, I'm going to seek out those blasted riders and slaughter every last one of them. I don't care what the autocrator thinks. They need to be exterminated, and from what I've heard, killing the riders will get rid of the dragons, too."

"Mrs. Mayer," Mrs. Klein said as she passed, pointing to the nearly empty bowl in my hand. "Move on to the next patient. We don't have time to chitchat all day."

Dammit. "Yes, ma'am," I said. I spooned the last bit of stew into the patient's mouth, then shoved the bowl on the lower shelf of the cart and moved on to the next. I wished I could have asked him if he knew where the dragons were being held, but I couldn't linger without creating suspicion.

As I moved on to the next patient, Lessie let out a long string of curses, her anger searing the bond between us. *"How dare he,"* she fumed. *"How dare he blame us for this, when it was his people that attacked us! If the Zallabarians hadn't provoked this attack, if they weren't trying to take our country, he wouldn't be lying in an infirmary bed, and his comrades would still be alive."*

"I know," I said, trying to keep my voice gentle even though I agreed with her. *"He's wrong, but keep in mind that he's also badly wounded, and possibly dying. He may not survive those burns."*

"I hope he doesn't," Lessie growled. *"I hope he dies slowly, in agony."*

The vehemence in her voice both surprised and saddened me. I hated that Lessie was hurting like this—she was still a baby by dragon standards. She should be playing with her fellow dragons, not mourning them or trying to rescue them. I wished we could go back to the way we were, when she was carefree and happy and mischievous. This war had changed me, but I hadn't fully realized just how much it might change her, too.

Who would we be when all this was over?

"I don't know," Lessie said, her voice soft now. *"I wish I could say*

I'm sorry, Zara, but I can't help the way I feel. It's not right, what's happening here. But as long as we're together, we'll be all right."

I held onto those words like a lifeline and pushed the sadness away. Luckily, I didn't have much time to dwell on my thoughts. The nurses ran me ragged the rest of the day, until the sun had long set, and Mrs. Klein finally pulled me off duty. When she offered me a cot from the shared dormitory the other nurses used, I nearly accepted. My feet and back ached fiercely, and I wanted nothing more than to collapse where I stood and never move another muscle again.

Instead, I thanked her, and took a horse-drawn cab, promising to return at the same time tomorrow morning. The gentle rumble of the carriage wheels lulled me to sleep almost immediately, and when we arrived, the driver had to come down from his perch and shake me awake.

"Come now, Miss," he said. "Let's get you inside."

He helped me from the carriage, and I sucked in a lungful of cold air. The brisk wind whipping down the street slapped some cold into my cheeks, clearing the fog from my head.

"Thank you," I said, pressing a coin into his hand. "I can manage from here."

I went inside, and the landlady took one look at me and gave a sympathetic cluck of her tongue. "You go on up to your room," she said kindly. "I'll have a bath drawn for you, and a meal sent up to your room."

"Thank you." I trudged past her and up the three flights of stairs.

By the time I reached the bedroom, my whole body ached, and I badly wanted to flop onto my mattress and pass out.

Instead, I went into the bedroom, closed the door, and dug out the magical earpiece from my luggage.

It took me three tries, but eventually Tavarian answered.

"Zara," he said, sounding both tired and relieved. "Did you make it safely back to Lessie?"

"No. I decided to stay in town." Sitting on a chair by the window, I gave him a quick rundown of what I'd been doing, and what I'd learned so far. "How are you?" I finally asked.

"Likely as sore as you," he said. "They put all the recruits through basic training—something I'd hoped to never undergo again," he added wryly.

I winced, remembering the fitness drills the academy ran us through on a regular basis. "That doesn't sound like fun."

"It isn't, but I'm doing a sight better than most of the others," he admitted. "I've also been given some literacy tests, and I believe the recruiters are considering me for some kind of clerical job."

I raised an eyebrow. "You're not planning on taking it, are you?"

"Of course not," he said with a chuckle. "I'd much rather be with you than stuck behind a desk."

His words warmed me, but I tried not to dwell on them. "Have you learned anything from the soldiers?" I asked.

"Not much more than you," he said with a sigh. "I've heard that some of the new recruits will be sent south for a special detail. It could be to guard the dragons, but I don't know for certain. I also heard they are looking for prison guard types—which, unfortunately, I am not, or I would try to get into that position if it meant being stationed wherever they're keeping the riders."

"As helpful as that would be, I'm glad you're not," I said pointedly, just in case he was thinking about trying to finagle his way into the job. "How much longer do you plan on staying?"

"Hopefully no more than a few days," he said. "I don't want to leave empty-handed, but if they try to assign me to a post, I will have to make myself sca—" He stopped abruptly, then lowered his voice. "Footsteps coming. I have to go. Stay safe, Zara."

Stay safe. The words echoed in my ears long after he disconnected. How often had he said them to me? I tucked the earpiece away just in time to hear a knock at the door. When I answered it, two maids came in, one with a tray of bath salts, pumice stone, and loofahs, and the other with a slice of meat pie and a glass of cider on a tray.

"Sorry we couldn't find something more, ma'am," she said as she set the food down on the table. "But the kitchen's closed up now."

"That's all right." I smiled, and the smell of meat and potatoes rekindled my appetite. I scarfed down the food as quickly as possible, and after a long soak in the tub, I crawled into bed and immediately passed out. But I was only asleep for a few hours when I was awoken by hunger pangs. Frowning, I sat up and placed a hand to my stomach. The meat pie had sated me at the time, but it wasn't nearly enough food after the day I'd had. I wrapped myself in a dressing gown and ventured downstairs to see if I could grab something from the larder. But it was locked up tight, as was the kitchen, and I didn't want to trouble the landlady. At this hour, close to midnight, she was probably asleep.

I retreated upstairs and rummaged through my luggage, hoping to find something to quiet my stomach long enough to fall back asleep. I only found a single biscuit, hard enough to break my teeth. Definitely not enough to sate me, even if I could chew it. Annoyed, I pulled on my clothes and ventured out to search for a nearby tavern. Some were still open at this hour, and it wasn't long before I came upon a squat wooden building. Music and light spilled from the open doors and windows. When I stepped in, the yeasty scent of beer mixed with the salty scent of human sweat assaulted my senses.

Thankfully, sweat and beer weren't the only things this establishment offered, and after sitting down at the bar, I was served a mug of ale and a plate of cheese, sausage, and bread. I munched on the food, trying to ignore the men's curious stares. I'd wrapped a dark cloak around me to hide my dress, and a scarf covered my hair, but I was still a woman alone at night. There was always a man around who tried to take advantage. As a treasure hunter dressed in pants and wearing my weapons openly, I usually managed to deter most of those. But in this guise, I was bound to attract trouble.

Sure enough, not halfway through my meal, a drunken soldier sat next to me at the bar, his nose ruddy and eyes droopy.

"'Scuse me, Miss," he slurred, jostling his arm against mine as he tossed a coin onto the table. "Mind if I buy a few hours of your company?"

I buried my indignation as I studied him. His uniform marked him as a lieutenant, which meant he could be a source of information. "You can buy me a drink," I said sweetly, pushing my empty mug toward him. "And perhaps we'll see where things go from there."

The man bought me another ale, and a dram of liquor for himself. I giggled and flirted with him, slipping in innocent questions as I touched his arm and surreptitiously plied him with more alcohol. "You look so strong," I said, squeezing his bicep. "Where are you serving?"

"I was stationed here at the garrison," he said around a hiccup, "but tomorrow I'm being sent off to a new post. A black hole with no women and only dour guards and prisoners for company." He reached over and squeezed my hand. "That's why I've sought you out, Miss. You're my last chance to get some before I leave."

I hid my grimace of disgust at the feel of his clammy fingers against my skin. "That sounds terrible," I said, my voice dripping with false sympathy. "Where is this terrible place? Kraug Prison?" Kraug was notoriously known as the place where Zallabar sent its worst criminals. It was a fortress located north of here, on a rocky, isolated cliff, nearly impossible to break in or out of, or so I'd heard.

"No, not Kraug," he said with a shudder. "Thank small mercies for that. I've been stationed at Mienar. It's an old, abandoned tin mine in the south that's been recently converted to a prison. Hidden deep in the mountains, dark, underground... hell on earth, in other words."

I questioned him more and managed to get a few details about the place before he trailed off, mumbling incoherently. I gently laid his head on the bar. He was already snoring by the time I slipped away, my mind churning as I quickly left the tavern and headed back to the hotel. The soldier had described Mienar as a warren of narrow passages barely wide enough for two men to walk abreast, and a frigid hell for both the prisoners and the guards. He also told me that the nearest village was Ostkarren, ten miles away—hardly an easy walk for a soldier who wanted a pint after a hard shift, he complained. It sounded like a good candidate for a dragon rider prison, and it was in the right direction.

Back at the inn, I fell into bed, my exhaustion pulling me under. But I woke with the sunrise, excitement thrumming in my blood at my discovery, and immediately tried to contact Tavarian. He answered on the second try.

"Give me some time," he said before I could say anything. "I need to feign an injury so I can get away and speak with you."

He disconnected before I could get a word in. Slightly put out, though of course I understood the need for secrecy, I reached out to Lessie instead. She awakened at my nudging, and her sleepiness quickly turned to excitement as I told her what I learned.

"That sounds very promising," she said, sounding in much better spirits than yesterday. "When can we leave? We should go immediately."

"I want to, but we need Tavarian first," I said. "He's still at the garrison, posing as a recruit."

Lessie snorted. *"We should just fly overhead and burn the whole place to the ground. What do we need to wait around for?"*

I shook my head, but my heart lightened—this was more like the Lessie I knew. *"I'd rather not accidentally barbecue Tavarian in the process, and besides, that would attract too much attention."* The magical earpiece buzzed, and I snatched it up. "That's him trying to contact me now."

I fitted the earpiece to my ear and answered. "You're free now?"

"Yes. I'm on my way to the healer's and taking my time." I could hear the smile in his voice. "I have good news for you."

"Oh?" I sat up, clutching the sheets beneath me. "Have you discovered where the dragons are being held?"

"As a matter of fact, I have." I wanted to cheer at the triumphant note in his voice, but I managed to get hold of myself before I woke the entire inn. "The dragons are in Treylin Valley, a green, hilly region to the south. I broke into the offices last night and found the information in several documents on the captain's desk. Unfortunately, I didn't have time to figure out where the riders are being kept. I had to slip away before I was caught by a patrol. There is little point in rescuing the dragons first—if the military is holding the riders, they can still murder the dragons, too."

I grinned. "You're right. I guess it's a good thing I found out where the riders are being held, isn't it?"

A stunned pause. "When? I thought you were going to bed after I spoke to you yesterday."

"I went out to a tavern to grab a late dinner," I explained, "and ran across a soldier who's being stationed at a prison in the mountains near a place called Ostkarren." I told Tavarian the scant description that the drunken soldier had given me. "He didn't confirm the riders were there, but it seems like a likely place."

"Then we must go there at once," he said. "I will slip away tomorrow night and meet you in the forest where Lessie is hiding." He sighed. "I'm nearly at the healer now. I must go."

He disconnected, and my heart pounded as I quickly dressed for the day. I was still sore from all the hard labor, but I hardly noticed the aches and pains now. We were finally getting somewhere! Part of me wanted to stay here at the inn, to plan and conserve my strength, but I didn't want to be missed, so I ate a hefty breakfast, then took a cab to the estate.

The morning was less hectic than the first one, as the flow of new patients had ebbed, but it was still very busy, and I hardly had a moment to catch my breath. The atmosphere was much the same—soldiers bitter against the Elantians and angry about the dragons, nurses sympathetic to their own but giving absolutely no thought to the Elantian wounded and dead left on that battlefield. Not that I was surprised—we were the enemy, after all—but it seemed unfair that I felt empathy for these mangled men while they felt none for my own people. By the time lunch break came around, all I wanted to do was get away from them all.

Mrs. Klein seemed to sense my dour mood. "Why don't you go take some fresh air outside," she suggested. "It'll help clear your head, get the stench of sickness out of your nose."

I nodded. "That sounds like a wonderful idea, thank you." I stripped off my apron and washed my hands, then headed to the mess to grab a plate of sandwiches and a cup of tea.

I took my bounty outdoors, into the overgrown gardens behind the manor. Even though the bushes and trees were in bad need of pruning, and the flowerbeds were overrun with weeds, there was still something charming about the wildness of the place. I found a dusty stone bench to sit on, beneath an old apple tree whose leaves were beginning to turn. The garden was still green, but tinged with strokes of gold and burnt orange, a sign of the coming winter.

As I ate my lunch behind the high, unruly hedges that offered plenty of privacy, I wondered if I should decamp now. Mrs. Klein would be disappointed but not surprised if I begged off, pleading a headache or some other malady. After all, by the nurses' own admission most of the gently bred ladies who came here did the exact same thing. Besides, did I really need to be breaking my back aiding the enemy?

I finished my tea and two of the sandwiches, then took the third one with me. Instead of going back inside, I decided to stretch my legs and walk the estate grounds. My treasure sense pinged, telling me there were some valuables on the grounds, but nothing interesting enough for me to bother digging up. Still, I followed the loudest one, and it led me into a small, ancient-looking temple hidden away in a thicket of trees.

I wonder what god or goddess you were built for, I thought as I drew closer. Once upon a time, I would have immediately headed for the treasure within, but my recent encounter with a deity left me wary of taking things from temples. Carefully, I placed my hand against one of the cracked pillars, tracing the carvings of strange creatures frolicking in an open meadow. My fingers fluttered over the hooves of a satyr, the wings of a fairy, the horns of an imp—

"Enjoying yourself?"

I jerked at the sound of a lazy male voice, and nearly dropped my sandwich when Caor stepped out from behind the pillar. How long had he been standing there, watching me? And why hadn't I sensed him in any way?

"Checking in on me?" I asked, trying to hide my shock.

He folded his arms. "I am. Have you made any progress searching for the other dragon heart pieces?"

I scowled. "You know I haven't. Isn't that why you gave me this ring, so you could spy on me from afar?"

"Yes." He didn't sound the least bit apologetic about it. "For all the good it's doing me. Don't you understand what's at stake here?"

"I know I need to rescue the other dragons before I do anything else," I snapped. "If you were smart, you would help me, so I could get back to looking for the dragon heart sooner. Can't you tell me anything?"

Caor considered. "What do you want to know?"

"Where the Elantian wounded and prisoners are being kept, for starters."

He shrugged. "That sort of thing does not concern the gods. You will have to discover that on your own. Except that you already have, haven't you?"

"Yes, and no thanks to you," I grumbled. I wanted to tell him that with this kind of attitude, it was no wonder these useless gods were forgotten, but I refrained.

Caor sighed. "I understand you want to rescue your friends, but the situation with Salcombe and the dragon god is much more important in the long run."

"I get that, but I have no idea where to even begin looking. Salcombe has all his notes and journals on the subject, while I have absolutely nothing. I can't go on a wild goose chase across the continent when I could be helping the dragons, which is at least something I *know* I can do."

"You don't have to go on a wild goose chase," Caor said. "I can tell you right now where the fourth piece is."

"You...what?"

"Salcombe is currently searching for it in Orbolia," he said, referring to a country at the very northernmost point of the continent. "He will soon discover that it is not, in fact, there, but was moved to Zallabar some five hundred years earlier. You absolutely must beat him to the next piece, and since you are already in Zallabar, you have a convenient head start."

Adrenaline surged in my veins, and for a moment I forgot all about the dragons and my current mission. "Here, in Zallabar? Where?"

"Barkheim, the capital. Only three days by carriage, though considerably closer by dragonback," he pointed out, waggling his eyebrows.

I did some quick calculations in my head. "If Salcombe is really in Orbolia, it will take him a week to get back here once he realizes the dragon heart isn't there," I said. "Plus, he may not immediately figure out where in Zallabar the heart is, *if* he even figures it out. After all, he was here looking for a piece last time that turned out to be in Traggar." Hope blossomed in my chest, and a grin tugged at my lips. "That's enough time for me to rescue the dragon riders and make it to Barkheim."

Caor growled. "How can you be so cavalier about this?" he demanded. "You should go retrieve the relic now. The Zallabarians aren't going to kill the dragon riders, at least not any time soon. They can wait!"

"Maybe, but I can't," I said firmly. I wasn't going to let the gods yank me around like this. After all, how could I even trust that Caor was telling me the truth? Maybe the Zallabarians wouldn't kill the riders, but they could be torturing them, squeezing out vital information that would give them even more of an edge in the war. I thought of Jallis again, and my stomach turned. What if he was one of those prisoners? He'd been with the other dragons at the western border, I was certain of it.

Caor gave a long-suffering sigh. "I wish I could help you, but the gods refuse to aid the dragons in any way after what has happened, and I will face severe repercussions from my more powerful brethren if I assist you in this."

I couldn't help it—I rolled my eyes at him. "For such powerful beings, you seem oddly limited. If the dragon god's heart is so important to you guys—and don't lie to me, I can tell that it is—then why don't you retrieve the pieces yourself?"

"Because this is your realm, not ours," Caor said. "We cannot work in the human realm without the help of willing inhabitants such as yourself. In our glory days, we had avatars and oracles to carry out our bidding, and through them, we were able to perform great miracles. But with humans having turned their backs on us for so many years, we're able to do little but watch. This is why we had to rely on our champion when Zakyiar invaded your world, and why it was such a devastating blow when your people chose to kill him."

Caor's voice was flat, but I caught a glimpse of anguish in his eyes, and I felt inexplicably guilty even though I had nothing to do with this mysterious champion's death. "You are our champion now, Zara," he went on, more softly now. "And you have only a few weeks at the most until Salcombe gets his hands on a third piece. If he does, he will become almost unkillable. You cannot allow him to succeed."

He inclined his head to me, and vanished.

"Dammit!" I cursed, smacking my hand against the pillar. A few remnants of plaster crumbled off it, and I hastily jumped back, remembering this thing was ancient. The last thing I needed was a stone pillar falling on top of me right now.

"Lessie," I said, pinching the bridge of my nose. *"I don't know what to do."*

"Yes, you do," Lessie said firmly. *"Caor and his ilk might be right about Salcombe, but you heard the god—they don't care about the dragons. In fact, they probably hope that the Zallabarians end up killing us all. I agree that finding the heart is important, but we can't allow our enemy to hold the dragons much longer. They have something planned, and I can feel it in my bones that if we allow them to go through with whatever it is, Elantia will never be able to recover."*

"Right." Dragon's balls, why did this have to be so hard? I bit my lip as I trudged back to the manor and got back to work. On the one hand, Caor's warning rang true, and supposedly the gods should know best. But on the other hand, they didn't exactly have a stellar track record. I'd read the few myths and legends that had survived—gods made terrible mistakes all the time. And I wasn't going to sacrifice the future of my nation when, by all accounts, there was no reason I couldn't help the dragons and *then* go after the heart.

Besides, if the soldier's description of the prison was as bad as it sounded, it had to be ten times worse for the prisoners. People held in such terrible conditions didn't last very long, and any dragon rider death would also mean the death of a priceless, magnificent dragon. If the gods couldn't recognize the value of these creatures, creatures my people had worked with for hundreds of years, that was their loss, I decided.

"Thank you again for your help today, Mrs. Mayer," Mrs. Klein said when I took off my apron for the last time. "I'll see you tomorrow morning again, at six a.m."

"You're welcome, but I'm afraid I won't be coming back." I gave her an apologetic smile. "I received a message from my husband this morning, ordering me to go back to our family home and stay with my mother-in-law while we await his return."

A few of the nurses scoffed that they always knew a fine lady like me would never stay for long, but most of them gave me hugs and sad smiles, sorry to see me go. To my surprise, I found that part of me was sorry to leave them. Even though I'd only known them for a short time, and they were serving the enemy, I felt bad leaving these women behind when they were clearly so desperate for help.

You can't save everyone, Zara, I reminded myself as I left the estate. *And especially not everyone from both sides.*

"Lessie," I said. *"I'm on my way to the inn to pack my things. I'll be headed your way as soon as I've had a decent meal."*

"Do you think you can come now?" Lessie asked, and I'm surprised at the terseness in her voice.

"Why? What is it?"

But Lessie didn't answer, and my heart pounded with fear. Anxious, I tapped on the roof, then stuck my head out the window and shouted to the driver to go fast.

"Lessie? What's happening? Are you under attack?" I could feel her fear, but it was a low-level fear, not the death-grip choking terror that you felt when your life was truly in danger.

A few tense moments passed before Lessie answered. *"Never mind. It's fine."*

"What the hell?" I burst out, relieved and angry all at once. "What's going on in there?"

"Humans come into these forests to pick mushrooms," Lessie said. *"I'm usually good at avoiding them, but two women walked right into my clearing. They nearly ran off to alert the town, but I've captured them, and they're not going anywhere."*

"How did you secure them?"

"With my claws," Lessie said smugly. *"I've got them both pinned to the ground, and I made it clear to the women that if they tried to make a run for it, I'd eat them."*

I shuddered, knowing it was true. I'd seen Lessie eat a whole human live once, in battle. *"Hang tight,"* I told her. *"I'll be there as quick as I can."* There might be more in the area, and Lessie could only hold so many humans. I had to get to her fast and get the hell out of there.

9

The cab dropped me off in front of the inn in record time, and I flew upstairs to pack my things. I settled the bill with the landlady, giving her the same story I'd told Mrs. Klein. Ducking into a closet toward the inn's rear entrance, I changed out of my nice dress and back into my farmer's wife outfit, then slipped out the back with my luggage in tow, leaving only the fancy clothes behind.

On my way out of the city, I stopped by the butcher and purchased an obscene amount of local sausages that smelled delicious, and several loaves of dark rye bread. I stuffed these into my bag as well, then set a brisk pace as I headed out of the city and toward the forest. It would take several hours to make the journey, but by that time it would be close to midnight, and Tavarian should have been able to slip away.

By the time I reached the valley, my shoulder ached from carrying so much weight, and my feet felt like they were on fire.

Luckily, I didn't pass any other foragers—not that I expected to see anyone looking for mushrooms in the middle of the night—and the two women Lessie had captured were still there, intact.

"Zara!" Lessie's tail thrashed in welcome, but she did not remove her clawed hands from the prisoners. I felt a twang of sympathy as I stared into their terrified eyes—a mother-daughter duo, judging by the similarities in looks and the disparity in age.

"Please," the mother said, her body trembling as she stared at me. "Let us go. We won't tell anybody what we saw."

"Yes, you will," I said calmly as I sat on a rock and pulled the pack of sausages from my bag. I tossed five straight into Lessie's waiting mouth, then pulled out my dagger and began slicing off pieces for myself to eat with the bread. "And I wouldn't blame you for it. But don't worry. I'm not going to kill you." I took a bite of bread and sausage, and suppressed a moan as the spicy, rich flavors saturated my tongue.

We sat for another hour in relative silence, Lessie and I eating the sausages while the women whimpered. Eventually I took pity on them and fed them a few bites. The younger girl looked like she was about to pass out from terror when I approached with my knife in hand, but when I offered a slice of meat, she took it eagerly, almost biting my hand in the process.

"Hey!" I snapped, then abruptly went silent at the sound of a faint male voice shouting. Was that Tavarian?

"Isla! Marla! Are you there?"

"Papa!" the girl sobbed, struggling mightily against Lessie's grip.

"Otto!" the mother cried."

"Dammit!" I cursed. I didn't see any lanterns yet, but that voice was far too close, and the women had just given away our position. *"Lessie, we have to go!"*

"What should I do with the women?" she asked as I vaulted onto her back. *"Should I kill them?"* She sounded a little reluctant, but I knew she would if I gave the order.

"No," I said with a sigh. *"Just let them go."* It wasn't their fault they'd stumbled upon a dragon in the middle of the woods, and I hated the idea of crushing this man's hopes just as he was on the verge of finding his family.

Lessie flexed her hind legs, and with a powerful beat of her wings, we were airborne. The women screamed as the gust of wind rained leaves and sticks and dust all over them, and I heard a cry of alarm from the man searching for them. But the sounds of their voices faded quickly, and two seconds later, we were gone.

Unfortunately, it was a clear, moonlit night, and my heart leaped into my throat at the sight of a solitary figure in a military uniform running straight toward us. Was that a crossbow on his back? My stomach clenched, and I instinctively hunkered down in the saddle. Crossbow bolts would glance harmlessly off Lessie's scales, but I wouldn't be so lucky, especially since my dragon rider armor was back on the airship. I was about to order Lessie to climb higher when she abruptly swooped down.

"What are you—" I shrieked, then stopped as we got closer. It was Tavarian! He raised a hand to hail us, and Lessie snatched him up in her claws, then shot back up into the sky, trying to find a bit of cloud to take cover behind.

"Are you all right?" I shouted down to Tavarian as I leaned over the side to get a better look at him.

I couldn't hear his response over the wind, but he gave me a thumbs up. His hair had come free of its usual ponytail and trailed behind him like inky banners in the night. There were shadows beneath his eyes that spoke of exhaustion, but despite that, his eyes were bright with triumph and relief. My heart lightened instantly as he grinned up at me.

We're going to be okay, I told myself. *As long as we stay together, we're going to be fine.*

We flew south for several miles, and then Lessie stopped near a moonlit lake so we could re-situate ourselves.

"Thank the skies you came back," I said, flinging my arms around Tavarian. He cinched his own arms around my waist in a tight hug, and I buried my nose in the crook of his neck, inhaling his scent. "I was worried we would miss you."

"Why did you leave so suddenly?" He stroked a hand down my hair, soothing me. "Did something happen?"

"Some locals discovered Lessie's hiding place." I quickly explained what had happened. "I know it would have been safer to kill them, but I couldn't bring myself to."

Tavarian sighed. "They will tell the garrison that they saw you, and the prison to the south may tighten up their security," he said. "But then again, it is always possible no one will believe their story. In any case, I don't fault you for staying your hand. Killing civilians in cold blood is very different from killing in self-defense."

I gave Tavarian some sausage and bread from my luggage, then helped him tie his own pack onto Lessie's saddle before we mounted up again. As Lessie continued to fly, I told Tavarian about my encounter with Caor, and what he'd said about Salcombe and the dragon god's heart.

"If what he says is true about Salcombe potentially becoming invincible, that is very troubling indeed," Tavarian said when I was finished. "I agree we cannot abandon our mission to rescue the dragons, but at the same time we also cannot allow Salcombe to recover a third piece. I wish there was a way we could attend to both things right away."

I hesitated. "Perhaps we could split up," I offered. "One of us could go to Barkheim, while the other continues on to the prison."

Tavarian shook his head. "Although I could fly Lessie while you go to the capital, she and I cannot communicate with each other, which will make it difficult for us to work together. And though I could go to the capital by myself, without your talent for sensing magical objects, searching for the piece of heart will be like looking for a needle in a haystack."

"Not to mention that there is no way I am flying anywhere without you, Zara," Lessie said sharply. *"We're sticking together, remember?"*

"Yes, yes, I agree." I patted her neck, trying to be reassuring, but frustration simmered beneath my skin, a writhing, living thing trying to claw its way out of me. No matter which choice I made, if I went east to Barkheim or south to the prison, I would still feel the heavy weight of guilt and dread, the terrible doubt that I was making the wrong choice. Why couldn't I catch a break, for once?

"Relax." Tavarian tightened his grip on my waist from behind, pulling me against him. "Don't beat yourself up, Zara. I know it's hard not to blame yourself for everything that goes wrong, but we're doing the best we can."

The best we can? An old memory flickered in my mind, and Salcombe's voice echoed in my ears. *"I don't care about your best. I care about results."*

But I didn't say anything to Tavarian, because he was right. We *were* doing our best, and against impossibly unfair odds, too. Who else from the Elantian army was out here in Zallabarian territory, risking their necks to save the dragons? Tavarian was the only council member who risked his own life. The rest of them had tucked their tails between their legs and fled south, away from the fighting. By now they might have left the country entirely, retreating to one of our island territories across the sea where they would plot and plan to take back the country, which really meant sending more men back to die while they sat in their homes, fat and safe.

You're damn right we're doing the best we can, I snarled, directing my anger not just at Salcombe's voice but also at the assholes who'd gotten us into this mess in the first place. If Tavarian and I failed, it wouldn't just be our fault. The blood would be on their hands, too.

Letting out my frustrations with a deep sigh, I finally settled against Tavarian, and for the first time in a long time, allowed myself to just relax. With Tavarian's spell cloaking Lessie's form, we didn't have to worry about being spotted, and Lessie's keen eyes would pick up anything important.

As we flew, Tavarian told me of his escape from the garrison. He'd had to use both his magic and his fighting prowess to get out. Apparently, some of the recruits had deserted earlier in the day, so they'd tripled the guard to stop any of the other draftees from running away.

It was such a clear night, Lessie had no trouble following the river southward, and then along a tributary that split off slightly east and led straight to the village near the mine. It only took us two and a half hours to reach it, but we didn't dare fly too close. While Tavarian's spell cloaked Lessie from sight, it could do nothing to prevent her from casting a dragon-shaped shadow on the ground, and even here they had cannons. Instead, we flew over the mountains to get a sense of the topography, locate the mine, and find a hiding place for Lessie. The mine was not visible from above, but the village was easy to make out.

"I'm tired of hiding," Lessie complained as we landed in a small, deserted valley about half an hour's walk from the village. *"I'm a*

dragon, not some little mouse to hide in a corner. I want to be part of the action."

"Trust me, the moment there is even a chance of action, I'll unleash you upon our enemies," I assured her as I hopped down from the saddle. "But first, Tavarian and I need to scout and infiltrate, which will be a bit difficult if we go walking around with the only free dragon in Zallabar."

Lessie huffed, then ambled off into the forest in search of game. While we waited for her to come back, Tavarian and I sat on a log and ate more of the sausage and bread. Though I'd bought quite a bit of it, it wouldn't last more than a few days between the two of us. We would have to augment it with whatever wild fruit or berries we could find in the woods if we wanted it to stretch.

"Zara." Lessie's urgent voice jerked me to attention, my hand on the hilt of my dragon blade. *"There is an area here, a few hundred yards north of the clearing, where I can hear underground activity."*

"Underground activity?" I jumped to my feet. *"Like what?"*

"People walking, talking. Some moans of pain." I could hear the excitement in Lessie's voice, even as her anger surged in the bond. *"I think it's the secret prison, directly below us!"*

I relayed this information to Tavarian, who'd been staring at me quizzically. "That would be quite a lucky break," he said, raising his eyebrows. "We should investigate the area, see if perhaps there is some hidden entrance nearby."

We waited until Lessie returned with a large deer in her claws, then took off toward the area to the north, following her directions. Ten minutes later, we were standing next to the large boulder she'd indicated as a landmark. I put my ear to the ground, wondering if I could pick up on the sounds, but I couldn't make out anything.

"Lessie's hearing is at least ten times stronger than ours," Tavarian reminded me. "If the prisoners are there, they will be dozens of feet beneath the ground. What Lessie hears is similar to how a cat senses mice scurrying beneath the floorboards."

We didn't see any obvious entrances, so rather than doing a thorough search of the area and risk being caught by patrols, Tavarian and I took cover in the dense, rocky terrain and kept a lookout. For several hours we saw nothing at all, but as dawn began to lighten the sky, four military men emerged from a large boulder a hundred yards from our position and walked toward the village.

"That must be the entrance," Tavarian whispered, so quietly that I almost didn't hear him. "Let's move west and see if we can't spot it from another angle."

We waited until the soldiers' footsteps faded, then skulked in the direction Tavarian indicated, darting between gnarled trees and rocky outcroppings. At first, the rock face behind the boulder appeared to be nothing but stone, but when I zoomed in with my goggles, I spotted a cleverly hidden door painted the exact same shade as the rock. It stood to reason that it would be well-guarded from the inside, and sure enough, my treasure sense picked up on enough weapons to indicate there were at least four armed soldiers right on the other side.

"We're not going to be able to break in without alerting the entire base," I whispered to Tavarian. "We need to find another way in."

We crept back to the clearing where Lessie waited, and went over what we'd found.

"If the mines are like a warren, as that drunken soldier told you," she said, *"then perhaps we can make our own entrance in a different spot or find other entrances that are less well-guarded. We should try searching for those now that it's daylight and they'll be easier to find."*

Tavarian and I did as Lessie suggested, splitting up while she guarded our belongings at the camp. About two hours later, I ran across a patrol and crouched behind bushes as they passed. Were we fools to camp here? Should we find a different location where Lessie would not be easily spotted? Tavarian's spell couldn't shield her on the ground—he'd told me that it worked by bending the moonlight and using the cloud mist to advantage, effectively blending Lessie's iridescent scales into the sky. Such a thing wouldn't do any good in the forest.

"I don't know what we did to deserve getting posted in this hellhole," one of the passing soldiers grumbled to his patrol partner. "These dark, damp conditions make my bones ache."

"Shut it, old man," the other one said, a teasing note in his voice. "You'd think that you're forty-five, not four and twenty, by the way you talk."

"I just don't understand why I signed up for the army if I don't get the chance to fight," the first man said, his voice growing farther away.

Some instinct told me to follow them, and I crept alongside the path, crouching behind the bushes and thankful for my spelled boots.

"We should be out conquering Elantia with our fellow soldiers, not watching these whiny dragon riders."

"Maybe," the other man said as they stopped in a small, secluded clearing. "But if we were out with the army, it would be more difficult for us to find the time and privacy to do *this*, wouldn't it?"

The soldier backed his grumpy patrol partner against the tree, and in the next second, they were practically eating each other's faces. My cheeks burned as they pawed at each other's clothing, but as the first man dropped his trousers, a keyring attached to his beltloop clattered conveniently to the rocky ground.

I hesitated, then crept to the other side of the clearing, doing my best to ignore the sounds the soldiers were making. Technically I didn't need the keys since I had my lock pick, but if Tavarian and I had to split up, it would be good for him to have a set. Heart pounding, I glanced through the leaves to make sure that the lovers weren't looking my way, and got *far* more of an eyeful than I wanted. Ducking my head again, I quickly darted my hand out, unhooked the keys from the man's belt—his trousers were pooled around his ankles—and whisked them behind the bushes.

At least someone around here is getting some. I crawled away, careful not to disturb any rocks or branches as I retreated from the amorous couple. These soldiers were proving my point that sex was a distraction—if they hadn't been so caught up in each other, I would never have been able to steal the keys.

Well that was a first, I thought as I got to my feet, far enough away that I was certain I wouldn't be seen. I'd stolen from all kinds of people, in all sorts of situations, but never from someone in the middle of a sex act. My lips stretched into a grin as I imagined the look on Carina's face when I told her all about it.

If you get the chance, a dour voice in my head said, instantly souring the mood.

I will *get the chance,* I told it stubbornly. I didn't care what the odds were—I would come back from this alive, and I would reunite with my friends.

I returned to the clearing, eager to tell Tavarian that we were close to the dragon riders and that I had the keys. Unfortunately, he wasn't back yet, and when I tried to contact him via the earpiece, he didn't answer.

"Tavarian told me to let you know that he's gone off to the village to make some inquiries," Lessie said. *"He should return in a few hours."*

"Oh." I sat down on a log, disappointed. *"I wish I'd known. I would have liked to go into the village."*

Lessie cocked her head. *"I felt your excitement earlier. What did you discover?"*

I fished the keys out of my pocket and dangled them in front of her. *"Keys. I stole them off a pair of fornicating soldiers. No idea how much they're going to help, since they lead to the front entrance,"* I added as I tossed them into the air and caught them. *"But it's better than nothing, I suppose."*

An hour later, Tavarian returned to the clearing. My stomach grumbled at the smell of food—he'd brought some welcome provisions, and I eagerly tore into some fresh bread and cheese while he told me about the trip.

"The soldiers go into the village fairly often, mostly to the pub," Tavarian told me. "Despite their patronage, the locals are not very fond of them. There have been more than a few reports of local girls being accosted by randy soldiers, and they often try to underpay the merchants. I asked around about the mine, but nobody seems to know why the military has taken it over. There was an old man who used to work there, and he says the mine was stripped of tin close to twenty years ago."

I shrugged. I pulled the keys from my pocket and tossed them to him. "I also found these today. Took them off that pair of patrolling soldiers who decided to take a tumble in the hay, so to speak. They were whining about having to guard a bunch of dragon riders, so we're definitely in the right place."

"Really?" Tavarian raised an eyebrow as he took the keys. "Your ingenuity never fails to surprise me. Do you know what these keys are for?"

My cheeks warmed at the compliment. "I don't know where all

of them lead to, but one of them goes to the metal door we saw earlier. The soldiers know the keys are missing," I added ruefully, "and the door is guarded from inside, so I don't know how much this helps."

Tavarian frowned. "I doubt they will be changing the locks anytime soon," he said. "As far as the guards, I might have a way around them."

"Oh, really?"

Tavarian pulled out a package of fresh fish from one of the bags. He roasted it over the fire as we talked strategy. We discussed several options, and then he drew out paper and ink and wrote a hasty note to his airship crew to follow Lessie back here. After darkness had fallen, we pinned the note to Lessie's saddle and sent her to deliver the message.

"Be careful," I said as I wrapped my arms around her neck in a brief hug. *"Tavarian's spell won't be able to shield you now."*

Lessie huffed. *"I've managed without the shielding spell for quite some time now."* She nudged my belly with her nose. *"Don't do anything stupid while I'm gone,"* she said.

I sighed a little as she took off, missing her already. "How long do you think it'll take them to get here?"

"If Lessie doesn't run into trouble or make too many stops, they should arrive just before dawn," Tavarian said. He unpacked his bedroll and rolled it out near the still-flickering fire. I'd been worried about making one, but Tavarian said it was necessary for the next part of the plan, and he'd used his magic to suppress the smoke and dim the light so no one from a distance could see it.

"You should lie down and rest a bit," he said, patting the bedroll. "I have to go forage for the right plants. I'll be back in a bit."

I nodded but ignored the bedroll, instead taking a seat on one of the logs and staring into the fire. I was tired, and I couldn't risk accidentally falling asleep on the mat when I was supposed to keep watch.

Luckily, Tavarian was back in less than twenty minutes with the plants he needed. "This is trellin," he said as he laid it out on the ground. He used his magic to dry the plants out, then took a rock and a flat stone and ground them into a fine powder. "Be very careful not to inhale," he said, as he poured the powder into a leather pouch. "When ground into a powder, this herb assaults the lungs and makes it very hard to breathe."

"That's your plan?" I arched an eyebrow. "To suffocate the guards?"

He shrugged. "Unless they already have weak lungs, the powder will only incapacitate them for an hour or two," he said. "It has no lasting effects."

"That wasn't what I was worried about," I said wryly. As much as I hated the idea of killing, this was war. Those soldiers would have no qualms about killing us—we couldn't afford to play nice. "I just thought it would be something like that sleeping gas Salcombe used."

Tavarian's face darkened at the mention of my old mentor. "Salcombe did quite a bit more than gas his victims to sleep."

I winced. "I didn't mean to imply that you're anything like him," I said hastily. "You're not. You're a good man, Tavarian."

"Do you really think so?" he asked, an odd note in his voice.

"Of course I do." I frowned. "Why would you think otherwise?"

He turned to face me fully, taking my hand in his. "We've been through a lot together, Zara," he said in that low, velvety voice that made my stomach flip-flop. "And in many ways, we've grown quite close. And yet, despite the attraction between us, you continue to hold me at arm's length. Why would that be, unless there is something about me that you find unpalatable?"

I squirmed like a guilty child beneath his penetrating gaze. "There's nothing about you that's 'unpalatable,'" I told him. "It's just that I don't really know what it is that's between us. And now that we're in the middle of a war and emotions are running high, I don't think I can trust my heart."

Tavarian regarded me silently. "You asked me once what I meant when I said I wanted all of you," he said. "In that moment, I was confused as to what you were asking. I thought that I'd been clear. But I've had to think, and I realize now that being raised as an orphan, and then by a man who only saw you as a means to an end, has made you wary of commitment. You want to take it slow. Keep things casual. Leave yourself plenty of time and space in case you need a way out."

His words struck too close to home, and I tried to pull away. "Tavarian—"

"But the truth is"—he tightened his grip on my hand, not allowing me to retreat—"I don't want to keep things casual. I don't want a mere tumble in the hay. You are the only woman I've ever told my secrets to"—his voice grew rough with emotion, stirring my own heart—"the only woman I've ever trusted to have my back. I don't want you for an evening, or for a week. I want you to be mine, completely, and I want to be yours. Until the day we follow our dragons into the great beyond."

"Oh." I stared at Tavarian, my mouth hanging open. No man had ever made such a declaration to me, and especially not with such breathtaking sincerity. "Is that all?" I asked in a strangled voice.

Tavarian chuckled. "You don't have to give me an answer now," he said as he brought my hand to his lips. I was mesmerized by the shape of his mouth as it brushed over my knuckles, sending sparks through me. "In fact, I'd prefer you think long and hard about it, because I don't do anything by half-measures. I want you to be completely sure before you say yes."

"Right." I scraped a hand through my hair, feeling dazed. "Umm, yeah. I'll think about it."

"Good." He squeezed my hand, then finally released it. "Get some sleep," he said, nodding toward the bedroll on the ground. "I'll take the first watch."

"Okay." Sighing, I lay down on the bedroll and stared into the fire. Tavarian crouched in front of it and retrieved the mortar with a stick, then took it out of my line of sight to pack the powder away for our break-in. I tried to close my eyes and sleep, but my heart was still racing from Tavarian's declaration. There was no room for interpretation for what he'd said—he wanted commitment, a permanent relationship. And for a man of his status, that meant marriage. And children.

Was that what I wanted? To settle down with a titled lord and raise his heirs? Of course they would be my children, too, and I would love them. Most women would kill for the opportunity. But I wasn't built the way most women were. I was a treasure hunter, an adventurer. I lived for the thrill of exploring new places, unearthing new finds. That didn't exactly mesh with the life of a titled lady, as I well knew from my experience in playing at one.

Oh come on, a voice in my head chided. *This is Tavarian we're talking about. He wouldn't force you to give up your passions just because the two of you got married. Besides, him being a titled lord doesn't mean very much given the state of the country.*

Right. Which was exactly why I shouldn't be worrying about this right now. How could I possibly make a decision about Tavarian when I had no idea what the future would hold?

Damn him for asking for a commitment, I thought grumpily as I tossed and turned in my bedroll. I could really use that tumble in the hay right now, if only to let off some of that steam and frustration. But I refused to lead him on, and after what he'd said, I knew I couldn't give him my body unless I was willing to give him my heart, too.

Despite my emotional turmoil, the crackle of fire lulled me into a dreamless sleep. It seemed like I was only out for a few minutes when Tavarian gently shook my shoulder, coaxing me awake.

"Come on, Zara," he whispered in my ear. "It's time to go."

"Huh?" I sat up and stared at him through bleary eyes. "But I thought I was taking the next watch."

He shook his head. "I let you sleep. You needed it." He rose to his feet and slung a pack over his shoulder. "Hurry. We need to get the prisoners out by the time Lessie returns with the airship."

I scrubbed a hand over my face, trying to banish the sleep, then strapped on my weapons and my pouch belt and followed Tavarian into the woods. I wondered if Tavarian was using a spell to silence his footfalls or if he was just really good at stealth. He made no sound even though the forest floor was littered with branches and roots and pebbles.

The clouds had shifted in the sky again, giving us more moonlight to see by. It was close to two in the morning, and as we suspected, there was no patrol about. In no time at all, we stood in front of the hidden door again, and Tavarian watched my back as I shuffled through the keys, trying to find the right one.

Here. I plucked the biggest key on the ring and carefully fitted it into the lock. It turned easily, and I nudged Tavarian to let him know, then gripped my dragon blade in my free hand. The moment the lock clicked, I threw the door open, and Tavarian and I rushed in.

Unlike the first time we'd been here, there were only two soldiers manning the entrance, both sleepy and relaxed. They jumped to their feet at the sight of us, drawing their weapons, but I extended my dragon blade, piercing the first one through the heart before he had time to strike. Tavarian blocked the second guard's sword with his own, then disarmed him and hit him on the side of his head with the handle. The man staggered into the wall, crying out for help, and Tavarian finished him with a slice across the neck, silencing him.

"Crap." My muscles were coiled as I crouched beside the bodies, quickly patting them down. The man's cry had echoed down the tunnel, loud enough to alert anyone nearby. But no one came, and after finding nothing of importance, we moved on.

Tavarian took a torch from the wall, and we silently made our way down the tunnel, ears pricked for any sign of an approaching enemy. But again, we heard no one. I suspected the entrance tunnel was far enough away from the main part of the mines that no one else had heard. There had been a cord hanging from the tunnel ceiling near the entrance, probably an alarm to let the others know if there had been a breach or if the guards needed backup. Without that, the others would be clueless.

Breathing a little easier, Tavarian and I carefully explored the warren of tunnels. The passages were very narrow, curving and twisting very suddenly, and the ceilings were so low in places that we had to crawl on hands and sometimes even elbows to get through.

It's a good thing I'm not claustrophobic, I thought. My time as both a thief and a treasure hunter had trained any possible fear of small spaces out of me.

Besides, Tavarian's presence was reassuring. He was strong and fast, and even more highly trained than me as a fighter and soldier. Regardless of the uncertainty surrounding our relationship, I was very thankful to have him on my side.

Eventually, we reached a rough-hewn staircase, and spent the next half hour descending through several steep levels. My treasure sense alerted me to a room up ahead, conjuring up an image of several sets of armor and weapons. I slowed, putting a finger to my lips to signal Tavarian to be quiet. Not that he wasn't already silent—the man moved like a ghost.

He nodded, and we crept toward the entrance of what turned out to be a common room. Peeking through a crack in the door, I saw five soldiers sitting around a table, drinking beer and making bawdy jokes.

"I'll take care of this," Tavarian mouthed. He pulled the handkerchief tied around his neck over his mouth, and I hastily did the same, moving out of the way as I realized his intent. Tavarian stuck his hand through the door and scattered a fistful of powder into the space, then hastily withdrew. I could feel the hum of power as he worked some spell, manipulating the air to circulate the powder through the room.

"Oi, did you hear that sou—" a soldier broke off, struck by a coughing fit.

"Wha—" the second soldier started in, too, and soon, the entire room was coughing. Satisfied, Tavarian shouldered the door open all the way, and we leapt inside, blades flashing. With a spin of my dragon blade, I severed two heads at once, then spun around and ran a third man through as he leapt at my back. Blood spattered the walls, the floors, our clothing as we quickly dispatched the afflicted men, who were in no shape to fight back. My flesh crawled at the sight of the blood staining my skin, and I hastily rubbed my hands on my trousers, wishing I could wash off the evidence of my crime.

It's not a crime, I reminded myself sternly. *They're the enemy.* I pushed my emotions to the side, forcing myself to be dispassionate. It was just blood. It would wash off.

"All right," Tavarian said as he stepped back. He was wearing all black, all the better for concealment, so I couldn't see a spot of blood on him. He cleaned his bloody sword on the back of one of the corpses, then sheathed it. "Where to next?" If he noticed my discomfort, he didn't mention it, and part of me was glad. I couldn't afford kind words or sympathy right now. I needed to harden my heart and stay focused on the mission.

"There must be a dormitory or barracks somewhere," I said, pitching my voice low so it wouldn't echo in the tunnels. Casting about with my treasure sense, I tried to narrow down the direction by searching for areas with items of value consistent with soldiers' quarters. There were three that could fit, so I picked one, and we headed in that direction.

My first guess was off. It turned out to be a common room for the officers, based on the nicer furnishings and the liquor cabinet, so we passed it and went onto the next. After twenty minutes and several tricky corridors, we came upon a heavy metal door at the end of a wide tunnel.

"Here," Tavarian murmured, pressing his hand against the door. The telltale hum of magic filled the air, and when he tugged the handle, the door silently glided open. We both peered in through the tiniest crack, and even if I couldn't make out the silhouettes of the bunk beds within, the sounds of snoring would have clued me in. Using my treasure sense, I tried to gauge how many men were in there based on the number of uniforms. Roughly twenty. Accounting for perhaps another ten more on guard duty, including the ones we killed, that would put the soldier population at maybe thirty-five, forty people.

Not very many, I thought. Which meant the prison population likely wasn't more than one hundred.

Tavarian seemed to come to a similar conclusion, for he closed the door instead of throwing powder inside. Even incapacitated, the odds were not in our favor against twenty trained soldiers. I found the key to the dormitory, locked the door, and broke it off. There. That would keep them busy for a while if they woke up, and I didn't have to stain my blade with more blood.

Yet.

Tavarian squeezed my hand briefly, and then we retraced our steps until we found another staircase. We descended several more levels, and between the echoing tunnels that picked up any motion and my treasure sense, we were able to kill two more patrolling soldiers without raising any alarm, and stuff their bodies into alcoves or small rooms.

"I think we're almost—"

A door opened to my right, and a half-naked man lunged out. I choked back a scream as the wild-eyed soldier slashed at my neck with the knife clutched in his fist, and felt a sting as the steel kissed my trachea.

"You!" I gasped, recognizing his thin face. It was the lieutenant I'd plied with alcohol the other night who'd given me the information about this place.

"Have we met?" the soldier sneered, but he didn't get in another word before Tavarian was on him. He slammed the man into the wall, but the soldier lashed out with his knife and ripped into Tavarian's arm. The sight of his blood spraying through the air made my own blood run cold, and the soldier started screaming, "Intruder alert! Intruder alert!"

Tavarian swore loudly, grabbing the man's knife hand and twisting until he dropped the weapon. He used his own dagger to cut the man's throat, then grabbed my hand and dragged me down the staircase. The sounds of pounding footsteps and shouting soldiers echoed from both above and below, and I gripped my dragon blade tight with one hand, grabbing Tavarian's shoulder with the other.

"Take the ones from above. I'll take the ones below," I shouted. Pushing Tavarian behind me, I lifted my blade just in time to see a soldier dart around the curving staircase. I jumped away from Tavarian so I wouldn't accidentally run him through, then extended my blade fully. It punched through not only the first soldier but also the one behind him, and I yanked it back with a grunt, trying to ignore the arc of blood.

A third soldier from around the corner cried out, but I didn't wait for him to regroup. Gathering my legs beneath me, I leapt onto the two bodies and rammed my blade into soldier number three before he could decide whether to retreat or regroup. There were three other men behind him, so I retracted my weapon to a more manageable length and met their swords with my own twirling blades. The dragon blade almost seemed to have a mind of its own, a seamless extension of my body, parrying and whirling as it sliced through the row of enemies as if they were mere stalks of wheat.

"Zara!" Tavarian rushed down the staircase, his silver eyes wild. "Are you all right?" The left side of his face was speckled with drops of blood, and his arm still bled profusely.

"I am, but you're not." Blood clung to my skin and clothes, but I refused to look. I grabbed his sleeve and used my knife to rip it off, then tied it around the wound in a makeshift tourniquet. "We need to get that treated."

"Later," he said, pushing past me. "The barracks doors won't hold for long if all this noise awoke the soldiers. We need to get the others out of here."

Fast as we could manage, we fleeced the dead soldiers of as many weapons as we could carry, then raced down the stairs and through another door. Not wanting to fumble with the key ring,

I used my magic lockpick to open the door. The stench of sweat, blood, and fecal matter hit me like a wave, but at the sight of the rows of cells, bursting with prisoners, a rush of relief flowed through me.

"Zara!" a familiar voice yelled, and my mouth dropped open as Jallis clutched the bars of the third cell to the left, desperate eyes locking with mine. He had ugly bruises on his face, and his cheeks were gaunt, as if he'd been underfed. "Dragon's balls, is it really you?" he shouted over the din of clamoring prisoners. They all wore tattered Elantian military uniforms, and all looked unwashed and malnourished.

"Yes! I'm here to get you out!" Tossing Tavarian the key ring, I used my lockpick to open the first cell on the left while Tavarian found the key to open the cell doors on the right. The first soldier popped out of the cell immediately, practically crying with relief, and his eyes widened when I shoved a sheathed sword into his hands.

"Take these," I said to him and the three others as they squeezed out of the cell. "We may encounter enemies."

I moved down the row, handing out weapons to the soldiers as I freed them. Most of them were really banged up, but a few were in bad shape, showing signs of torture. All were suffering from severe dehydration. Their sorry state made my blood boil with rage, but I forced it down, determined to stay focused.

Eventually, I reached Jallis's cell. The moment I released him, he pulled me into a quick, hard hug.

"Thank the skies," he whispered hoarsely into my hair. "I thought we were going to die in here."

Once upon a time, the feel of his arms around me would have made my knees go weak and my heart flutter. But now, I only felt a wave of sympathy for him. "I'm glad you're okay," I said, handing him a short sword. "There are more weapons up the stairs on a few dead soldiers. Take some men and go collect them. We need as many people armed as possible."

"Can you use your treasure sense to locate the armory?" Jallis asked. "I could take a few men to break in there, and there might be enough weapons for almost everyone."

I closed my eyes for a moment, reaching out with my treasure sense. Sure enough, there was a room full of weapons two floors up. "Go quickly," I urged, and gave him the location. "We'll meet you on the floor above with the rest of the riders."

As Tavarian and I released the rest of the soldiers, we posted the armed ones in front of the prison entrance, then quickly triaged those who were wounded or sick. Tavarian's face was pale from blood loss, but he rallied his strength and used his magic to heal the worst ones just enough so they could walk out of here. The dragon riders were astonished, but they wisely saved their questions for later.

"Zara!" Kade, Ullion, and Daria, the three cadets who'd been sent to the Traggaran Channel camp with me, fought their way toward me. "We thought we'd never see you again," Kade said, his eyes too-bright. "I'm sorry we weren't able to do anything when Roche had you imprisoned. She knew we were your friends and she had men watching us like hawks. Will you forgive us?"

I grinned. "Are you kidding me? I'm just happy to see you guys are both alive." I slapped Kade and Daria on the back. "If you guys are feeling guilty, don't worry about it. I'm about to put you all to work."

Ullion saluted. "We're more than happy to serve. What can we do?"

"Kenrook." A soldier interrupted us as he approached, looking apologetic. I blinked at the halo of unruly bright curls that surrounded his head, which were remarkably similar to my own. But then again, I wasn't the only redhead in Elantia. "I'm Captain Haldor Savin, and I want to apologize for doubting you back at camp. Many of us believed Colonel Roche when she said that you turned traitor, but no traitor would have risked her neck to save us like this."

"I'd like to apologize as well—" another soldier began, and my face grew hot as the room was suddenly filled with shouts and sobs again. Gods, I wasn't sure if I could take this, not now. We needed to get out of here!

"Enough!" Tavarian barked, his stern voice cutting through the din. "You can thank Zara later, once we're out of here. Right now, we need to move before more guards come upon us."

Turning back to Kade, Daria, and Ullion, I posted them all as team leaders along with me and Tavarian. I then organized the riders into five teams, roughly twenty-five each. "Stick to your team leader and follow their orders," I said. "The corridors are narrow, so we move single file. Don't wander, don't make pit stops for any reason. We march until we've cleared the surface."

The soldiers nodded, and I led the way while Tavarian brought up the rear. As we made our way through the corridors, I grabbed more torches and passed them on to the team leaders to light the way for the others. My heart pounded as we approached the armory. To my relief, Jallis and his men had successfully broken in and were waiting for us by the open door.

"Zara." He saluted me as I approached, and I swore at the sight of his blood-soaked shirt. He and the three men with him were banged up, though at least none of them were among the dead bodies on the ground. "We've secured the armory. Harder than I thought," he added with a grunt.

We managed to make it up to the second level of the mines when I heard a distant crash, followed by the sounds of shouting. "Run!" I yelled, moving aside so the others could rush past. "Jallis, take the weak and the wounded and get them the hell out of here!"

Jallis looked like he wanted to stay and fight but did as I asked. Even after raiding the armory, a good third of our soldiers remained unarmed, so they went ahead with Jallis in the lead while the others rallied around me to form a barrier in the corridor. A jolt of worry hit me as Tavarian came to stand by my side, his bloodied hands gripping the hilt of his sword.

I glanced sideways at his wounded arm. "You should have joined the others."

He rolled his eyes. "I'm not an invalid."

"You're going to be if you lose more blood."

And then there was no time to talk. The twenty-odd soldiers who'd been locked in the barracks burst into the corridor, which was wide enough for us to stand three abreast. Gritting my teeth, I cut into the soldiers with two long, forearm-length daggers, not wanting to risk my dragon blade in such close quarters. The smell of blood mingled in the air with screams of pain and rage, and though my fellow soldiers were malnourished and weakened, they attacked and overwhelmed the guards with a surprising amount of vehemence.

The soldiers, quickly realizing they were outnumbered two to one, tried to beat a hasty retreat. But the dragon riders chased after them like a crazed pack of dogs, ripping into them with their blades and bashing their heads against the walls. The enemy's battle cries turned into wails and pleas of terror that turned my stomach, but I forced myself to keep my heart hard. These men and women had been through hell at the hands of their captors. They had every right to take vengeance on the enemy.

A distant explosion echoed from somewhere above us, and everybody paused. "What was that?" several of the soldiers shouted.

One of the enemy soldiers gave us a bloody grin. "That's our failsafe," he said, his words slurred around his swollen tongue. "We have orders to collapse the mine if it's compromised."

"Shit!" I grabbed the arm of the nearest Elantian soldier, who was on the ground, still mid-stab as he straddled his victim. "We have to go, now!"

Even as I said the words, the walls trembled.

"Now!" I roared, charging for the stairs. The other soldiers dropped the few remaining enemies and followed behind me, and I had to pump my legs faster than I'd ever thought possible to keep from getting trampled. As I darted through another tunnel and up another landing, large chunks of rock rained down. My heart plummeted as cries of pain echoed in the tunnels—the soldiers were being struck by the rocks raining down from the ceiling. "Come on!" I yelled, ushering people past while trying to avoid getting struck myself.

It seemed to take forever, but we finally reached the corridor that led to the front entrance. I sobbed with relief at the sight of moonlight spilling through the open door. I burst into the clearing, lungs heaving. Tavarian stumbled out after me, and I grabbed his uninjured arm and hauled him away, giving space for the stragglers to come out behind us.

"Zara!" Jallis rushed over to me, his face pale with shock as he took me by the arms. "What's going on in there?"

"Cave-in," I coughed. The air inside the mines had filled with dust from the crumbling walls, and even pulling the neckerchief up around my face hadn't been enough. "Some kind of fail-safe explosion if the mines are compromised."

"Those bastards," Jallis fumed. His eyes widened as he looked toward the line of soldiers, many of whom sported bleeding wounds from their heads and shoulders. "Do you have any medical supplies?"

"In those bags over there." I pointed at the bags of provisions Tavarian had procured from town, thankful nobody had stolen them while we were gone.

Jallis nodded, then strode away, commandeering the healthy soldiers to assist the injured.

WE DRAGGED everyone as far from the mines as possible in case there was any chance of further explosions or more booby traps, not stopping until we reached the clearing.

Tavarian put on a good show, but I could tell he was flagging. His gait had slowed and the stern mask he usually wore was crumbling, giving way to lines of pain etched into his face.

"Come here," I said when he started toward one of the injured soldiers lying on the ground. "You've done enough. You need to rest."

"What about you?" he demanded, even as I led him to a tree. "You're wounded too." His silver gaze lingered on the cuts on my face and arms, and though he couldn't see it, I had a feeling there was a darkening bruise on my ribs from where one soldier had landed a good kick.

"My injuries are minor, and I didn't just expend a bunch of energy healing twenty or so people," I said. Placing my hands on his shoulders, I looked up into his face, then stood on tiptoe and pressed a light kiss to his lips. Instantly, I felt the tension in his body melt, and I almost laughed when he slid his hands around my waist.

"Down, boy," I said, applying pressure to his shoulders. He was so weak that he went down easily, and I helped him rest his back against the tree trunk. "You need to rest. I mean it."

"Okay." His eyes were already fluttering closed, but he grasped my hand as I started to pull away. "Don't leave me here," he said sleepily.

I smoothed a stray lock of hair from his clammy brow. "I won't leave you," I promised. *Ever*, I wanted to say, but I knew I couldn't promise that, so I sealed my lips on the word before it could escape.

I stood up as Tavarian slipped into sleep, and turned to see Jallis watching me thoughtfully.

"Need something?" I asked as I strolled over to him. He was crouched beside a wounded blonde, wrapping a haphazardly cleaned and stitched gash in her side with gauze.

He shook his head. "I'm just thinking about how Lord Tavarian healed all those people." He glanced down at the woman, whose eyes were closed as she gritted her teeth against the pain. "She was deathly ill, coughing her lungs out every night for the past three days."

Her eyes opened, a pain-filled blue that made my heart wrench. And yet she smiled at me. "Now it's just a slight cough," she said in a voice like sandpaper. "I thought I was going to rot away in that cell. Instead, I got to run my sword through the guard that raped me when I was first brought here."

Any sympathy or horror I'd felt while watching my fellow soldiers mow down the enemy vanished instantly, and I crouched next to the woman to clasp her hand. "You fought well, soldier. Thank you for helping me get everyone out alive."

But everyone didn't make it out alive. As I walked through the clearing, which wasn't nearly large enough to fit everyone, I talked to the soldiers and tried to get a head count even though I wasn't sure exactly how many prisoners had been there. I learned from Captain Savin that five had died in the cave-in, and another three had perished from injuries or sickness during their incarceration. My heart was sick with the knowledge—not just that the soldiers had died, but that their dragons had died with them. I could just imagine how the other dragons would have felt, watching their comrades suddenly keel over as their partners passed, terrified and angry that they could be next and there was nothing they could do about it.

The only saving grace is that at least the cave-in killed any remaining soldiers. But even that might not be completely true. There could have been a few soldiers who had gone into town, or who had escaped from other exits. I warned the other soldiers to be on their guard.

While Tavarian and the other injured slept, I took watch with Jallis and the healthy soldiers, rotating in three shifts through the night. Although exhaustion tugged at my mind, I insisted on doing my shift, preferring to sit up in one of the tree branches, high enough that I had a perfect view of the horizon. Dawn would be here soon, and would hopefully bring Lessie as well. I could feel her getting closer through the bond, though she was still too far away to make contact.

The tree branches below me rustled, and I glanced down as Jallis climbed up. My shoulders tensed—I wasn't sure if I was ready to talk to him alone, not yet—but I leaned my head back against the trunk and kept my expression relaxed as he clambered onto the thick branch next to mine.

"Hey." His voice was soft, almost tender, but he didn't reach out to touch me. "Are you all right?"

"Am I all right?" I tilted my head to the sky, considering. The stars were numerous tonight, a twinkling blanket of white fire that was as dazzling as it was remote. The past few weeks had been a wild ride. Sure, I'd bloodied my hands, witnessed unspeakable suffering, lost good men and women, and walked through bloody fields full of dead people, but I'd also thwarted a dangerous political alliance, helped Zuar City prepare for war, dodged a nasty attack from a colonel who'd wanted to throw me in prison for life, and found and freed the dragon riders. My ribs might be hurting, and my skin might sting from cuts and bruises, but my heart was full. For the first time in a long, long while, I saw hope as I looked at the lightening horizon.

"I'm good," I finally said, turning to face him with a smile. "Pretty damn good."

Jallis nodded, a slight smile coming to his own lips. "I'm glad to see it. You seem...different. Less angry, more confident in your skin as a soldier and a dragon rider. I know you hate the military,

Zara, but the way you carried out this mission proves that you're a born leader. You're a rising star, and all the other riders respect you now."

"Yeah, and it only took saving all their asses to make it happen." My voice turned bitter, my smile sliding off my face. "Is this all you care about, Jallis? That I'm being a good little soldier now?"

"No!" He jerked upright, a chagrined look on his face. "No, I didn't mean that at all. I was just trying to compliment you." He sighed. "But I can see that anything I say is going to be twisted through the lens of your hatred for the military."

I sighed, my heart softening. "I don't hate the military," I said gently, reaching out to place my hand atop his. "And I don't hate you either. It's just that after everything that's happened, I can't help but be resentful. It isn't just about what Colonel Roche did to me," I said before Jallis could interrupt. "It's about the state of our country. If our military wasn't so stubborn and ignorant, and had adapted our warfare technology to the changing times, we wouldn't be about to lose our home."

Jallis nodded. "You were right about everything, Zara," he said. "I was wrong to discourage you from speaking out. I should have backed you...hell, I wanted to back you. But I didn't want to get strung up for it the way you did. I was a coward." His gaze dropped, and he looked genuinely ashamed.

"You weren't a coward. You were just being sensible and following the rules." I withdrew my hand. "I can't even really blame you, Jallis. You've been preparing for a military career your entire life. Of course you would follow protocol and try to stay in line. But I'm not built that way. I grew up in an orphanage, on the streets. I got my bread and butter from stealing, and then plundering temples." A little shiver crawled down my spine as I said the words, remembering Caor. Had the gods been watching every time I took from one of their sacred buildings? If so, why had they chosen me, when I'd desecrated their sanctuaries so often?

Jallis smiled crookedly. "We're from different worlds, for sure. But that doesn't mean we can't be friends, and as your friend I should have backed you." He cocked his head. "You know, the last time I saw you, you were being dragged to the colonel's office in chains. How did you end up out here, on a rescue mission?"

"It's a long story." But we had all night, so I told it to him—how Lessie had broken me out, how the two of us had flown to Zuar City to help with the preparations, and how after I'd been caught, Tavarian had come to my aid like a knight in shining armor. "We pretty much came straight here after my court-martial was over," I finished. "It took us some digging, but we eventually tracked down the location of the prison, and here we are."

"Amazing." Jallis shook his head. That thoughtful look was back in his eyes, but it was tinged with a hint of jealousy now. "Things are...different, between you and Lord Tavarian now."

I raised an eyebrow. "Are they?"

"I've seen the way he looks at you," Jallis countered, "and you kissed him earlier. Are you in love with him?"

"Love?" I sputtered. "Don't be ridiculous. I've been too busy chasing after you and the other riders to have time to even *think* about a relationship, never mind love."

Jallis folded his arms. "There is no set amount of time that it takes to fall in love with someone, and war tends to stir up all kinds of tensions between people. Besides, from everything you've told me, it sounds like the two of you have been through quite a lot together."

"I don't know," I said, feeling a little awkward. The last person I expected to be talking about my feelings for Tavarian with was Jallis. "I... I think I could love him, maybe. I know I like him, and he likes me." That last part was a severe understatement, but I was hardly going to tell Jallis that. "Do we really have to talk about this?" I finally whined, throwing up my hands.

Jallis laughed, and just like that, the tension between us vanished. "No," he said softly. "We don't have to talk about it. We don't have to talk about anything. I just want to be here for you."

"Thanks." I gave him a warm smile, and we sat in companionable silence, our eyes fixed on the horizon. I wondered if Jallis still thought he had a shot with me. After everything that had happened between us, I'd never be able to think of him in a romantic way again, but I didn't feel like spoiling the mood by shoving that in his face right this second. After all, he was still my friend, and a damn good soldier at that, judging by the way he'd taken command today. As long as I treated him like a friend, I didn't see why we couldn't continue this way.

"Zara," Jallis said, just as I dozed off. "Look! It's Lessie."

My eyes popped open, and I grinned at the sight of my dragon flying directly toward us, with the airship in tow. *"Lessie!"* I cried.

"Zara!" Her joy was palpable through the bond. *"Where do you want us to land?"*

I considered for a moment. *"As close as you can, but not in the clearing. It's filled with soldiers."*

"You rescued them then." The bond swelled with pride. *"I had no doubt you and Tavarian would succeed."*

Jallis and I climbed down, and I went to wake Tavarian. "Lessie's back," I said as I gently shook his uninjured arm.

"Mmm." He opened his mercurial eyes, still foggy with sleep but not pain. One of the soldiers had cleaned and stitched his wound last night, and for all I knew, Tavarian might have already used magic on it to lessen the pain. "She brought the airship?"

"Yes. It's landing nearby. You should go and consult with your crew."

Tavarian ambled to his feet. He still seemed weak from using so much magic last night, so I ordered two soldiers to accompany him just in case he ran into any trouble along the way.

I turned back to the team leaders, who were already up and about, and asked for a report.

"Nothing out of the ordinary," Kade reported. "None of our patrols caught sight of any enemy soldiers wandering the area or approaching the hidden entrance to the mines."

"Excellent." I turned to Daria. "What about you, Lieutenant?"

She smiled. "Everyone has survived the night. At least everyone who made it out of the tunnels." Her smile faded. "We lost so many, Commandant."

I tried to ignore the way my stomach flip-flopped at the title. "Stop calling me that." The soldiers had unanimously elevated my rank last night and started referring to me as Commandant—not an official military title, at least not in Elantia, but it was still the last thing I wanted.

"We can't," Ullion said. "We have to call you something, and private doesn't seem appropriate considering what you've done."

I sighed. "Then just call me Zara." I raised my voice so everyone in the clearing could hear. "We're not just a platoon of soldiers. As far as we know, we're the only dragon riders left on this world." My heart ached as I thought of Rhia, and I hoped to gods that wasn't true. "We're a team, a family, and we need to treat each other that way. Whatever personal grievances any of us might have against one another, it's time to forgive them. Our entire focus needs to be on rescuing the dragons."

"Do you have a plan for that?" Savin asked. "I can feel the general direction my dragon is in, but he's too far away to communicate with."

"Lord Tavarian has uncovered intelligence that suggests the dragons are being held in the Treylin Valley," I told him. "We plan on going there next, and any of you are welcome to come along so long as you are able-bodied and won't slow us down."

The soldiers shouted questions all at once, and we spent the next hour hashing out the details. Tavarian returned from the ship bearing a map and showed the soldiers where Treylin was. They all agreed they felt their dragons in much the same distance and direction. All but the most severely wounded agreed we needed to travel there immediately, before the army found out the riders escaped and went to the valley to slaughter their dragons.

I also briefed them about the invading force sweeping through Elantia and the importance of recovering the dragons so we'd have a chance at fighting back. Aside from Jallis, whom I'd told last night, none of them knew about the second army or the impending attack on Zuar City, and many were dismayed to hear that so much of Elantia had been conquered already.

"This situation is intolerable," Captain Savin said, "and even more reason why we must make haste. By your leave, Zara, I will take a contingent of men east, toward the valley."

"Wouldn't it be easier to load us onto that airship?" another soldier asked.

Tavarian shook his head. "The airship is not large enough to accommodate all of you," he said. "I will take as many as I can, but the wounded must take precedence. The safest course would be to transport them to Ruisin, while the rest of you head for the valley."

That made sense to me. Ruisin was another neutral country that bordered Zallabar on the opposite side from Elantia.

"Once we've freed the dragons," Tavarian announced, "we will all meet up in Ruisin and decide our next course of action."

Decided, Captain Savin rounded up all able-bodied men and women—roughly half the remaining riders—and they prepared to march out. I was impressed with his initiative, and grateful he was taking the problem out of my hands. Tavarian had his crew bring what fresh clothing he had aboard the ship to distribute amongst the most needy, since they were all wearing tattered uniforms. Then he, Jallis, and I helped the crew assist the sick and injured onto the ship.

"I'll be going with Captain Savin," Jallis told me once the last of the soldiers were on board. "I figure it'll take us two days' march to reach the valley. You and Tavarian will fly ahead on Lessie, I assume?"

I nodded. "We'll scout ahead, make sure the way is clear, and if we can, we'll free the dragons on our own."

"Good." His gaze drifted to Lessie, who watched us nearby. "How she's grown," he said with a wistful smile. I knew he was remembering our first flight together on the back of his dragon, Kadryn.

"She can hold her own," I said with a little grin, then gave him a light shove. "Get going, soldier."

Jallis grinned back at me, then trotted back into the woods. I sighed in relief that I finally had a minute to myself and went to hug Lessie.

"I thought you'd forgotten about me," she teased as she curled an

arm around me, bringing me close as I tried to put my arms around her neck. She'd gotten bigger again. My arms had trouble spanning the underside of her neck now. *"Is everything okay with you and Jallis now? You two seem friendly again."*

"We had a long talk last night," I said as I stroked her scales. "He knows how much he messed up, and I think he understands where he's at now."

"Too bad for him," Lessie said, and I was surprised to hear the sympathy in her voice. *"You two could have been a good match if he wasn't so immature. But then again, I always preferred Tavarian."*

I snorted. *"Matchmaking now?"* But a smile tugged at my lips. Now that we'd managed to rescue the riders without killing ourselves, I was starting to feel a bit more hopeful that we'd actually come through this alive. Which meant Tavarian and I might have a future to talk about.

Maybe.

"When will you be ready to leave?" I asked, pulling back to have a look at her. She didn't seem injured in any way, and I felt no pain in the bond, but I could tell she was exhausted. *"I know you need to rest after such a long flight."*

"I do." She opened her mouth on a yawn, loud enough to shake the leaves and make a few of the crew members look sideways at her from the deck. *"I flew there without stopping, and then back again, so I need to rest three hours, at the very least. The valley doesn't seem all that far according to that map."*

I left Lessie to her nap and returned to the deck, where Tavarian was consulting with the ship's captain. I waited nearby until he finished.

"Lessie says she needs a few hours before we can take off," I told him. "Is the ship leaving now?"

"They will wait for nightfall," Tavarian said. "I gave the crew members some gold to purchase clothing and provisions in Ruisin when they arrive. They'll have to sleep on the ship, which is a bit cramped for so many passengers, but they'll manage."

I nodded. "The trip will be dangerous." I glanced at the sky. It was bright blue today, with only a few puffy clouds. "Hopefully, there will be more cloud cover by nightfall." There was always a chance they might run afoul of a Zallabarian airship on the way, and unlike them, our ship wasn't outfitted with guns.

"I know, but thankfully it isn't far." He cupped my cheek in his hand and gently traced the bags beneath my eye with his thumb. "You're exhausted, Zara. Go catch a few hours of sleep below deck. I'll come wake you in a little while."

I went below deck, intending to do as Tavarian suggested. But the sounds of terse commands and pained moans reminded me that the cabins on the ship had been commandeered as a makeshift hospital to treat the wounded. Poking my head into the mess, I saw that the men and women who required treatment had been laid out on the tables. Riders and crew members worked tirelessly, stitching wounds, applying poultices, and wiping fevered brows.

"Hey." I snagged the sergeant who was serving as our medic by the elbow as he rushed past. "What's the situation? Are these life-threatening wounds?" Some of the riders had been seriously injured during the escape, and there had been some who were already ill or injured when we'd broken into the compound.

"Mostly, no," the soldier said. "Some fevers and infections, but we have the supplies to treat them. I think almost everyone in here will recover."

"Good." A thought itched at the back of my mind, and suddenly I remembered the amulet resting against my chest beneath my clothes. "Is there a patient here called Rurian Vanar?" Or perhaps he was outside in the tents, amongst the uninjured?

The medic frowned. "As a matter of fact, there is. The patient over in the corner." He jabbed a finger toward a bed on the far side of the room. "He was the worst case. His leg was shredded during the battle, and the Zallabarians did nothing to treat his wound. It's a miracle he survived imprisonment and got out of the mine. Hopefully we cut the leg off in time to prevent sepsis."

Wincing, I nodded at the medic, then made my way over to the patient. He was only a few years older than me, with silver-blond hair and youthful features that were mercifully relaxed in sleep. A blanket covered most of his body, but I could tell which leg he'd lost—the left one was propped up by a pillow to encourage blood circulation, and had been cut off at the knee.

I stopped by Rurian's bedside, hesitant to disturb him. I could see bits of the old man in his features—the strong brow and jawline, and the shape of his nose. I reached behind my neck to unclasp the amulet when his eyelids fluttered open. Deep brown eyes flared wide when he caught sight of me.

"Commandant." He began to push himself upright.

"No, no." I dropped my hands so I could gesture him back down. "Please don't get up. You need to rest." My gaze flickered to his amputated leg, then back up to his face. "How are you feeling?"

"I've been better," he admitted as he leaned back against the pillows. His face was a bit wan, I noted, the lines tightening with pain. "But all in all, glad to be alive. Is there something I can help with? I'm a bit limited, as you can see, but if there's anything I can do I'm glad to pitch in."

"I'm actually here to deliver something from your father," I said with a smile. I unclasped the amulet from my neck and handed him the chain. "I accidentally ended up paying him a visit at his estate when I was out searching for surviving dragons. He told me he was worried about you and that he wanted me to bring this to you and make sure you got home safe."

Rurian's eyes gleamed with tears as he took the amulet. "Pa," he whispered, clenching his fist around the jeweled metal. He closed his eyes briefly, then looked up at me. "How was he doing?"

"He and Temerion are fine," I said gently. Or at least they were when I last saw them. The Zallabarians could have found them, but I didn't see any point in bringing that up. "Just worried about your safety, like I said. He was very insistent I give you this amulet."

Rurian gave me a crooked smile. "Pa always was superstitious."

I arched an eyebrow. "Maybe, but that amulet has real magic in it. I can sense it."

"Is that so?" He considered it for a long minute, then handed it back to me. "If that's the case, then you should take it."

"Me?" I held up my hands. "No way. Your father would have my hide!"

But Rurian grabbed my hand before I could back away. "Look," he said as he pressed the amulet into my palm. "If this thing really does have magic, then you need it more than me. Right now I'm safe and comfortable and out of the fighting. You're about to go and rescue all of our dragons, and if you don't succeed, the rest of us will die anyway. I have no illusions about what the Zallabarians will do once word gets out about our escape—they'll slaughter them all."

My stomach turned leaden as icy fear chilled my bones. "I'm hoping we can get to them before the rest of the military has been alerted."

"Me too. And that's why I'm giving this to you." He curled my fingers around the amulet, then gave me another smile. "On loan, of course. Wouldn't want to upset my Pa. You can return it when you come back with the dragons."

"All right." I put the amulet back on, and as it came to rest against my chest once more, I felt as if a great weight was settling on my shoulders. No pressure, right? "I'll be back with this," I told him.

"I'm counting on it."

After I finished my visit to the makeshift infirmary, I caught a few hours of sleep in one of the few beds that was still open. The moment Lessie announced she was recovered from the trip, Tavarian and I packed our bags and mounted up. Thanks to his cloaking spell, we didn't need to wait for nightfall, so we headed directly for the valley.

"You know," I said sleepily as I leaned against Tavarian's chest, basking in the warmth of his body. I was too tired to fight the urge, especially now that the hardest part of the mission was past. "If Zallabar's goal was to keep the dragon riders alive, they were doing a piss-poor job of it. The prison conditions were terrible, and if we'd arrived a few days later, they would have been too weak to move."

I felt Tavarian nod from behind me. "As it was, there were already too many deaths," he said. "Three soldiers is not that many, but three dragons out of such a small population is very large indeed. Perhaps our enemies were working at cross-purposes. I suspect that some of the higher-ups want to keep the dragon riders alive, for whatever reason, while the people manning the prison did not."

"That doesn't surprise me," I said. "More than once I've overheard Zallabarians complaining that the military should have killed off the dragons, that they're too dangerous to keep alive." I supposed their hatred and fear came from all those previous wars, when we used the dragons against Zallabar.

"Well," Tavarian said, a wry note in his voice, "as much as I am glad that they were not killed, those citizens are right. Dragons are too dangerous to keep alive as prisoners, and they are going to learn that very soon."

I grinned, his words lightening the last dregs of worry that had settled on my heart. Trusting Lessie and Tavarian to alert me if anything went wrong, I finally allowed myself to fall asleep. It was amazing how safe I felt with Tavarian's eyes on me. I'd never really been much of a cuddler in the past, preferring to leave my lovers' beds as quickly as possible after a tryst—or kick them out of mine—but I could easily see myself lounging around in bed with Tavarian, sleeping in as we lazily explored each other's bodies.

The thought inspired some pretty heated dreams, and I was pretty annoyed when Lessie woke me up. *"Mind out of the gutter,"* she said. *"We're close."*

I sat up in the saddle, shaking the sleep from my brain. We were completely surrounded by thick, white clouds, but as Lessie dipped below the cloud line, the hazy image of a verdant valley came into view. My heart soared at the sight, then immediately plummeted when I spotted the strategically placed cannons.

"There are dozens of them," Tavarian said after I'd lent him my goggles for a better view. "We are safe, thanks to the illusion spell, but I cannot extend the spell to the rest of the dragons since they are on the ground. Anyway, I would not be able to shield more than two or three. We need to figure out how to get them out without risking their wings being shredded by cannon fire."

"Lessie," I said. *"Can you reach out to the dragons and find out what's going on?"* We were still too far out to see them and had no way of knowing whether they were chained or caged.

"I'm talking to Kadryn right now," Lessie said, her voice electric with excitement. *"He says that they are fine, aside from the dragons that died last night, and are relieved to hear their riders have escaped. They were worried that the Zallabarians were just starting to kill them off."* A flash of rage lit Lessie up from the inside, fueling my own anger. *"They have not been chained, but the cannons are manned twenty-four hours a day by fresh soldiers on both sides of the valley."*

I relayed the information to Tavarian. "We could always go around to one side and destroy the cannons," he suggested. "That may allow the dragons enough leeway to make a break for it."

"How is that going to work?" I argued. "If Lessie comes within striking distance, she'll be too low to the ground and the spell will fail. We'll be pulverized."

"Cannons only work if the person manning them is alert enough to fire," Tavarian pointed out. "If we can hit them with the choking smoke, we can incapacitate them long enough to destroy them. I can use my magic to direct the smoke at them without putting us within striking distance."

Tavarian reached for the pouch of powder to do just that, but before he could, I felt Lessie stiffen beneath me. *"Cover your ears!"* she warned, and that was all the warning we got before an earsplitting roar pierced the sky.

"Ahhh!" I screamed as I clapped my hands over my ears. Or at least I thought I screamed—I couldn't actually hear anything but the ringing in my ears, which was so loud I thought my head was going to explode. *"What the hell is going on?"* I demanded of Lessie.

"The dragons are using their collective roar to incapacitate the soldiers," Lessie said excitedly. *"A genius move! Look at the soldiers, Zara. They can't stand it!"*

I risked my eardrums for a split second to pull my goggles back on, and sure enough, the soldiers manning the cannons had all dropped to the ground, clutching at their bleeding ears as their faces twisted into identical expressions of agony. My heart soared as a horde of dragons in all shapes, sizes, and colors rose from the valley, spewing fire at the cannons even as they beat their wings as hard as they could to get away. Two cannons, which were somehow miraculously still manned—perhaps the soldiers were deaf—fired, and Lessie screamed in rage as one dragon's wing was shredded. Tears sprang to my eyes as it plummeted to the earth, and I briefly wondered if his rider was on the ship, or with the contingent of soldiers headed this way. Would he drop dead in the middle of the forest, or lying on the deck of the airship?

A few other dragons were wounded by the cannons—I could see the streams of blood—but they beat their wings ferociously, and their fellow dragons helped where they could. Tavarian let out a sigh of relief once the dragons had cleared the cannons, and we joined the horde in the sky, releasing the spell so they could see us.

"Several of the dragons demand that I teach them this invisibility trick," Lessie said. *"Do you think I should let them think it's me, and not Tavarian?"*

"You can do whatever you want," I said. "We just helped save their asses."

After a quick consultation, the dragons agreed to fly southward, toward Ruisin. Tavarian switched over to Kadryn's back so Lessie wouldn't have to carry so much weight, and together we escorted the wounded dragons from the rear while the stronger ones led the formation.

Even though I couldn't understand the dragons, I could feel their joy and elation vibrating through the air, and it was infectious. I could also feel their grief at the dragon who'd been shot down, but most of that was eclipsed by the sheer relief of finally being free, and knowing that their riders were safe. Whatever drowsiness I'd felt before vanished, and I spent most of the ride back smiling.

"Do you think that the Ruisins are going to be unhappy when they see close to a hundred dragons fly across their border?" I asked Tavarian.

"Undoubtedly," he said, giving me a wry smile. "But we will deal with that when the time comes."

We were about an hour and a half into our ride when half of the dragons suddenly veered sideways, then plummeted straight toward the forest. *"They've sensed their riders below,"* Lessie told me as two of the wounded we'd been escorting followed suit. *"Should we all stop, or should the rest of us keep going?"*

I thought of Jallis. *"Let's make a quick stop here,"* I told her. *"I want to consult with the other riders."*

We landed just outside the woods, and a few minutes later the riders burst from the tree line, whooping and cheering. Part of me wanted to tell them to shut up and stop drawing attention to us, but the rest of me was happy to see the dragons and riders reunite, and besides, we'd already alerted anyone nearby when our host landed. The dragons whose riders had gone on to Ruisin kept watch while the others embraced their riders, and Tavarian and I gave them a good ten minutes to bask in the joy of being together again.

"Jallis." I approached him where he was standing with Kadryn, stroking his dragon's green hide as if he'd expected to never touch him again.

"Zara." He grinned, then broke away from Kadryn to pull me into a brief but heartfelt hug. "Thank you so much for doing all this." His eyes gleamed with tears as he pulled back. "I didn't realize how hard it would be, being away from my dragon for so long, or how emotional I'd feel at seeing him again. I can't imagine what you must have gone through when you and Lessie were separated in Traggar."

"It was tough. But I'm glad everyone's reunited again." I glanced at the nearby village, knowing someone there would be sending word that a large host of dragons was spotted. "We need to get into the sky again and meet up with the rest of our party in Ruisin. It's only a matter of time until the Zallabarians deploy an army to come after us, especially with the way they've been recruiting."

Jallis nodded. "I'll get the men in the air," he said. "You take the rest of the dragons and lead on."

We took to the skies again in two groups: Jallis led the dragon rider pairs while I led the dragonless ones. Tavarian had switched to yet another dragon, a beautiful ruby red female called Kiethara, who Lessie quickly became fast friends with. I smiled as I glanced sideways at Tavarian, noting the wistful look on his face. He had to be thinking of Muza, his own dragon.

When we finally crossed the Ruisin border, I felt the dragons let out a collective sigh of relief at being free of Zallabarian territory. But we'd only been flying for fifteen minutes before another dragon approached. My eyes widened as I saw the rider on its back, and I slid my goggles onto my nose to get a better look.

"It's Rhia and Ykos!" Lessie said as my goggles focused on them. I caught the telltale gleam of Rhia's chestnut hair, and Ykos's golden scales were unmistakable. *"And she has passengers?"*

"Huh?" I looked closer, and sure enough, there were two small children tied to the saddle. *"What's going on here?"*

Rhia hailed me with a wave, and I told Jallis and Tavarian to escort the remaining dragons to where the airship had landed while I went to meet Rhia. The moment Lessie landed, I jumped to the ground. Rhia did the same, and in the next second, we were in each other's arms, sobbing and laughing.

"Oh, Zara!" Rhia cried, tears streaming down her face. "I was so worried I would never see you again!"

"What's happened?" I asked, pulling back so I could look at the children. They were still clinging to the saddle, their eyes wide as they looked at Rhia and me. "And who are these two?"

"Their mother is one of the dragon riders who was taken," Rhia explained. "Lieutenant Serina Caron. Do you know if she made it out?"

I wracked my brain. "I think so," I said slowly. "She definitely wasn't among the dead. But why did you bring them to her? Surely they would be better off left at home."

Rhia tensed. "I think we should have their mother here before I tell you the story."

We took to the skies on the backs of our dragons, and flew to the airship, which was camped in a large field several miles outside the nearest village, plenty large enough for the dragons to make themselves comfortable but far enough away from civilization that one would have to come out on horseback to investigate.

We landed near the airship, and I smiled again as a second wave of dragon riders rushed out to meet the rest of the dragons. As a willowy brunette in her forties sprinted toward a large, jet-black dragon with blue streaks, the two children broke away from Ykos and rushed toward her.

"Kian! Alias!" the woman cried in alarm when she saw her children. She dropped to her knees and took them into her arms, joy warring with confusion. "What are you two doing here?"

"Mama, mama!" they cried giddily as they hugged her back, burying their faces in her chest. "We got to ride a dragon!"

"I can see that."

"You're Lieutenant Caron?" Rhia asked as we approached.

"I am." The woman's eyes, a deep green that matched her sons', flashed. "Are you responsible for this? Why would you bring my sons into such danger?"

Rhia glanced back at me. "Can you get Tavarian and Jallis? They'll want to hear this too."

I nodded. "They should be on the ship. Let's head up there together. We can meet in the salon."

"I'll be along in a moment," Lieutenant Caron said. She tried to keep her voice even, but I could hear the swell of emotion in it clearly. "I... I need a moment with my dragon. And my children."

"Of course."

Rhia and I went to collect Jallis, who was conferring with Captain Mirkor, the highest-ranking officer who had been on the ship with the wounded. Tavarian had apparently procured tents for the soldiers, and they were busy assigning stations, berthing, and rations to everyone. "Jallis," I said. "You're needed on the ship. Important meeting."

"Of course." Jallis excused himself, then turned to us. A grin lit up his face as he looked at Rhia. "It's good to see you, Lieutenant Thomas."

"You too, Jallis," she said. Once upon a time she might have blushed—back at the academy, Jallis was one of the most popular guys—but now she merely smiled as we fell into step together. "Glad to see prison hasn't dimmed your smile."

As we walked to the airship, Jallis and I gave Rhia a quick rundown of everything that had happened. We quickly found Tavarian, who greeted Rhia warmly and did make her blush. After the lieutenant arrived with her children in tow, we adjourned to the salon.

"All right," Caron said when she was finally seated, pinning Rhia with a frank stare. The children were playing on the floor nearby with a set of wooden figures Tavarian had produced from nowhere, and two crew members were setting out plates of simple fare for us to eat. "Tell me why my children are here and why Lord Tavarian and Lieutenant Jallis are so interested in this matter."

Rhia took a deep breath. "I was sent to Zuar City to bring news about the advancing army to the government, but by the time I arrived almost all the military and civil authorities had already decamped. I was told by the last few officers to deliver a warning message to a unit further west, and not to return to the capital because all hope was lost." Pain flashed in her eyes. "I could hardly believe we were giving up, but I'd seen the invading force with my own eyes, and knew that Ykos and I would die if we stayed. So I did as I was ordered."

"That's terrible," Lieutenant Caron said, "but my children weren't in Zuar City. What does this have to do with them?"

"I'm getting to that," Rhia said tersely. "After I delivered the warning, Ykos and I headed south to see if there were any other dragon riders I could join up with. But that part of the country was in the process of being brought under Zallabarian control, and it was all Ykos and I could do to keep from getting blasted out of the air by those infernal cannons." Her eyes flashed. "Eventually we found a dragon rider's estate to lie low in, where Ykos could hide in the barn, but a few days later the Zallabarians came to the house with a list of residents. Your house," she said to Caron.

The lieutenant's face paled. "No."

Rhia nodded sympathetically. "Since I wasn't on the list, I pretended to be a maid. They specifically asked about your boys, and we were lucky that we'd already hidden them away because they planned on taking them."

"Taking them?" Caron said indignantly. "For what? Is it not enough that they had us and our dragons? They have to take our children, too?"

"I think I know why," I said slowly, the pieces clicking together in my mind. "If the Zallabarians were planning on breeding the dragons, which is what I heard, then they'd need potential candidates to bond with them. By taking small children of dragon rider heritage, and grooming them into loyal Zallabarian soldiers, they can turn the dragons into formidable weapons."

A ripple of disgust and horror went through the entire room. "The Zallabarian army wants to breed its own dragon riders?" Jallis demanded. "But they hate dragons!"

"It's the most logical explanation," Tavarian said. "Why else would they go through so much trouble to capture our dragon rider force when they could have slaughtered us all with the cannons?"

"They didn't tell us the reason they wanted to take the children," Rhia said, "but what you're saying makes sense. They told your husband and grandparents that the children would not be harmed, but they refused to say how long they would be gone or what they were going to do with them. When your husband claimed the children were visiting a relative, the soldiers immediately searched the property. I sent a warning to Ykos, and he and I dispatched the soldiers. Two of them managed to get away, so we took the children and flew away before reinforcements could be called."

Caron's face, which had been white as a sheet, turned red as color rushed back into her cheeks. "Those bastards," she fumed. "They've probably taken their failure to capture my children out on my family. Did you manage to take the dragon eggs with you?" she asked. "There were two on the property."

Rhia shook her head. "Your family didn't mention them, or I would have tried. But we had to get out of there quickly, so I didn't think to ask."

"Fools," the woman muttered on a sigh. She glanced toward her children, and her gaze softened before she turned back to

Rhia. "I owe you a great debt. Thank you for bringing them to me."

"You're more than welcome," Rhia said warmly. "I'm just glad you were here. I had no idea where to look, but Ykos and I were close to the Ruisin border when he sensed the dragon host flying this way. Naturally, we went straight to you."

The lieutenant thanked Rhia once more, then gathered her children and took her leave.

My entire body ached from lack of sleep and all the traveling, and I wanted nothing more than to find an empty bed and fall into it. But now that the soldiers were settled and out of harm's way, we needed to get more information, so I called in Major Savin and asked him and Jallis to give us a full report, after describing briefly what we already knew.

"So, you saw the battlefield, did you?" Savin asked. "It was gruesome, wasn't it?"

"Very," Tavarian said. "And there were an astonishing number of Elantian dead, especially compared to how few the Zallabarians lost. How did this battle start?"

"We were ambushed," Jallis said grimly. "The night before the battle, the Zallabarians dropped gas bombs on our camp and incapacitated us. It's actually pathetic how easy it was for them to round us up while we were choking and gasping for air. Once they had us secured, they were able to coerce our dragons to come quietly. I think a few managed to escape and participate in the battle, but I'm guessing by the look on your face that they didn't survive."

I shook my head. "There were ten dead dragons on the battlefield, by my count," I said sadly. "Likely the ones you're talking about."

"What about that one dragon rider pair we saw flying with the fleet?" Tavarian asked, turning to me. "I believe Lessie told you the dragon's name was Leeras?"

"Leeras?" Savin bared his teeth in a snarl. "The rider's name is Fillian, and he's a traitor. Daria said that she was able to communicate with her dragon for a brief period of time, and he told her Fillian was the one who approached them and gave them the Zallabarians' demands. He was allowed to take his dragon and go free, while the rest of us were put in chains."

I clenched my teeth. "Bastard. I wonder if he was in on it the entire time, or if the Zallabarians got him to turn right then."

"Either way, he's a traitor," Jallis pointed out.

Very true.

"We all want revenge against the Zallabarians," Savin went on, "but I have to admit that with most of the country occupied, I'm not sure what we *can* do. Unless you and Lord Tavarian have a plan in mind?"

We were all silent for a long moment. "Although Zara and I originally intended to use the dragons to help defend Zuar City, I fear we are too late for that," Tavarian said. "And I see very little point in taking the dragons back to Elantia just so they can be slaughtered. What we need is an army of our own, with technology that not only matches but also surpasses the Zallabarians'."

Savin slumped in his chair. "I agree, but where would we get the engineers, the resources, the men? I've seen their new technology firsthand—they have steam-powered vehicles in addition to those shrapnel cannons, and other war machines that we had never faced before. How can we compete with that?"

"I don't think that we should count the dragons out just yet," Jallis said. "They are still useful for guerilla warfare, and if we can figure out a way to avoid the cannons more effectively, they can still fight."

"We might try to find a country who is willing to ally with us," Tavarian said, "and who has the necessary resources. I don't yet know who that would be, but in the meantime, we need to focus on keeping the dragons safe and, if possible, increasing their population."

Jallis frowned. "We only have five female dragons left. That could take hundreds of years."

To my surprise, Tavarian smiled. "I have an idea about how to get around that—" A sharp rap on the door cut him off.

"Lord Tavarian," the ship's captain said, a little red-faced and out of breath. "There are officials from Ruisin here to see you. They're...umm...rather insistent."

Tavarian sighed. "Send them on in."

The captain disappeared, then came back a few moments later with three middle-aged men dressed in colorful suits.

"Good evening," the one in the middle said to Lord Tavarian. He was a balding man with a bit of a pot belly, but his broad shoulders and proud posture told me he'd once been in very good shape. "I am Mayor Pitkin, and these are my secretaries, Mr. Coyle and Mr. Bardin. I understand you are in charge and this is your airship?"

"It is my ship." He gestured to me as we both stood. "My name is Lord Varrick Tavarian, and this is Zara Kenrook." He quickly introduced the others in the room as well.

"A pleasure." The mayor's thinning lips suggested it was anything but. "You have quite a large group of dragons here with you, Lord Tavarian. Why are they here?"

"We recently rescued them, and their riders, from a Zallabarian prison," I said, refusing to be ignored. "They're exhausted, so we've stopped here to allow everyone to rest and recuperate from the ordeal."

"Why Ruisin?" Bardin challenged. He had straight, shoulder-length blond hair and a reed-thin frame, and I didn't like the way his eyes narrowed on us. "Why not return to your own borders?"

"Because we've been invaded," Jallis snapped, "and you already know that, so I'm not sure why you're beating around the bush." The vehemence in his voice was unexpected—Jallis rarely lost his temper. "The Zallabarians have conquered nearly all of Elantia, and there is no place near the border where we can safely rest our dragons for the night."

To my surprise, the mayor's severe expression softened, just a fraction. "While I understand your plight, and sympathize with the state of your country, we cannot allow you to keep these dragons here. If Zallabar discovers we are providing refuge for you, they may very well attack us."

"Zallabar is already going to attack you," Tavarian said, his voice as smooth and unhurried as if we were discussing the weather. "Come, Mayor Pitkin, you know that it's a strong possibility. Those bags beneath your eyes and the lines on your face tell me you've likely had quite a few sleepless nights thinking about it and trying to prepare. Rather than hunkering down and waiting for the inevitable, why not ally with us? Someone needs to take a stand against the Zallabarians before they've taken over the continent."

The mayor gave Tavarian a dubious look. "Even if that were so, Ruisin is a small country. An alliance between us would not make any difference against the might of Zallabar. Besides," he added, "our farmers are terrified for their sheep and cows. We depend very heavily on our livestock, and we don't need our dairy cows stressed and unable to produce milk because of your beasts."

"They're not mindless beasts," I argued. "If we tell them to leave your livestock alone, they will."

"Even so, you cannot remain," the mayor insisted. "I will allow you to stay one day and night, but come tomorrow evening you must leave our lands, or we shall be forced to arrest you."

"Arrest us?" Savin exclaimed, but Tavarian held up a hand.

"Understood," Tavarian said. "We appreciate your kindness and generosity."

Tavarian personally showed the mayor and his retinue out. The moment the door closed behind him, Savin and Jallis started grumbling. "*Arrest us*," Savin fumed, raking a hand through his messy curls. He was in desperate need of a trim and a shave, as were most of the male soldiers we'd recovered. "How do they plan to do that? If anyone tried to take me away again, my dragon would burn them to a crisp."

"So would all of our dragons," I said, "but where exactly is that going to get us? The whole reason we're stuck in this mess is because of our history of bullying and coercing our neighboring countries into doing our bidding. Using our dragons to force the Ruisins to help us will only send the message that we're the same old bullies we've always been and strengthen the Zallabarians' position that we deserve to be wiped off the map. Any chance of forming an alliance with a larger country will be ruined."

"We know that, Zara," Jallis said heavily. "It's just that this is so hard to swallow. It feels like we've been kicked out of our homes with nowhere to go."

"I know something about that," I said with a wry smile. "I grew up as an unwanted orphan, remember?"

"Right." Jallis's expression flickered briefly, as if he felt guilty. "But you've found a home with us now, only to lose it again."

"I've found that home is less about where you're at, and more about who you're with," I said lightly. Though Salcombe had put a roof over my bed and food in my belly throughout my teenage years, I'd never felt like his house was my home. My first real home had been the Treasure Trove, the place Carina and I had invested our hearts and souls into, that we'd built up into a thriving business despite the odds against us. And then later, Dragon Rider Academy had also become a home, not just because I was amongst my own kind for the first time in my life but also because that's where Lessie, the most important companion in my life, was.

Savin laughed. "Your short time in the military hasn't beaten the romantic out of you," he said. "I can't decide if that's a good thing or not."

I shrugged. "Compassion and rationality each have their uses," I said. "Too much compassion can lead you to make stupid decisions that risk the welfare of the group, but too little can result in dehumanization, which leads to horrors and atrocities."

"See?" Savin laughed. "You're like a damn poet."

Tavarian chose that moment to stick his head back in. "We need to inform the others of the change in plans," he said.

We went out to the deck railing and called for an assembly, then addressed the crowd and told them the news. The riders were understandably angry about the local mayor's ultimatum. "Where are we supposed to go, then?" one of them shouted. "Do we just fly from country to country like beggars until we can find someone who isn't cowed by Zallabar and is willing to take us in?"

"There actually is a place that might work," Rhia murmured in my ear. "A place that might not only be a refuge but also might house a weapon we can use to fight back."

"What?" I grabbed her arm and pulled her aside, Tavarian and Jallis following. "Why did you wait so long to mention this?"

Rhia blushed a little. "Ykos mentioned it while we were flying here, and with all the excitement I forgot to tell you beforehand," she said apologetically. "Apparently, his grandsire told his father that there is a tremendously dangerous and potent weapon hidden in the isle of Polyba."

"Polyba?" Tavarian said, sounding extremely interested. "That's one of our island territories. But why would it be there? Does your family own land there?"

"No," Rhia said. "Ykos's grandsire belonged to the Grier family. They had a secret estate on the island, and they hid the weapon there, then erased the existence of the estate from the family ledgers so no one would ever go there. Of course, Elantia was safe and powerful back then, and I doubt they ever imagined such a weapon would ever be needed again."

"That's all well and good," Jallis said, "but what kind of weapon is this? Who knows if it still works after all this time? And if it kills indiscriminately, it may not do us any good."

"I don't know, but it doesn't really matter," Rhia said. "Polyba is far enough from the coast that the Zallabarians won't be able to see it from land, and Ykos says it's also sparsely populated and partially inaccessible due to the mountainous terrain and thorny plants. Only the southern tip is habitable."

"If it is large enough for a dragon population of this size, then I don't see why we can't make that our temporary base," Tavarian said. "So long as there's enough food and resources for all of us. Once we find this mysterious weapon, we can determine if it's any good against modern technology, and if it isn't, figure out a different plan."

We announced our plans to go to Polyba to the dragon riders—though we left out the news of the possible weapon, since it was unconfirmed. The dragon riders cheered, and I was happy to see their faces brighten with hope. I could only pray to whichever gods were listening that Rhia was right, and that Polyba was the safe haven we were looking for.

10

I spent the night sleeping under the stars with Lessie, and the next morning, rose early to grab a sponge bath and a change of clothes from the ship. On my way out the door, I ran into Tavarian, who asked if I would like to head into town with him for breakfast.

"Do you think the locals will welcome us there?" I asked dubiously. "The mayor made it pretty clear that he wants us gone."

Tavarian smiled. "Gold is still gold, regardless of who it comes from," he said. "And despite what the mayor may have said, the local businesses were happy indeed when the crew came into town yesterday to purchase provisions. Unfortunately, they only purchased enough for a few days, and I would like to stock up on some more things, especially if we are going to be settling on an island."

"Good point."

I followed Tavarian on deck to find the crew preparing for take-off. After a quick chat with the captain and with the soldiers running the camp, we lifted off, headed for the town. It only took a few minutes to get there, and once we landed, Tavarian and I went straight to an inn and ordered a lavish breakfast. Stuffing myself with rich, fresh-cooked food was like paradise after living off bread, cheese, and dried meat for days.

"Tavarian," I said as we ate. "Do you know much about Polyba? You seemed to recognize it when Rhia brought up the name."

"I've only seen it on maps," Tavarian said. "I admit I didn't pay much attention to it, since, as Rhia said, it seems to be a mostly uninhabitable land, with no sizable government for us to contend with. If there truly is a powerful weapon hidden on it, I have no doubt you will pick it up immediately with your treasure sense."

"That's true," I said, "but the weapon isn't the only thing I have to worry about. I'll need to head back to Zallabar first so I can retrieve the piece of heart before Salcombe gets to it."

Tavarian scrubbed a hand over his face. "You know, with everything that's been going on, I completely forgot about the heart," he said, sounding bemused. "Has Caor contacted you since the last time you told me about him?"

"No." I tapped the ring on my right hand, wondering if he was listening, or if he was off on some other kind of godly business. What exactly had the gods been doing all these years anyway? Did they float on clouds or lounge around in palaces in their realm? Or did they have cities to govern and wars to fight in their own territories? Surely, they must have found some way to keep themselves busy after they'd turned their backs on us.

"Anyway," I said, "considering we're still fairly close to Zallabar, I think it makes more sense that I head for Barkheim now, while you go with the others to Polyba." I twirled a curl of my hair around my finger, watching the way the sunlight glinted off the red strands. "I'll join you there once I've retrieved it."

"Is it really such a good idea for you to go on your own?" Tavarian asked. "You will be in the heart of enemy territory, and Lessie will not be able to help you should you run into any trouble." He gave me a stern look when I opened my mouth to argue. "I know you'd prefer to involve as few people as possible, but you need me for the illusion spell to keep Lessie cloaked, if nothing else. We will just have to trust Rhia and Jallis to keep things under control. Besides, it is not as if they need us to lead the way."

"True." I nibbled on my bottom lip as I considered what might lie ahead for us in Barkheim. "You know, even if we do get our hands on the dragon heart piece, what then? Do we lock them away again and hope someone doesn't find them in the future?"

"That does seem to be our only option," Tavarian said. "Those pieces are impossible to destroy. If the old mages, who were much more powerful than the modern mages of today, couldn't manage it, then I don't see how we could do it now."

I puzzled over the problem as we shopped for supplies and loaded up the airship. In the privacy of my quarters, I tried summoning Caor with the ring, but if he heard me calling, he ignored it. Frustrated, I ripped it off my finger and flung it across the room. To my annoyance, it bounced off the wall, then zipped straight back onto my finger.

I snarled. "What's the point of having this if it's only a one-way device?" I flopped onto the bed, barely resisting the urge to curse Caor and all the other gods. Did they have some kind of plan to destroy the pieces of Zakyiar's heart? Were they ever going to share that plan with me? Or was I just going to be kept in the dark, only allowed to see one foot in front of me while they cackled and rubbed their hands over whatever mysterious long game they were playing?

When the ship landed, I called Jallis, Rhia, Savin, and the other team leaders into the salon. "Let's get everyone loaded up onto the ship who's still too weak to fly on their mounts," I said. "You guys need to be out of here by dusk."

"What do you mean 'you guys?'" Rhia demanded. "You're not coming with us?"

"No, and neither is Tavarian." I explained about the piece of the dragon's heart we needed to retrieve, leaving out the parts about Caor. I trusted Rhia and Jallis enough to tell them, but the others, who didn't even know about Salcombe's mad quest, would have a hard time wrapping their heads around the idea that the old gods actually existed.

"Are you serious?" Kade said when I'd finished. "Those myths about the dragon god's heart are real? I thought they were just stories."

"Oh, they're real," I said. "I've come across three pieces, and they are incredibly dangerous." I didn't tell them that I hadn't seen them with my own eyes. I'd been able to use my treasure sense to conjure up images of them when I'd sensed them nearby, and that was good enough.

What would it feel like when I finally got my hands on one? Would I feel a heady rush of consuming power, as Salcombe no doubt did whenever he handled one? Would the dragon god try to corrupt me? I shuddered at the thought, hoping that wasn't the case. Tavarian hadn't seemed affected even though he owned a piece, though I doubted he'd handled it much. Maybe the dragon god's power only worked on people who already had questionable moral character.

You're a thief, Zara. People don't get much more questionable than that.

I finished the meeting with the soldiers, and then we spent the next six hours breaking down camp, going over inventory, and loading the ship.

Lessie bid farewell to Kadryn, Ykos, and Kiethara, nuzzling each of them. Tavarian and I stood side by side as we watched the entire column of dragons take off as one, with the airship following behind. Lessie escorted them for the first few miles, like an honorary vanguard.

"It's really an amazing sight," I said, my voice hushed with awe as I stared at the dozens of dragons disappearing into the cloudy evening. Scales of all hues caught and reflected the waning sunlight, making the sky look as if it was covered in a shimmering rainbow.

"It is." Tavarian put his arm around my shoulder. "We'll see them again soon."

I leaned into his side, drawing strength from the solid warmth of his body. I couldn't believe I used to think Tavarian was cold and unfeeling. He seemed to be able to sense what I was thinking or feeling, even when I wasn't sure myself, and more often than not knew just what to say to put me at ease.

Isn't that what every girl wants in a life partner? a sly voice whispered, and I shook my head.

Tavarian glanced down at me. "What is it?" he asked, his black eyebrows drawing together in puzzlement.

I smiled. "I was just thinking how fortunate it was that Salcombe sent me to rob you and not another dragon rider," I teased. "If not, I might have ended up making out with one of your fellow councilmembers instead."

Tavarian's face twisted up into a scowl that was so comical, I almost burst out laughing. "Enough teasing," he said, tugging at my hair so that my head tilted up to look at him. He turned to face me, and then his lips were on mine, hot and demanding. My hands instinctively fisted into the front of his shirt, and as his addictive scent filled my head I nearly forgot all about my resolution not to sleep with him until after this war business was done.

And when, exactly, is it going to be done? the same voice whispered. When I'd finished collecting the dragon heart pieces? When I'd stabbed Salcombe in his own cold, dead, twisted heart and chased down every last one of his minions? When we finally took our country back and drove Zallabar from our borders?

And what if none of that ever happened?

Tavarian tightened his free arm around me, pulling me closer as his tongue slipped between my lips. *Take it,* his body seemed to say as he deepened the kiss. *Take it all, before it's too late, and we find ourselves afloat in a sea of regrets of our own making.*

I nipped at his lower lip in answer, and the groan he rewarded me with reverberated through my body and straight down into my toes.

The sound of flapping wings interrupted the moment, and I threw a hand up as Lessie landed, spraying us with dust and grass. *"I would say get a room,"* Lessie said, sounding highly amused, *"but the rooms just flew off, and we need to get going."*

Tavarian reluctantly drew back. "We're not finished here," he murmured, briefly caressing my swollen bottom lip with his thumb. And then he stepped away, heading to Lessie's side so we could mount up.

11

Lessie flew swiftly as she arrowed toward the Zallabarian border, unhindered by the need to exercise caution thanks to Tavarian's cloaking spell. We had packed fairly light for this trip. We wore our civilian clothes, though I had trousers under my skirt to make riding easier, and in addition to food and gold, Tavarian had also brought a fake beard and mustache. It was necessary for him to wear the extra disguise, he explained, since he was well-known in Barkheim from his many diplomatic missions to the capital.

We flew through the night, stopping in another clearing at dawn so Lessie could rest and hunt, and Tavarian could recharge his magical energy. I kept watch as both of them slept, intending to sleep in the saddle when we took flight again.

I managed to make it a few hours before my bladder's needs made themselves known. Standing up, I reached out with my treasure sense to make sure no one was nearby, then quickly darted into the forest to take care of business. I was just adjusting my trousers when I caught a flash of light to my left.

"Who's there?" I whirled around, a dagger in my hand. The bushes rustled, and a hand darted out, strong fingers wrapping around my upper arm.

"Let me go!" Fear jolted through me, and I lashed out at the arm with my dagger, but the blade struck only air. I tried to pull back, but the hand's grip was too strong. It yanked me through the bush...and into a bustling city.

"What the hell!" I cried, looking around. My heart pounded wildly as my head spun. The sudden change of scenery was messing with my head, making me dizzy and nauseous. "Where am I?"

"Barkheim," Caor said, his voice raking down my spine like sharp claws despite his lazy tone. He leaned against a pillar. We stood outside a small temple sandwiched between two towering buildings. "I don't know why you're upset. I've saved you two and a half days of travel time."

"Maybe I don't like being teleported against my will," I said through gritted teeth. Barkheim? The capital? I pressed the palm of my hand against my clammy forehead. The sounds and smells of the city battered my skull—sweat, charcoal, perfume, urine—and my treasure sense was going haywire. Taking a deep breath, I focused on dimming the cacophony of chimes and gongs in my head. The sound reduced to a very faint melody, almost indistinguishable from the noisy city, and my headache receded a little.

Caor shrugged. "You would have said no if I'd consulted you. Better to seek forgiveness than ask permission, right?" He gave me a cheeky grin.

I bared my teeth at him. "You're lucky I was wearing my pack, or I'd be screwed right now. And what about my friends? Tavarian and I were already on our way here. He would have been invaluable. And not to mention my dragon! She is carrying the luggage, and all our money! I only have a few coins on me."

Caor wrinkled his nose. "You can't exactly go hunting in a city like this on the back of a dragon, and I would never use my magic to aid one. As for Tavarian, he is not the one we have chosen for this quest. You are. Therefore, you are the one we've transported, period."

I opened my mouth to rail at him, for such "help" that was worse than useless, but he vanished, unfairly getting in the last word. "Asshole!" I shouted at the sky, uncaring that several citizens had stopped to stare at me in the street. "You could at least throw me a bone if you're going to strand me here!"

Something hard bonked on my head. Swearing, I threw up my hand to shield my head, then paused as the item bounced off my skull and landed on the ground. A gold coin, I realized dimly as I crouched in the dirt. Enough money to put food in my belly for a week while I figured out what to do next.

Would have been nice if you'd dropped a bit more, I thought as I pocketed the money. People were still staring, and I gave them an apologetic smile, wondering if they'd seen Caor. With my luck, he'd only made himself visible to me, making me look like a crazy person talking to no one. *Yeah. Definitely not forgiving you.*

Realizing I'd drawn way too much attention to myself, I skirted the side of the temple and disappeared into the alley behind it. Reaching into my pack, I dug out a scarf and wrapped it around my head to hide my red hair. Hopefully there had been no guards nearby to hear me shouting in Elantian, but as far as I knew I'd already been compromised. I needed to disguise myself.

Which I could have done easily, if I had access to the rest of my luggage, I grumbled. I wondered if Caor could hear my thoughts from wherever he was, or if it only worked if he was talking to me. Not that it mattered. He and the rest of the gods clearly didn't care if they were inconveniencing my life. If this mission wasn't so important I would have flipped them the bird and walked straight out of this city.

Instead, I stepped into the street, then asked a man standing outside a shop where the nearest market was. Barkheim was a very rich city, so there were quite a few shopping districts. I located one five blocks away and found a stall selling colorful dresses. After I'd changed into a purple one that matched my scarf and had skirts voluminous enough to hide my weapons, I bought some grilled sausages and vegetables from a vendor. The hot, greasy food filled my stomach and took some of the edge off my anger so I could finally think.

I guess I ought to start searching now, I thought as I glanced up at the sky. It was mid-morning, still fairly early in the day, but Barkheim was an enormous metropolis, twice the size of Zuar

City. That was a lot of ground to search, and unlike last time I'd searched a city for a piece of heart, I didn't have a dragon to ferry me around. As I devoured my second sausage, several steam-powered bicycles ripped through the streets, their helmeted riders hugging the vehicles with their entire bodies as they gripped the handlebars. I felt a twinge of envy and briefly wondered if it might be worth it to steal one, just to get around faster.

You'd probably kill yourself. I sighed as the voice of reason asserted itself in my brain. I'd never driven a steam-powered vehicle before and had only ridden in one a few times. One of these days I would learn how, but now was not the time.

Finished with my food, I wandered the streets for a bit until I found a travel agency. The woman inside was chatty, and more than happy to provide me with a map of the city for a small fee. I told her that I was a Warosian traveler visiting the city with my husband. "The poor man is holed up sick in our hotel room," I said with a sad smile. "I'm afraid he ate something that didn't agree with him. I spent all day yesterday nursing him, but I didn't come all the way out here just to sit in bed the entire time, did I?"

"Of course not!" the woman exclaimed. "Warosia is a long way to travel from indeed. I'm a bit surprised you and your husband decided to come, what with the war going on. Tourism has dropped significantly since it started. I'm fairly certain that if you wanted, I could get you a tour of the city for half price," she said hopefully.

I was about to refuse her, then thought better of it. "What kind of tour?"

"An omnibus one." She plucked a pamphlet from her desk and handed it to me. "It's quite nice, sitting on the upper levels of the vehicle. Raises you up out of the stench some and allows you to see everything. Normally it's five coppers, but I could give it to you for three."

I dug the money out of my skirt pocket. "When does it leave?"

An hour later, I sat on the upper level of a large, two-tiered steam vehicle. It lumbered through Barkheim's streets like an oversized bear, coughing great gouts of steam from the pipe jutting out from the rear end. As the woman had promised, sitting on the upper level did alleviate the stench of the city somewhat, though it did nothing about the noise. There were enough seats to easily fit fifty or so people, but only a third were filled, mostly by Zallabarians visiting the capital from different parts of the country.

As we drove through the streets, the driver prattled on about the different districts, giving us a brief history about them and pointing out any historical landmarks and buildings. There was some kind of horn attached to the front of the two-story bus, allowing his voice to easily carry to those of us sitting up top. I listened with half an ear, but mostly I focused my treasure sense, filtering out countless lower value items as I methodically searched for the piece of heart. The omnibus stopped frequently to let passengers on and off at pick-up points, slowing the journey considerably, but it was still much faster than traversing the city on foot.

"And this here is the garden district," the driver said as we stopped at the corner of a well-kept street. The houses here were much nicer than the townhomes and apartments we'd seen so far, and as I stared, something reverberated along my treasure sense.

Could it be the dragon heart? It was faint, almost as if it had been muffled, but there was something familiar enough about the sound that I jumped out of my seat and raced down the stairs and into the street. The omnibus left me behind in a choking cloud of steam, and I hurried away into the neighborhood.

As I walked uphill, passing street after manicured street, the houses and the plots they sat on grew progressively larger. Within twenty minutes, I'd progressed from nice single-story homes to large, multi-storied mansions sitting on several acres of land. The signal also grew stronger, solidifying into that familiar, yet still somehow muffled, bell gong. I was getting closer to my target!

I wondered if some kind of spell masked the sound. That would make sense, considering that each one was supposed to be guarded by a mage family. The last piece Salcombe and I found had been buried on an estate, locked away in a magically sealed box. The estate itself was owned by a mundane family, as the mages who'd owned it had died out, but I had a feeling the ones who guarded this piece were alive and well.

I was running various break-in scenarios through my head when a large iron grille came into view. I quickened my pace until I reached the street corner, then stopped under a gallery's awning to study the area. The grille spanned the entire length of the street, as far as the eye could see in either direction, with a towering gate in the middle large enough to admit two carriages side by side. The gate was manned by eight guards wearing fur hats and starched uniforms with brass buttons, and more guards stood watch along the grille at one-block intervals. I swallowed at the sight of their weapons—each held a musket against his shoulder, plus a pistol and sword at his belt.

Rather than approaching the guards and asking them if they could pretty please let me in, I turned left and went into the first coffee shop I could find. Like everything in this district, it was an upscale establishment, with gleaming brass accents and highly polished wooden tables. My stomach growled at the scent of sugary pastries, even though I'd eaten an hour ago.

This close to lunch, the place buzzed with activity, but I managed to squeeze into a seat by the window where I could observe the guards. Beyond the gate, even grander houses lined a wide avenue—mansions that far surpassed Tavarian's floating estate and most of the mansions on Dragon's Table. I wondered who was occupying those estates now—I assumed Zallabarian officers had taken them over. I sincerely hoped Rhia's family had chosen to flee rather than remain at Dragon's Table, but what if they hadn't? Would the invaders force them out of their ancestral home? I wished I'd asked Carina to keep an eye on them, but in my hasty departure I hadn't thought to ask.

"Excuse me," I said to the serving girl when she came to deliver my coffee and pastry. "But can you tell me what's beyond that gate?"

"Hmm?" The girl glanced out the window. "Oh, that's where the Autocrator and the other bigwigs live," she said, and though her voice was pleasant, there was just a hint of disdain in it. "This gate didn't use to be here, but when the Autocrator moved into his new residence he ordered it built. It's been up for a few weeks and it's quite a nuisance!"

I thanked the girl, then sipped my coffee as I considered her words. If the members of the Zallabarian government lived here, why would the piece of dragon heart be so close to them? Presumably it belonged to a mage family, like the others we knew of. But a mage living so close to the Autocrator seemed odd, considering the Zallabarians were not fond of magic in the least. Perhaps this was like the other estate, where the original mage family that had kept the relic safe had died out, and a different family had moved in, none the wiser as to the extremely powerful artifact buried on their land.

But how did that explain the muffling spell? I was almost certain there was one, because at this distance the signal should have been loud enough to rattle my brain. On the other hand, I had very little understanding about how magic worked. If a box could be enchanted to remain shut long after the owner had passed, then perhaps a muffling spell could remain active as well.

I finished my snack quickly, then headed out. I nodded to the guards directly across the street with a pleasant smile, then proceeded to take a leisurely stroll around the entire perimeter. It took me an hour to walk around the blasted thing at the pace I was going, but I confirmed that the gate made a complete circle—or rather, a square that spanned some thirty blocks—and that the piece of heart was definitely within the perimeter.

Damn. I leaned against a tree on the sidewalk and chewed my lower lip as I considered the obstacle. If I'd had Lessie with me, she could have dropped me onto a rooftop at night, especially with Tavarian's cloaking spell to shield her from view. But thanks to Caor, that option was moot. I would have to find a way in.

But how? Sneaking past the gate wasn't really an option, not with all those guards. Perhaps if they only had swords I would risk it, but those firearms made it far too risky. They could shoot me down before I got more than ten steps within the compound.

The one upside was that Salcombe would also have a very hard time breaking in. Then again, knowing him, he probably wouldn't need to. He would just finagle an invitation from some politician he was friends with, likely the same person who'd helped him get his false citizenship papers.

Could I do the same thing? Worm my way into someone's good graces and hope they'd invite me to a party? I didn't have the money to buy the proper wardrobe, but maybe if I could steal enough for one good outfit, I could pose as a noblewoman.

The idea of returning to my thieving ways was enough to make my stomach tense with dread. As I passed through another square, several shop windows held signs, all with similar messages: "Congratulations to our heroic conquerors of Elantia!" I gritted my teeth. The signs were a welcome reminder that these people were the enemy, and I could not afford any sympathy for them.

This shopping district was much fancier, with higher-end shops lining the square, and vendors selling all sorts of exotic foods, clothing, jewelry, and art. It also meant there were wealthier shoppers, and I used my treasure sense to home in on the fuller pockets. An especially arrogant-looking officer caught my attention, and as he haggled with a merchant, I slipped past and relieved him of his wallet.

I turned the corner before he could catch a glimpse of me, then nabbed a second purse and a local newspaper on the way out.

With my spoils tucked away in my skirt pocket and the newspaper wedged beneath my arm, I left the wealthy district and secured a room at a boarding house a few blocks away. The lodgings were modest but clean, and the neighborhood safe enough that I felt comfortable laying my head on the pillow. I kicked off my boots and sat on the bed. Propped up against the pillows, I opened up the newspaper to see if I could learn anything useful.

As I expected, the newspaper was full of propaganda. I skimmed past the fluff and ego-inflated pieces, hunting for real information, and was dismayed to find that we'd lost the battle just north of Zuar City. I'd resigned myself to the idea that we would, but the numbers were horrific—eight thousand dead on our side, while the Zallabarians had only lost three thousand. A good show considering how badly we'd been outnumbered, but that didn't change the outcome.

The city was taken.

Our country was lost.

Fighting against the swell of tears in my throat, I forced myself to keep reading. The Elantians had handed over the capital without further resistance, and a group of them had been appointed to work with the Zallabarians to ensure a peaceful takeover of the country. The names mentioned included some of the previous councilors who had not fled the city after all. Barrigan, the antique shop owner who'd tried to drive me out of business, as well as the traitorous dragon rider we'd seen flying with that fleet of Zallabarian airships, were on the list of collaborators working with the invaders.

"Curse them," I growled, clutching the newspaper tightly. The paper began to tear, and I forced myself to take several deep breaths to calm myself. Once I was no longer seeing red, I read the article a second time to make sure I hadn't missed anything. Thankfully, there was no mention of violence occurring in the city itself. Judging by the way the Zallabarians had treated the farmers at the border, and the fact that the battle had taken place well outside the city, it was safe to say that the citizens had been spared. I hoped Carina and the orphans were safe, and that the soldiers hadn't looted the shop.

I finished reading the newspaper and found little else about the state of Elantia. There was, however, another article of interest —a piece covering a dispute between Traggar and Zallabar, both of which wanted to grab Elantia's overseas colonies. Since Traggar had the larger navy, they clearly had the advantage, but Zallabar was taking an aggressive line. As far as the writer was concerned, if Traggar had wanted those colonies, they should have joined with Zallabar when they had the chance, not spit on the impending alliance simply because their spoiled brat of a king had such a thin skin.

"Bastards," I muttered to myself as I tossed the paper aside. Squabbling over our territories like a pack of dogs fighting over the leftover bones of a carcass. It was disgusting and disheartening in equal measure, but at least I contented myself with the knowledge that Traggar was an obstacle for Zallabar. Perhaps King Zoltar would choose to make war against Zallabar now, rather than waiting until the Autocrator was ready to strike, and that would weaken both of them.

But that didn't really do anything for us now, I thought tiredly as I buried myself under the covers. I tried reaching out for Lessie one more time, but though I could faintly sense her distress, she was still too far out of range to talk with.

Hurry, I told her through the bond even as my mind slipped into sleep. I didn't know what was coming next, but my gut told me I couldn't do this alone. I needed my friends.

12

Aside from a trip to a seamstress to order two new gowns with the money I'd stolen, I spent most of the day sleeping, trying to readjust to a normal day schedule. I woke up on the third morning feeling largely refreshed, but also restless. The outfits I'd ordered were ready, so I went to pick them up. They were beautiful dresses—a lavender day gown of muslin with striped silk, and an evening gown of rich, emerald green satin. Hoping I didn't need more than that, I changed into the day dress, pulled my hair into a casual up-do, and slipped my feet into a pair of fashionable but sturdy boots. These dresses were more form-fitting and less forgiving than the frock I'd been wearing, and I was only able to bring a single dagger and my lock pick. I hated the idea of leaving my spelled boots and dragon blade behind, but there was no way I could walk around with all of my things.

Luckily, there was a solution for that, I thought as I closed the door behind me. I fished out my lock pick from my purse, then used it to lock the door. The moment the lock tumbled into place, the keyhole glowed briefly, signifying the spell was in place. I'd only used the lock pick for this purpose a few times, but the spell would hold against anyone who tried to break through the door. I'd tested it multiple times, and no amount of lock-picking skill or brute force could overcome it. As long as no one broke through my window, my belongings were relatively safe.

Wanting to gather more intelligence about the gated area, I ventured back to the wealthy district. I stopped in at a dainty cafe that was obviously frequented by the rich, judging by the elegant chairs and tables and pricey offerings. The coffee was atrociously expensive, and I'd already had some at the boarding house, so I settled for a scoop of ice cream and a glass of lemonade instead.

The cafe had a selection of the day's papers available to patrons, so I snagged a copy of the *Barkheim Times* and took it with me to a small table in the corner. Unfortunately, there was nothing of note today, but I continued to scan the paper anyway, hoping some kind of inspiration would strike. One report detailing a fire that had broken out in one of the poorer districts made me wonder if I could create some kind of disaster as a distraction, then slip through the gates while the residents were being evacuated. But that would still require getting in...

A familiar voice tugged on my attention, and I glanced up to see a middle-aged man in military uniform enter the shop with a slender woman on his arm. My mouth dropped open. It was General Trattner, the former Zallabarian ambassador I'd met in

Traggar! I'd befriended him when I posed as Salcombe's wife, Lady Trentiano, back when we were frequenting the Traggaran court. A stab of guilt pierced my heart as I remembered how I'd tricked him into enraging King Zoltar, but I pushed it aside. It had been a necessary deception, and I didn't regret the outcome.

General Trattner seemed to sense my stare, for his eyes locked on mine the moment the doors closed behind him. I hastily covered up my shocked expression with a smile, and rose from my chair to greet him.

"Lady Zara!" he exclaimed, a genuine smile lighting up his features. Trattner was a distinguished man in his late forties, a bit soft in the mid-section, but with a strong, stocky build that told me he'd been a formidable warrior in his youth. "What a pleasant surprise. What are you doing here in Barkheim? Is your husband with you?" His eyes darted around the shop, searching for Salcombe.

Dragon's balls. What to tell him? "Oh, he's at some gentleman's club somewhere," I said with a vague wave of my hand. "Is this your lovely wife you've told me so much about?" I turned to the woman next to him, executing a small curtsy. She was of a similar age to Trattner, but far better looking, with silver-blonde hair and skin the color and smoothness of fine china.

"Yes. Renate, this is Lady Zara Trentiano, the woman who I conversed with during some of those interminably boring parties. Lady Zara, this is Renate, my wife."

"I'm so pleased to meet you," Mrs. Trattner said with genuine warmth. We shook hands, and though her hand was delicate, I was surprised by the strength of her grip.

"And you as well." I hesitated, then gestured to my table. "Would you like to join me? Or are you in a hurry?"

After assuring me they weren't, the three of us sat down. A server came along, and Trattner and his wife both ordered coffee and pastries. "I'm glad to see you looking so well," I said, eyeing his uniform. Was it wrong that I was relieved to see he hadn't been demoted? "I was worried that you might face repercussions from the Autocrator after the unfortunate events that transpired in Traggar. In truth, I feel terrible about what happened."

"Oh, that is all behind me," Trattner said. "It isn't your fault that my tongue wagged so freely, and besides, we ended up doing fine against the Elantians without Traggar's help."

"Indeed." I kept my voice light even as anger bubbled in my gut. "I suppose you are rather lucky that the Autocrator didn't need the alliance after all."

"My cousin knew the alliance was a long shot anyway," Mrs. Trattner said. She hooked her arm around her husband's and leaned into him with a small smile. "I, for one, am happy Andras is home safe with us again." She gave Trattner's arm an affectionate squeeze. Andras? Was that his given name? I'd never thought to ask.

"Your cousin?" I blinked. "Do you mean the Autocrator?"

"I do." Her smile widened. "Why, would you like to meet him?"

"Oh no." I tried to keep the alarm out of my voice even as my heart hammered in my chest. The absolute last thing I needed was to draw the attention of the most powerful man in the land. "I was just curious. General Trattner never mentioned it."

"That is because my wife's connections are the least interesting thing about her." Trattner smiled warmly at his wife. "She is also a noted antiquarian scholar. One of the many, many reasons I fell in love with her."

"I remember you telling me that your wife was a historian." To my relief, we quickly fell into that topic, and eventually got onto the subject of treasure hunting. Mrs. Trattner seemed to think it was a wonderful thing that all the ancient temples were being unearthed. The artifacts within held so much information about how people from those times lived, including technological marvels that could be used to advance Zallabar's own technology.

"What do you think about the old gods?" I asked, thinking of Caor once more. "Do you think they were real, and that excavating their temples and taking their treasures is a desecration? Or are they figments of our ancestors' imaginations?"

Mrs. Trattner shrugged. "I tend to keep an open mind about these things," she said. "I have heard stories of curses befalling treasure hunters who opened up the wrong temple, but those may well be rumors or coincidence. The existence of gods would explain why magic exists, and also perhaps why so few mages are left, since the gods are no longer worshipped."

That last sentence gave me pause. "You think magic is dying out because humans have turned away from the gods? That it isn't because mages are persecuted in many countries? Or in the case of Elantia, transformed into something else?"

"Ah, you mean the dragon riders." Trattner wrinkled his nose. "I'm not certain the gods have anything to do with it, as there are countries where magic is thriving. It is a good thing that Elantia is not one of those countries. They would have been much harder to conquer."

"Right." I forced a smile as I dug some coin out of my purse to pay for my ice cream. "Well, it has been lovely talking to you both, but I really ought to find my husband now. We have a few calls to make this afternoon."

"Of course," General Trattner said, rising as I got to my feet. "Do tell your husband I said hello."

"Actually," Mrs. Trattner said, "why don't you bring him along to our house tomorrow night? My husband and I are having an informal buffet dinner with a group of history enthusiasts we meet with every few weeks. It is our turn to host this month, and I think you both would have a grand time with us."

"I'll have to ask my husband and make sure that he doesn't have any other plans, " I hedged, "but I for one would be delighted. Where in town do you live?"

"Here, in the Garden District," Mrs. Trattner said. "Unfortunately, we are on the other side of that stupid gate, but I'll be giving the guards a list of admitted guests."

Yes! I crowed internally. "Please do put my name on the list," I said, trying not to sound too eager. "If I can convince my husband, we will definitely be there."

I bid the Trattners farewell, then left the shop, my blood sizzling with excitement. Finally, I'd caught a break! I'd just have to tell them my "husband" was ill when I arrived, then slip out early before the others left so I could scope out the rest of the neighborhood. In my evening attire, with my hair and face properly done, no one would question a gently-bred lady out for an evening stroll.

What a stroke of good luck, I thought, staring up at the sky. It was clear and sunny today, and the air was crisp, hinting at the coming winter. Things had fallen into place so perfectly that I wondered if my meeting with Trattner was the result of divine intervention. I twisted the ring on my finger as I thought of Caor, but if the messenger god heard my thoughts, he gave no sign.

On my way back to the boarding house, music and shouting drew my attention. Quickening my pace, I entered a square and froze. It was filled with Zallabarian soldiers. The soldiers had thrown off their hats and were dancing in the square with civilians, and ribbons and banners were strewn across the square. "Victory! Victory!" the messages shouted. "Long live Autocrator Reichstein!"

A husky soldier grabbed me around the waist and pulled me into a lively dance. I was so bewildered that I didn't think to refuse him. "What is going on?" I shouted above the music, even though my sinking heart already knew.

"We won!" the soldier shouted, jubilation all over his face. "Elantia has given us their unconditional surrender!"

My stomach soured, and whatever optimism I'd enjoyed earlier evaporated. I managed to get through the dance without stabbing anyone, then quickly hurried away, my eyes burning with tears.

"Lessie?" I called frantically, needing to talk to someone, *anyone*, who would understand. But there was no answer, and my mind was in such turmoil that I couldn't even tell how far she was. Once more, I was surrounded by the enemy, with no one I could trust or lean on for support.

Was this always how it was going to be? That I would fight, over and over, to be reunited with my friends, only to be ripped away and thrust into the heart of danger once more?

Don't dwell on it, I told myself firmly, blinking back the tears. I quickened my steps toward the boarding house, trying not to think about the sounds of celebration spreading throughout the city as more people heard the news. Soon, throngs would fill the streets throughout the capital, and I didn't want to be anywhere near them. I'd learned a lot about discipline in the military, but I didn't think anyone was capable of watching the enemy celebrate the death and subjugation of their own people without wanting to set the whole city on fire.

One thing at a time, Zara. I would go to General Trattner's house tomorrow night and figure out how to steal the piece of heart. And then I would get the hell out of this city and back to the people I loved.

13

The next evening, I dressed in my finery, then hired a steam car to take me to the gated district. I winced a little at the expense—I hadn't really paid attention to how much these things cost when Salcombe ferried us around—but paid up anyway, knowing that Lady Trentiano could hardly afford to show up at the gates on foot. I was playing the part of a wealthy noblewoman tonight, and I had to carry it off perfectly.

Riding in the steam car was a luxury experience. The entire conveyance was painted lacquered black and upholstered with butter-soft leather. As I sat back in my seat, I marveled at how quickly the world zoomed around us. The steam car moved several times faster than a horse, and yet it felt as if I was hardly moving at all.

We came to a smooth stop in front of the gate, and I watched through the windows as one of the guards approached the driver's side door. The driver rolled down the window and told the guard my name. The guard checked the list to make sure I was on it, then gestured for me to roll down my window. I swallowed a little as I did so, then smiled pleasantly as I allowed the guard to study my face. Had Trattner provided descriptions of the guests to check against?

After a minute, the guard ordered the others to open the gate. "A guard will escort you to General Trattner's home," he said, then turned to the driver. "Please follow behind him, and mind the speed limit."

I was about to ask him how we would be following another guard when we were in a steam car, when a smaller steam engine whistled up ahead. A uniformed guard waited on the other side astride a steam bike. Once the gates were open, he turned the bike, kicked off, and shot forward, leaving us room to follow behind him.

I was immediately envious.

We followed the steam bike at a fairly sedate pace, which allowed me plenty of time to study the other houses. They were all grand estates boasting towering manors and acres of manicured gardens dotted with fountains and sculptures. But as we passed one with a gold-plated fence above a marble balustrade, my treasure sense buzzed excitedly.

This is the place, I thought as the gong reverberated through my head. *This is where the piece of heart Caor sent me after is hiding.*

"What a gorgeous house!" I exclaimed to the driver as I leaned forward a little. "Do you have any idea who it belongs to?"

"I believe Baron Fersel lives there, my lady," the driver said. "He is a close advisor to the Autocrator, whose own house is located just behind it. It is an even more splendid property, at least in my opinion."

"I'm sure it is," I murmured, and marked the location in my memory as we drove past. I counted the number of streets and houses until we rolled to a stop in front of General Trattner's house. His mansion, located two blocks to the left and ten houses down, wasn't as grand as the one with the dragon heart piece, but it was still much nicer than any place I'd ever been invited to.

"Lady Zara!" Mrs. Trattner exclaimed when the footman showed me in. "I'm so glad you could make it. Please, let me introduce you to my children." She rose from the pastel green couch where she was sitting next to her husband, and the other people in the room rose as well. A son and two daughters, I noted, all but one grown-up. Mrs. Trattner introduced them as Hans, Heidi, and Hannah. Hans, she said proudly, was an officer in the army, while Heidi was married to the minister of finance, who was not here tonight. Hannah had yet to have a proper coming out, but once she did, they were confident she would have many suitors.

"I can see your mother prefers 'H' names," I said with a smile after Mrs. Trattner introduced me in turn and invited us all to sit again. "It's a pleasure to meet you all."

"And you." Hannah, the youngest at perhaps sixteen, smiled shyly at me. "Father tells us that you have an interest in ruins?"

"I do." And just like that, we fell into animated conversation. The easy way I was able to converse with General Trattner and his family was as disturbing as it was a relief. There was no need to pretend interest in them, but it was also far too easy to forget they were the enemy and would have me jailed if they suspected even an inkling of my true identity.

"Where did you get that pendant?" Heidi asked with sudden interest, pointing at it. I'd pinned it to the collar of my gown, thinking that the copper went quite nicely with the emerald silk.

My hand fluttered to the copper pendant. "It was given to me by a friend. Why do you ask?"

"We've seen those pendants on ancient temple reliefs," Heidi said eagerly. "They appear to have been worn by the temple priests. Would you mind if I have a look?"

"Certainly." I unpinned it from my collar and handed it over. If the Trattner girls could tell me more about it, all the better.

The Trattners passed it amongst themselves, tracing the odd geometric symbols etched into the copper as they oohed and ahhed. "I would be careful with this, Lady Zara," General Trattner said as he handed it back to me. "Old relics like this, especially ones that belonged to priests or were used in ceremonies, often have a touch of magic in them."

"I will," I promised as I slipped the chain around my neck again.

Heidi looked like she wanted to say something more about the amulet, but before she could, two ladies and three gentlemen were shown into the room. Mrs. Trattner got to her feet, and we all followed for another round of introductions.

"Lady Zara, this is Baron Niklas Fersel," Mrs. Trattner said as she introduced me to a tall, handsome man in his forties. He had golden hair and deep brown eyes, and looked very distinguished in his fitted suit and goatee. "Baron Fersel, this is Lady Zara Trentiano, visiting from Warosia with her husband."

"A pleasure." Baron Fersel took my hand and pressed a perfunctory kiss against the back of it. Despite the glove I wore, I felt an unmistakable zing at the contact—this man was a mage, I was certain of it. The baron's eyes widened briefly, and I forced myself not to tense up. Had he sensed something about me, as well?

Dammit. I certainly hadn't planned on meeting the man I was going to rob tonight. How was I going to get around this? Could I slip out before he went home for the evening, and retrieve the piece of heart before he arrived?

I tried not to betray my nerves as we all settled in, this time to talk about a historical dig some two hundred miles west of the capital. Apparently, it had been put on hold due to the war, and now the archaeologists in charge were fighting to keep the site preserved. Most of the men and women present agreed that something needed to be done. The archaeology team needed the funds to hire guards so treasure hunters and criminals would not plunder the site.

At no point in the conversation did any of the others betray any knowledge of Baron Fersel's magic. So, it was a secret, then. I wondered what the Autocrator would think if he knew that one of his closest advisors was a magic user. Would he cast him out? Or would he find a way to use the man's talents to his advantage? For all I knew, he already had.

"I hear the archaeologists have already uncovered several magical artifacts," Heidi said with enthusiasm. "But they are keeping the nature of these artifacts tightly under wraps, until the publication of their report."

"It's too bad my husband couldn't make it tonight," I said, eyeing Baron Fersel out of the corner of my eye. "He has quite an interest in magical artifacts."

"Does he?" The Baron's eyes sharpened, but before he could say more, General Trattner interrupted.

"Can't make it?" he asked, looking concerned. "Did something change?"

"I'm not sure what you mean," I said, my pulse skittering in my veins. What did he mean, had something changed? I'd already hinted that Salcombe might not be able to make it.

"Oh, I ran into Lord Trentiano in the market today," Mrs. Trattner said gaily. "He said that he was more than happy to put aside his engagements for the evening to attend the party—"

"And so I am," Salcombe said, stepping into the room. He was in his Lord Trentiano persona—a picture-perfect representation of a healthy, handsome male in his forties, not dissimilar to Baron Fersel with his dark hair and fine clothing. The women in the room immediately began to titter as I stared, unable to hide my shock. "Zara," he said warmly as he came over to me with arms outstretched. "You look lovely tonight."

"Thank you," I said. "This is an unpleasant surprise," I added under my breath as I embraced him. He wore some kind of cologne that made me think of fresh ocean breezes, and his body felt strong and whole. But beneath all that I could sense the stench of death and decay lurking just beneath the surface.

What price was Salcombe paying in exchange for this glowing sense of health and vitality? Was the rot I detected coming from his heart? His soul?

Salcombe's grip tightened on me, fingernails digging in just slightly. "I must thank you," he murmured, "for getting me an invitation. It would have been infinitely more difficult to steal the piece of heart without one. I suppose it is a good thing that the blow I dealt to your head didn't kill you after all."

I wanted to wrench myself from Salcombe's grip and pummel him, to rail at him for all the terrible things he'd done to me. Instead, I gracefully slipped away, and returned to my seat between Mrs. Trattner and her daughters. As I sat down again, I noticed Baron Fersel watching me intently once more. Did he suspect something? Salcombe and I had only passed a few seconds in conversation, nothing more.

The bell rang for dinner, and we all filed into the dining room where an endless buffet awaited us. I dutifully piled my plate high with rouladen, *kartoffelpuffer,* and other Zallabarian dishes that would have normally made my mouth water, but the food tasted ashen in my mouth. I spent the evening talking to Trattner and his wife, mostly, while doing my best to ignore the way Salcombe effortlessly charmed everyone with his good looks and conversation. He even managed to reel Baron Fersel into a lively discussion about magical artifacts, and there was no way that I could butt in without looking extremely rude. At the rate he was going, I wouldn't be surprised if he finagled an invitation to the man's house before the end of the night!

I wasn't sure the situation could get any worse, but shortly after dinner, once we'd adjourned to the sitting room, another guest was brought in. "Uncle Zilos!" Heidi and Hannah cried, jumping up from their chairs to throw their arms around him.

The man chuckled warmly as he embraced his nieces, and I studied him closely. Though he was dressed in fine clothes, they were simple—dark brown trousers with a white linen shirt and waistcoat, and sturdy boots. Well made, but not ostentatious. He sported a thick head of mahogany hair and a handlebar mustache, and his face was handsome in a pleasant kind of way. He chatted with the girls for a few minutes, then went to greet Trattner and his wife.

"Autocrator," Trattner said. "What a wonderful surprise! I hadn't thought you could make it."

My blood turned to ice. Autocrator? As in Autocrator Reichstein?

The Autocrator chuckled. "My wife is hosting her monthly women's society dinner, so she's kicked me out of the house and ordered me to find company elsewhere." He glanced around the room, and his eyes landed on Salcombe. "Who is your guest, Renate? I don't believe we've been introduced."

"Oh! This is Lord and Lady Trentiano." Mrs. Trattner waved us over, and Salcombe immediately stepped forward, hooking his arm around mine as he did so. I allowed him to drag me over to the Autocrator and locked my face into a pleasant smile to hide the murderous surge of emotions threatening to overcome me.

"I met Lady Trentiano in Traggar..." General Trattner gave the Autocrator a brief account of our history together. The dagger carefully hidden in the folds of my skirt seemed to be burning a hole into my leg, and my fingers itched to grasp it. At this distance, would I have time to stab Reichstein before I was restrained or killed? Surely my own death was worth it if I could cut the head off this snake. The man was responsible for the death and enslavement of hundreds of dragons and tens of thousands of Elantians.

"Don't." I nearly toppled over in shock at the sound of Caor's voice echoing in my head. The ring on my finger warmed, and my palms instantly grew sweaty. *"You will not be able to kill the Autocrator and escape unscathed, and you still need to get the remaining pieces of the dragon heart. If you fail, the dragon god will rise again, and he is worse than a thousand Reichsteins."*

"Why don't you just give me some divine juju so I can kill him without repercussions?" I snapped at him once I'd regained my wits. But Caor didn't answer, and I cursed inwardly as the warmth of the ring faded. As usual, he only spoke when he wanted to.

"Lady Zara?" Mrs. Trattner's voice jerked me back to the conversation. "Are you feeling all right?" she asked, her eyes round with concern.

"I confess I feel a bit faint," I said, passing a hand across my brow. "Do you mind if I take a bit of air?"

"Of course." Mrs. Trattner took a step toward me and took my arm. "I'll escort you."

"No, that's quite all right." I gently pulled my arm from hers with a smile. "Sometimes I get overwhelmed with crowds and need a moment to collect myself. I'll be back in just a minute."

I slipped away from the group before anyone else could object, relieved that Salcombe didn't insist on following me. I suppose he couldn't do so without being rude now that I'd expressed my wish to be alone, which was the point. I exited the sitting room and turned left, then opened a pair of double doors at the end of the hall. The moment the chilly evening air hit me, I let out a huge sigh of relief. Curling my hands around the balcony railing, I leaned out and took in deep lungfuls of air, trying to calm my thundering heart.

Go now. Caor's voice was in my head again. *While Salcombe is still occupied.*

I glanced over the railing. It was a two-story drop from here to the ground, and the thorny rose bushes below did not look like a convenient place to land. Dammit. Over at the street beyond the fence, two guards patrolled. This neighborhood was well-lit; they would see me in an instant. I would be better served exiting through one of the servants' entrances.

I turned around to do just that, and ran straight into a hard male chest. "Lady Zara!" Baron Fersel exclaimed in his deep baritone, strong hands gripping my upper arms to steady me. "I do apologize for my clumsiness," he said as he released me.

"No, no, the fault was mine." I gave him a strained smile. "I was just about to head back into the party."

"Were you?" He arched an eyebrow. "It looked more like you were preparing to flee the house altogether. Are you quite all right?"

"I'm fine," I said quickly. "Why do you ask?"

Baron Fersel frowned. "Your affairs are your own, of course, but I couldn't help noticing how very tense you became when your husband showed up. Not to mention that you arrived separately to begin with. Are you in some kind of trouble, Lady Zara? Anything I can assist with?"

I hesitated, wondering if I should just brush the man off and escape. But he'd had his eye on me all night, and for all I knew he could put some kind of tracking spell on me once I left. The last thing I needed was for him to trace me all the way back to his house and catch me breaking in.

But what kind of story could I tell Baron Fersel that he would believe? I could try to tell him that Salcombe was a wanted criminal, but he was wanted by Elantia, not Zallabar. And besides, any attempt to throw Salcombe to the wolves would result in exposing my own identity, and I couldn't risk that.

"I should let you know that the pendant I wear helps me discern whether someone is lying or telling the truth," Baron Fersel said when I didn't answer. He tapped a star-shaped pin on his lapel that twinkled with tiny rubies. "It is quite useful for my line of work. If you don't wish to confide in me you don't have to, and there is no need for you to make up a story when I can detect falsehoods. Even so, I can't help but find both your and your husband's behavior to be rather suspicious."

I sighed, hooking a curl of hair around my ear as I looked up at him. "The truth is, Lord Trentiano's behavior has troubled me for a very long time. We have known each other since my childhood, and the more time that has passed, the more obsessive he has become with dragon artifacts. Most recently, he has fallen prey to a fatal obsession to locate the pieces of the ancient dragon god's heart and use them to resurrect him. This quest has quite ruined our relationship, to the point that the last time we were together he hit me hard enough to cause a serious brain injury. Luckily, I managed to get proper treatment, but as you can understand, I've been fleeing him ever since."

Baron Fersel's expression went slack with shock, and I hid a smile. Technically, I hadn't lied about anything, merely omitted a few details. "So, the man has been pursuing you all this time, even though he's tried to kill you?"

"It's...a complicated situation," I told him. "I don't want to end up back in his clutches, and yet I cannot allow him to succeed at his quest. I know it seems crazy that these dragon heart pieces exist and that they could be used to resurrect a god, but they are very real."

"I see." The baron was silent for a long moment as he scrutinized me. I could tell he was intrigued, but he was clearly unwilling to discuss such a sensitive topic with me openly, especially at a party where anyone could overhear. "I think, Lady Zara, that we should continue this conversation somewhere else," he finally said. "Would you allow me to take you back to my residence?"

Yes! "If you must," I demurred, lowering my lashes in an appropriate imitation of a modest woman. "But won't the others be scandalized?"

"This...situation that you bring up is much more important than any scandal." Fersel grasped my upper arm and steered me gently but firmly back inside. "But if you are so concerned, we need not tell the others of our departure—"

"Our departure?" Salcombe asked in a loud voice as he stepped into the hall. To my horror, the general and his wife were right on his heels, along with the Autocrator himself. "Just where are you going with my wife at this hour, Baron Fersel?"

The baron tightened his grip protectively around my arm. "The lady tells me that she is not feeling well," he said evenly. "I have offered to escort her home."

"Thank you, but as her husband that duty falls to me," Salcombe said tersely as he took a step forward. His eyes gleamed with rage, though he hid it behind a sympathetic smile. "Come, darling—"

"Don't you 'come, darling' me!" I shrieked, slapping his hand away. Salcombe actually recoiled, more from shock than anything else, but it was still a satisfying reaction. "You know very well why I asked Baron Fersel to take me home instead of you," I said dramatically, jabbing a shaking finger in his direction. "You may not be aware of this, Autocrator, but this man is a bully and an abuser. He nearly killed me the last time we were together, and will surely succeed if I remain in his presence for much longer." I turned to the Trattners, who looked shell-shocked, and curtsied. "Thank you very much for your hospitality, but I really must go. I'm very sorry to have brought such trouble to your home."

I whirled on my heel and dashed for the stairs before either Salcombe or the others could get in a word edgewise. Salcombe shouted after me, but his words were drowned out by a cacophony of shouted questions and exclamations. For everyone else in attendance, the evening had suddenly become *very* interesting.

I hoped the scandal I'd just created would buy me enough time to get into the baron's house, steal the heart, and get out before Salcombe caught up. The rage in Salcombe's eyes was unmistakable. He was done suffering my attempts to thwart him. If he got his hands on me again, I was dead, and how could any divine intervention or magic save me when he had the wrath of a god behind him?

14

"Thank you so much for getting me away from there," I said as the baron showed me into his foyer. It was just as grand as the outside, with a black marble floor and high arched ceiling, the center dominated by a large, expensive table boasting some kind of abstract sculpture wrought of gold and silver. "I'm not sure what would have happened if I'd stayed there."

"You likely would have been just fine on your own, to be honest," the baron said with a shrug as he divested himself of his coat. He handed it to the waiting butler, along with mine, then ordered the man to make sure the guard around his estate was tripled. "The Trattners seem very fond of you and have no small amount of influence. I'm sure they would have happily had him arrested."

I shuddered. "You don't know my husband," I told him. "He can be frighteningly persuasive."

The baron said nothing as he escorted me down the hall and into the library. We sat at a large, polished oak desk by the window, and he poured us both three fingers of brandy, then handed my glass to me.

"Now," he said as I sipped. "Tell me exactly why I shouldn't order both you and your husband imprisoned right now."

I nearly spewed my drink all over his desk. "Imprisoned?" I squeaked. "Why would you do such a thing to me? I just told you that I'm the one who's trying to thwart this mad quest of his. I want nothing to do with the dragon god!"

"Perhaps," Fersel said as he tapped the arm of his chair. "And yet, my intuition tells me you have not been entirely truthful. There is something you aren't telling me about this."

What, you mean the fact that I've been given a divine mandate to hunt down the piece you have by a bunch of sulky gods who will barely lift a finger to help me? "I have told you everything you need to know," I said coolly as I folded my hands in my lap. "I have no idea why you wish to make an enemy of me, but I will not allow you to bully me any more than I will allow my husband. If you insist on arresting me for a crime I have not committed, then I will have no reason to keep my lips sealed. I will tell everyone about your true nature."

"My true nature?" Fersel asked, and I had to commend him for his incredible self-control. Aside from a slight flicker in his gaze, he gave absolutely no sign that my words had distressed him.

"Yes." I allowed my lips to curve in a small smile. "I have some small ability of my own, and I can sense that you are a mage. Just like I can sense that you have a piece of the dragon heart buried two floors beneath the house. In the cellars, I presume?"

Fersel's handsome features tightened with anger. "You seek to blackmail me, then?"

"No." I held up my hands, imploring him to listen. "I merely seek your help in keeping this dangerous artifact out of Lord Trentiano's hands. He already has two of the pieces in his possession, and they have given him heightened strength and charisma, as well as the ability to heal grievous wounds. If he should get his hands on the piece you hold, he will become unstoppable."

Fersel gave me a wary look, then sighed as he leaned back in his chair. "You are right that I am a mage," he admitted. "I am a descendent of one of the original families that sealed Zakyiar's relics away all those centuries ago. My family has denied our magic for centuries and changed our name numerous times in an attempt to disappear from history, and yet it is not the first time someone has traced us here. How did you find out my secret?"

"Lord Trentiano is a highly accomplished researcher and scholar," I said. "He also has quite a bit of money. Between the two, and the fact that he can likely sense the other dragon heart pieces thanks to his partnership with the dragon god, I don't think it was all that difficult for him."

Fersel's expression turned downright grim. "Then there is nothing for it," he said, pulling open a drawer. "I will have to kill you both."

He pulled a pistol from his desk drawer, and my heart dropped when he trained it on me. "Wait!" I shouted as I dropped to the ground, and the sound of the gunshot echoed in my ears, a miniature explosion that made my skull vibrate.

"Don't make this difficult, Lady Zara." The baron's chair scraped back, followed by heavy, methodical footsteps. "It's nothing personal, but it is my duty to protect the dragon heart piece. Two lives is a small price to pay, and if what you say is true, I will simultaneously thwart the dragon god. Surely that is worth your life?"

"You asshole," I growled, giving up any pretense of ladylike manners. Grabbing one of the chairs, I straightened up and ran straight at Fersel, using the piece of furniture as a shield. Wood splinters ripped through my skin as he fired at me, but I ignored the pain and used the chair to drive him straight into the wall. His next shot went wild, and I winced as the window behind his desk shattered. If his gunshots hadn't already alerted the guards, that would.

"Get off!" he roared, flinging his hands out. Magic sizzled in the air, and I gasped as an unseen force barreled toward me. But before it could connect, the amulet flared with blinding white light, erecting some kind of barrier around me. It repelled the magic, sending it soaring toward the ceiling, and I jumped back as a small chandelier went crashing to the ground.

"What *are* you?" Fersel sputtered, his face slack with astonishment. He and I lunged for the pistol at the same time, and I tackled him around the legs, taking him to the ground. The two of us tumbled across the carpet, away from the firearm, and I cried out as the baron pinned me to the ground and started raining blows down on me. I crossed my arms over my face to block them, but he still managed to get a few blows in, and each one hurt like a bitch. I could feel more magic sizzling in the air, but my amulet continued to glow, repelling his attempts to ensorcel me.

"Get him off," Caor said urgently. *"You have to get him off!"*

"Could use a little help here!" I shouted. But as Fersel shifted his weight, I felt the press of my dagger against my thigh.

What the hell. I dropped one of my arms and stretched it to the left, then bucked my right hip in the same direction, throwing Fersel off-balance. He let out a rather unmanly squawk as I used the momentum to flip us over, and before he could get his bearings, I yanked the dagger from my skirts and plunged it into his chest.

Fersel's roar of pain was nearly loud enough to shake the walls. "Y-you," he croaked, eyes wide with shock and agony as he stared up at me. Blood bubbled out of the corner of his mouth, and a wave of guilt hit me so hard that tears stung my eyes. I hadn't wanted to kill the man. He'd just been doing his duty, the duty passed on by his ancestors through the millennia. I'd just wanted him to help me. And now he was dead.

He's the enemy, Zara. He works for the man who slaughtered thousands of your people.

The sounds of shouts echoing from the courtyard spurred me into action. I yanked the dagger from Fersel's chest, wiped it on his shirt, then gripped it in my right hand as I hurried out the door. There was no point in hiding his body—the guards would have seen the broken window, and would find the blood on the floor. I needed to get downstairs, retrieve the heart, and get out of here.

As I ran down the hall, cursing my decision to trade out my spelled boots for these noisy ones, my ring began to warm against my skin. *"Don't worry about the guards,"* Caor said. *"Just get to the heart."*

I did as Caor said, barreling down the hall as I followed the heart's distinctive signal. The front door burst open, and I whirled around as guards came running into the house on the heels of the butler, who had undoubtedly gone to fetch them. But to my surprise, they headed straight upstairs, their eyes skipping past me as if I were no more interesting than the paintings mounted on the walls.

"My magic cannot shield you for long," Caor barked. *"Go!"*

I raced to the end of the hall, then yanked on the handle of a heavy wooden door that I hoped led to the basement. It was locked, so I shoved my lock pick through the keyhole and twisted. The keyhole flared as some spell activated, trying to resist the pick, but after a few seconds the lock clicked open. I wrenched the door open and grabbed a lamp from a side table, then rushed down the stairs into the darkness.

"Come on, come on, come on," I chanted as I methodically searched the cellar. It was ruthlessly organized, but though the signal was loud enough to make my brain ache, I couldn't find the piece of heart.

Focus, Zara, I told myself. *Clear your mind, and pinpoint the location.*

I stopped in the center of the room and took a deep breath, trying to clear my head. The sound of footsteps thudding upstairs and servants wailing wasn't helping things, but I forced myself to block it all out and focus on the object I was looking for.

Where are you? I asked it. *Show yourself.*

I felt a strong tug come from a patch of floor that was covered in sacks of flour. *There?* I strode over to the spot and grabbed the closest bag, then began tossing them clear of the space. Soon enough, a trapdoor came into view. I grasped the chain, and it began to glow coal red. My amulet flared at the same time, counteracting whatever magic was in the chain, and with a mighty tug, I yanked the trapdoor open.

Below the floor was a large chest enclosed in a four-foot gap between the floorboards and the ground. I used my lock pick on the magical padlock that held it shut, then flipped back the lid to reveal a black box carved with silver runes nestled amongst some other valuables. There were no seams or handles of any kind, no way to open it, but I didn't need to. I could hear the call coming from within clear as day, and as I stared, an image of a large, roughly cut chunk of black diamond swirled into my mind's eye.

The piece of heart was in this box. I was sure of it.

The footsteps began to draw closer, and I hastily grabbed the box and flipped the chest lid closed, then dragged the trapdoor in place. There was another staircase at the other end of the cellar, and I rushed over to it, then began to climb toward the double doors that I was certain led to the outside entrance.

"You!" a male voice cried. "What are you doing down here?"

Dragon's balls! I lunged for the doors, but they were locked from the outside and refused to budge. Heart in my throat, I spun around, the bloodied dagger in my free hand, and leapt from the staircase down onto the approaching guard. I stabbed him straight through the heart even as I took him down, and the light in his eyes went dark as we hit the ground.

"Mandel!" Three more guards raced down the stairs, and I jumped up, holding my dagger aloft. It was three against one, and with only a single weapon at my disposal, the odds weren't looking good. Not to mention I was hampered by the box under my arm, which I didn't dare relinquish.

"Drop your weapon," one of the guards snarled as he advanced on me. I might have if I thought they were going to take me alive, but the murderous look in his eyes told me otherwise. Instead, I tightened my grip and sank into a defensive crouch, prepared to fight to the death.

"Zara!" Lessie's voice burst into my head, and I nearly dropped the dagger. *"Get down, now!"*

15

The sound of wood splintering diverted the guards' attentions, and I dropped to the ground just as Lessie released a huge gout of flame into the cellar. My stomach turned as the scent of roasting flesh and burning hair mingled with blood-curdling screams, and I glanced up to see the guards on the ground, rolling to try and smother the flames, which were already spreading to the flour sacks. It was only a matter of time before they reached the rows of wine kegs on the opposite side, so I jumped to my feet and darted across the room before I was caught up in the conflagration.

Lessie didn't wait for me to reach the top of the stairs—she snatched me up in her grasp and took flight. Terror speared my chest at the sound of cannon fire, but Lessie executed a perfect barrel roll, then pumped her wings even harder, propelling us several hundred feet in mere seconds. A feat she would have never managed just a few months ago.

The air around us shimmered, and I gasped as patches of

Lessie's body disappeared, mingling with the night sky. "Are you all right?" Tavarian shouted from above, and my heart soared at the sound of his voice.

"You came for me!" I cried, happy tears stinging the corners of my eyes.

"Of course we did!" he shouted, and though I couldn't see him, I could hear the exasperation in his voice. "We had to, once we figured out where you'd gone. Though the next time you decide to take a shortcut, some advance warning would be appreciated!"

Laughing, I finally settled into Lessie's grip, allowing my body to dangle in her clawed hands as she flew. The wind rippled through my hair as we soared through the night sky. Even though my silken gown did nothing to protect me from the elements, I savored the sting of icy air against my skin.

We didn't stop until we were well outside the city limits, far away from the reach of cannons and pistols. Lessie landed in a clearing barely wide enough to accommodate the three of us, with trees that towered high enough that we would not be easily spotted by airships. Gently, she laid me down on the ground, and I groaned as the exhilaration from the past few hours deserted me, leaving me spent.

"Zara!" Tavarian was at my side, his silver eyes gleaming in the moonlight. His face was the picture of anxiety as he gripped my hand, an emotion I was unused to seeing from him. "Are you all right? Lessie and I flew as fast as we could to get here, but communication between us is severely limited, and I had no idea what sort of trouble you were in."

I smiled, then held up my hand. The black box containing the piece of heart was clutched in my fist. "Caor decided it was taking us too long to get to Barkheim, so he spirited me away when I went into the woods to relieve myself. Tonight, I finally got into the house of the mage who was guarding the piece of heart. I managed to steal it, but I was about to be skewered when you arrived."

Tavarian swore. "Those blasted guards," he said, his eyes flashing with anger. "If we'd been but a moment later, you would be dead. What good is it for you to be their champion if they don't care about your welfare?"

"On the contrary," Caor drawled as he stepped from the tree line. I jolted upright, nearly slamming my forehead into Tavarian's. His own eyes had gone wide with astonishment, and I remembered this was his first encounter with the god. "If not for a little divine intervention on my part, Zara would have died. That amulet is a handy little thing, isn't it?"

"No kidding." I traced it with my finger. "What are these exactly?"

"Protection amulets, given to our priests and priestesses to call upon us in times of need." Caor's lips quirked into a half smile as he canted his head at me, long hair spilling to the side. "I suppose since you are our new champion, it is fitting that you wear one. The amulet will not protect you from physical assaults, but it should shield you from all but the most powerful magical attacks."

"And the invisibility?" I asked. "Was that the amulet, or you?"

Caor shifted his weight from one foot to the other, and I got the distinct sense that he was uncomfortable. "Gods have the ability to pass amongst humans unseen if they choose," he said. "I lent you that ability for a few minutes so that you could get into the cellar. It's not something I do often, so I'd prefer you didn't mention it to the other gods."

I snorted. "You mean I'm going to meet the other gods someday?"

He winked. "Perhaps," he said, reaching up into the air. I blinked as he pulled my leather pack from seemingly out of nowhere, then tossed it to me. "I came to return this to you, since you're in no position to retrieve it yourself."

I caught the pack, then set it to the ground and allowed Tavarian to help me to my feet. "Will you trade it for this?" Tavarian asked, holding out the box to Caor. "Now that we've retrieved it, it needs to be destroyed. Surely one of you gods have the power to do so. We certainly do not."

But Caor shook his head, taking a step back. "I do not dare touch such an unholy object myself, lest it corrupt my power and turn me against my fellows. You are right that no human or mage in this world currently has the power to destroy the relic. It must be unmade by a god of equal strength."

"Okay, so how do we do that?" I demanded. "Is there someone we can summon to take care of this?"

Caor laughed. "The gods do not answer to summons. They must be called upon, at the right time and place." He scratched his chin for a moment, considering. "Your best option is to go to the Forge of Derynnis. He is the ancient god of the Underworld, and his fires are hot enough to destroy most anything magical. I believe that if you can convince him to cast the piece of heart into his forge, that will be enough to unmake it."

"The Forge of Derynnis?" I shook my head even as the scholar in me perked up, fascinated by the prospect of more lore. "I've never heard of it. Do you know where it is?"

"It is located in the side of an active volcano, on an island in the middle of the Byrgonian Ocean."

"The Byrgonian Ocean?" Tavarian echoed. "That's several thousand miles south of here!"

"It is quite a distance," Caor agreed. "A long journey even by dragonback." He eyed Lessie, who had been glaring at him since he'd appeared, with some distaste. "I imagine you would object if I transported you there without your friends, so you should handle your affairs quickly and start the journey as soon as possible. In the meantime, I will petition Derynnis myself and see if I can get him to help you."

I scowled. "You mean there's a chance he won't?"

Caor shrugged. "He's rather capricious, and as a god of the Underworld does not value mortal lives all that much. Even so, he is your only hope, so be on your best behavior when you do finally reach the forge. He does not suffer fools."

With that dire pronouncement, Caor winked out of sight.

Lessie let out an exasperated huff that wholeheartedly mirrored my current mood, and I coughed as a cloud of smoke shot from her nostrils. *"This dragon heart business seems to have become infinitely more complicated ever since the gods got involved,"* she grumbled at me.

"Maybe, but we have no way of destroying these pieces unless the gods help us," I pointed out. To soften the sting of my words, I wrapped my arms around her neck and leaned into her warm body. "Thanks for saving my hide again, by the way. You're getting pretty good at flying in to rescue me in the nick of time."

Lessie snorted. *"A skill I've been forced to develop, thanks to these mad missions we're constantly running."* But she wrapped her foreleg around me and made a purring sound deep in her throat that made my whole body vibrate.

I glanced over my shoulder at Tavarian, who was watching us a little wistfully. *He must be missing Muza,* I thought. Now that Elantia was in such dire straits, would Tavarian call Muza out of retirement? After all, the council was in no position to prosecute either him or his dragon for their earlier desertion. But then again, I had a feeling there was more to Muza's disappearance than what Tavarian had revealed. There was still a secret he was sitting on, one that I would have to worm out of him someday.

But now wasn't the time. Now, he needed comfort, just as much as I did.

I let Lessie cling to me for another moment, then gently extricated myself from her embrace and walked over to Tavarian. He opened his mouth to say something, but I ignored him as I wrapped my arms around his neck and stretched up on tiptoe to kiss him. I pressed the entire length of my body against him as our mouths met, and a gasp escaped my lips as a jolt of energy arced between us.

Lessie huffed again, but this time there was something distinctly amused in her tone. *"I'm going to hunt for dinner,"* she said as she took flight, buffeting us with a gust of wind. *"You had better have your clothes on by the time I come back."*

I might have laughed, but Tavarian took that moment to shove his hands in my hair and deepen the kiss. I moaned as his tongue tangled with mine, and opened wider to let him in, to savor the taste and feel of him as I poured weeks of desperation, frustration, and longing into the kiss. Desire flared inside me like a wildfire, scorching my veins and disintegrating all of my reservations.

"I thought you didn't want to do this," Tavarian panted as I yanked his shirttails from his trousers. "I thought I was a distraction."

"You are a distraction," I grumbled as I shoved my hands underneath his shirt. Smooth, taut muscles rippled beneath my fingers, and I had to stop myself from shredding the shirt entirely. I'd seen him shirtless once before, and though I'd tried to put the image out of my mind afterward, I'd secretly decided it was a crime against humanity for someone as well built as Tavarian to cover up something so perfect.

"But," I went on, pulling back just enough to look into those swirling silver eyes, "I also crave you more than a treasure hunter craves gold, and since I am a treasure hunter, that says a hell of a lot about how I feel about you."

"And?" He raised an eyebrow. "How do you feel about me, Zara Kenrook?"

I sucked in a breath. "I want the same things you want. I want to be yours, and I want you to be mine. Forever, until we follow our dragons into the great beyond."

He smiled as I tilted my head back, and this time when he kissed me it was slow and sweet. Looping my arms around his neck, I allowed him to take the lead, and he gradually deepened the kiss until we were both trembling with pent-up need.

"You deserve better than to be taken up against a tree, Zara," he panted, pulling back to look at me with that molten gaze of his. "Especially for our first time together."

I rolled my eyes. "While I appreciate the sentiment, please spare me your chivalry. We're alone, we're in neutral territory, and we've got a dragon watching our backs. If now's not the perfect time, I don't know when is, and if you don't make love to me, I might very well explode."

Tavarian's eyes flashed, the last of his restraint falling away in a blaze of lust. "You certainly have a way with words," he said, and then there were no more words between us. He backed me up against the nearest tree trunk and proceeded to kiss me senseless. Now that we'd given ourselves permission, we clawed at each other like wild animals, stripping each other bare as we dropped to the forest floor.

When we finally made love, clothed in nothing but moonlight and shadow, our bodies glowed with shared passion. Our breaths mingled in the crisp night air, scented with bergamot and leather and the natural pine aroma of the forest. It was a paradise of our own making, and I reveled in every touch, every gasp, every swell of sensation as we pushed each other toward an endless wave of bliss.

Spent, we snuggled together, lying on a bed fashioned from our discarded clothing. There were bedrolls in Lessie's saddlebags, but we were so reluctant to leave each other's company that we didn't even want to stir long enough to make a fire.

"That was pretty incredible," I said, smiling at Tavarian as I tucked a lock of inky hair behind his ear.

"It was." He skimmed his hand along the curve of my hip, stirring my blood even though we'd just finished. "Hopefully incredible enough to inspire a round two?"

"I don't know," I teased as I traced his bicep. I loved the hard ridges and planes of his body, and wished we had more time so I could explore him further. "I think you might have been a little *too* good. Good enough to keep me satisfied for the foreseeable future."

Tavarian smirked. "That's a first," he said, his lips brushing against my forehead. "I've never had a woman tell me I was *too* good in bed."

I laughed. "I should have known that comment would only inflate your ego," I said as I rose onto my knees. Tavarian's eyes darkened as he took in my naked form, and he reached up to hook an arm around my waist, drawing me atop him.

"Zaaaaraaaaa." Lessie's sing-song voice echoed in my head just as Tavarian's lips met mine. *"I'm on my way back now with two juicy bucks for dinner."*

I groaned, and Tavarian chuckled, the rumble of his chest sending vibrations through me. "I assume that's Lessie, on her way back now?" he asked as I rolled off him.

"Yes," I grumbled, searching through the pile of clothing for my underwear. I picked up his shirt and was about to toss it to him, then decided better of it.

"Zara," Tavarian said, sounding highly amused as I slipped the garment over my head. "As much as I like the sight of you in my clothes, your blouse and corset aren't going to fit me very well."

"No, they're not," I said with a grin as I handed him his trousers. "But I've decided that if we're going to sleep together, you need to be shirtless as often as possible."

He arched an eyebrow as he pulled on his trousers. "Wouldn't that be considered a distraction?"

"Yes." My grin widened. "The best kind of distraction. And now that Caor is sending us on a harebrained quest to find the god of the Underworld, I've decided I need as many good distractions as I can get to keep myself from losing my mind."

Tavarian chuckled, shaking his head. "We'll be fine, Zara," he said, pulling me into his arms again. We both turned our heads to the sky as Lessie came into view, a powerful, winged silhouette in the silver sky. "After everything we've faced so far, convincing a death god to help us should be a walk in the park."

I really hope so, I thought as Lessie landed in the clearing, kicking up dust and wind. Tavarian and I moved forward to help her with her catch, taking one of the bucks' hind legs to skin and roast while Lessie devoured the remaining meat. With any luck, Rhia and Jallis would have safely led the others to Polyba by now and were working on settling the island. We would go there first, help them get situated, and see if there really was a secret weapon that would help us drive the invaders out of our land.

"And then we get to venture into the Underworld," Lessie said, her voice rife with sarcasm. *"Isn't that going to be grand?"*

To be continued...

Zara and Lessie's adventures will continue in Test of the Dragon, Book 5 of the Dragon Riders of Elantia series! Head on over to Amazon to grab your copy today!

Did you enjoy this book? Please consider leaving a review, even if it's just a single sentence. Reviews help authors sell books, and the better a book sells, the faster its sequel gets written. Plus, they make the author feel warm and fuzzy inside. And who doesn't want that? :)

ABOUT THE AUTHOR

JESSICA DRAKE is obsessed with books, chocolate, and traveling. When she's not binge-watching Lord of the Rings or jet-setting around the world, she can be found chained to her computer, feverishly working on her next project. She loves to hear from her readers, so feel free to drop her a line at jessica@authorjessicadrake.com.

Printed in Great Britain
by Amazon